PUCK IN THE OVEN

MAINE MAULER HOCKEY SERIES

ZOE BETH GELLER

KINKY INK PUBLISHING

Puck in the Oven

Maine Maulers Hockey Series Book 5

Zoe Beth Geller

ALL THE FEELS ROMANCE

You can also visit me on Facebook and Amazon.

Please visit my website at zoegellerauthor.com

❀ Created with Vellum

FREE BOOK!

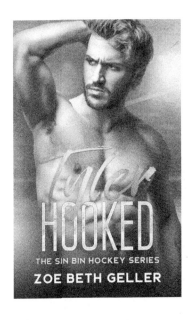

Tyler: Hooked
This is the prequel to the Sin Bin Series, a collection of 10
college hockey romances that are somewhat connected.

PLAYLIST

https://open.spotify.com/playlist/6e9jtWr5eApnqbɪaIdnjvv

Ex's and Oh's (Elle King)
Perfect (Ed Sheehan)
Love You Like That (Dagny)
Love Story (Taylor Swift)
Waking up in Paradise (feat. North Mississippi All Stars)

DEDICATED TO NIKITA

I rescued you from the cage,
But, you are the one who saved me.
It's a routine we had, saving each other. Each year with you
was a gift.
No matter when I walked, your head was always at my knee.
You never went to bed before me.
When it came time to let you go, I could not say goodbye.
You were the companion who never left my side.
So, in the end, I told you how much I loved you, and
I would find you—one the other side.

Nikita
June 20, 2010-July 8, 2022

1

Kal

"Hey, Korky, throw me some soap," I holler as I toss my empty squeeze bottle over the shower door. The locker room reeks of sweat even though our training facility is one of the best in the league, given the fact Madison Square Gardens was built in 1968.

Granted, I'm in awe of the great legends who have skated there. The NHL, with over one-hundred years in existence, and the Boston Sharks, who were the fifth team added to the league.

Ugh.

The Sharks left me with bad memories I can't erase. The loss to them last season in the semifinals hit me professionally and personally. Being booed by fans is a memory one never forgets.

The Sharks would be the only thorn in my side if I didn't have a trail of ex-girlfriends who all hoped to become the Mrs. Fat Chance on that. I tell them I'm not in it for the long haul, however, they still try to change me.

A tube of blue toothpaste flies over the door, landing on my wet toes. "What the fuck!"

Luc is laughing; other comments circulate. Garbled voices mix with the running water. Shit. I hope my entire day isn't one of 'stuff' occurring. Those are days where one incident after another occurs, culminating into layers of frustration. These are the tiny annoyances in life which make me want to go back to bed and say, "Do over."

I slide the shower handle to off and open the door. I step out, reach for the towel on the hook, and use it on my hair. After that, I use it to dry my face, and bleach from the laundry service embedded in the cotton infiltrates my nostrils. I glance about the room. We're all in various states of dressing.

Today, we practiced on different lines focusing on making smooth transitions to set the puck up for shots on goal. I can only hope we do better with passing in the slot in our next game.

What to do after practice is anyone's guess. We're in our hometown of the ever-growing Camden Bay. For some of the guys, this is the jump-off point for them to hook up with their girlfriends, others will appreciate the family time.

I can't imagine working kids into our routines. It's one reason I always wear a condom. I'm not getting a surprise Father's Day card. Yuck on the kids. What scares the shit out of me, is there is only one word which can irrevocably change my life. Once it's out of the box, it can't be undone. The word is...

Pregnant.

I move the towel over my back and leave my damp hair to air dry. No need to fuss with it. I'll have to shower and style it later, as we're required to dress appropriately for games. Personally, I'm not in the mood to dress up today.

However, we constantly make the headlines with our suits. I have no desire to be known as the best dressed man on the team. Luc is so damn tall, I don't know how he finds pants long enough to cover his ankles. Alexandre, he's another freaking Canadian who tends to wear his pants too short, which makes me wonder if it's how they wear their trousers up there. I'm not one to check out other men's legs in general. I mostly notice it if he's walking in front of me to the bus, or from paparazzi pictures as they circulate on social media.

Who wants to see a man's ugly ankles sticking out between svelte fabrics and our handmade leather shoes? We're expected to look like a billion bucks, every media outlet, along with our team photographer, will be taking pictures of us walking to our jet, our coffee in tow. The Mauler's love to post us on our team's social media site. It's mandatory we are picture worthy.

Alexandre is a great man. Who am I to make fashion critiques? I'm not a fashionista by any means. Besides, isn't that title reserved for the women we date? The ones who send us the bills for their shopping sprees when they spend a day in a city away from home as they wait for our night game?

I'd say Blake is the ugliest, but that's just me. Rachel seems to differ. But then again, we always pick on our best friends the most.

My stomach grumbles. I've burned through everything I had in the tank. I'm a human eating machine, and I can eat four times a day easily. I'm surprised the guys don't have a food group named after me. Maybe being nicknamed Bagel is close enough.

"Who's up for lunch?" I announce enthusiastically. I don't want to wait until I'm hangry. On game days we time our eating and sleeping. No one eats too close to a game. Most of us take a nap, too.

"I've got to get home," Justin volunteers with a sardonic smile. Knowing his wife's reputation, it's no wonder he's not thrilled to be going home. She's a handful. Plus, he's got three kids. I understand his commitment to having a private life. Besides, his sons are on hockey teams and his daughter figure skates. With three kids, keeping them all together at the ice rink makes perfect sense to me. I'm sure it becomes cost efficient at some point.

"I'm in." Finn pulls his jeans up and zips them before he tugs a team polo over his head and toned torso.

"Me, too," Sean chimes in, followed by Alexandre and Blake.

"Great. That makes five of us. What do we want?" They know I'm a human garbage disposal, anything will do.

"Not shit food," Blake throws it out there. Sure, the man's got a personal trainer on staff who handles all his nutritional supplements to keep him in top notch shape. However, we're best friends.

He opens his locker and grabs his leather bag of smell good shit. He groans as he pulls out a cherry flavored Jell-O shot in a tiny white pouch with the color showing through a circle cut out.

"Fuck. Who the hell did this?" he quips. I'm probably the first suspect on his list.

Finn snickers. I'm sure it's relief washing over him, similar to a cooling gel after a facial where his pores have been steamed.

"It wasn't me," Alexandre chimes in.

"I fucking know it was you, Kal," he says with a boisterous distaste in his mouth left from a warm shot of vodka, sugar, and food coloring.

Maybe I poke the bear too many times. I shrug my shoulders. "It's the world we live in."

"Yeah, we'll see about that," he grumbles as he spritzes himself, even though we're only going out for lunch.

"Fine. What do you guys want? I'm starving," I state, anxious to get going. I'm a foodie, and I get around. I have places to eat, waitresses I know, and I've been known to hit a few strip clubs before big games.

"I'm good with burgers," Finn suggests, "how about the new place around the corner? I hear it's good."

"Stan's Sports Bar and Grill?" I quip. Leave it to me to have the low down on useless facts others don't care about. And when they need to know such things, they come to me.

It's not always fun to be me in the press, especially when Hockey Scoop magazine gets a whiff of dirt on me. They have an uncanny ability to know what I'm up to all the time. I should check my car for a tracker.

"Great." Blake concurs.

I tug my jeans on, shove my feet into loafers as soft as butter. Thank God for Italian leather, I do love nice shoes. I grab my team polo shirt from my locker and throw it on with little regard for the wrinkles.

WE'RE at a table in the bar and grill surrounded by TV screens checking out the lunch time vibe and waitress' showing cleavage and displaying nice smiles. Of course, I'm looking at their nice facial features. . . well, after I check out the entire package and make sure I catch a glimpse of them as they walk away.

"You don't have to be such a man whore, Kal," Alexandre snickers and pretends to be disgusted by my shameless social life as he diverts his eyes from me and gives his full attention to the extensive menu.

I check out our waitress' cute ass. "That takes the fun out of it. Hell, you're married, not dead. Well, some of us aren't married," I defend myself. I make a note to stop being the poster man for bachelors. Maybe it's a genetic defect, I don't care to be tied down longer than a year. It's difficult for me to discern if my commitment issues are from my dad being such a dipshit, or my mom, who worked her ass off to support us kids.

I can imagine wanting someone to come home to at night. Right, and I love the Easter Bunny, too. No way is anyone going to interrupt my down time watching other hockey teams and golf. My time is me time, bring me another beer, please. Women are like the Stanley Cup, I keep them a while but at the end of the year, they are always returned to their original home.

Our waitress, Sally, according to her name badge, returns, and I order the loaded tater tots for the table. Those are always yummy no matter where they are served. How can anyone screw up a deep-fried potato?

This joint hasn't been open long enough for me to have a waitress familiar to me. Usually, waitresses stand around and talk, banking on a larger tip because they appear to be genuinely interested in what I'm saying.

The specialty burger looks good, and Blake orders one as well. Good. I order before making a trip to the men's room. I hope the guys don't pour hot sauce in my drink on general principal.

Hell, with me, they'd be more likely to order me a caffeinated drink with a shot of tequila. The only thing saving my ass today is the fact we're playing Boston tonight. It's less likely the team will screw with me now.

Ugh. If only I could delete the memory of washing out to them in the first round of playoffs. They went on to beat the Toronto Twisters in the finals and were rewarded with the Stanley Cup. We were taken out by the best team in the league, but it does nothing to take the sting out of one fact. We weren't good enough.

This year, we have Simon on D and Colton Cermak, he's a great D-man too. He was in contention for the James Norris Trophy before he joined us and is one of the few players on the team to ever make it to the semifinals numerous times. He has experience we can use this year.

On the way to the bathroom, I make a detour to the kitchen where I talk to the chef and Sally. My plan is to ruin Blake's burger, and Sally will bring a second burger to him when the prank is over.

"Remember, he's the one to my right," I instruct Sally as I slip money in her hand.

"Sure, as long as no one complains about me, I'll do it," she replies with a smile.

I convince her she'll be fine, it's just what us jocks do.

I return to the table and banter with the boys. Our loaded tots arrive. I dip mine in the sriracha sauce, enjoying the spicy flavor on my tongue.

"These are crispy, they did a good job," I comment. Blake turns his nose up at the dip.

"How do you eat that?"

"Practice," I say to fuck with him. My stomach is a galvanized steel drum. Blake eats his tots with sour cream and the others lap up what's left of the spicy mayo as our waitress swings by to refill our drinks. She informs us our food is on the way.

I glance at my watch. I have a few hours to kill before my

nap. At home, I'll watch some shows I have in my queue and fall asleep like a baby.

Alexandre mentions how his wife is craving sandwiches loaded with dill pickles.

"There's a way to prevent all that, y'know," I tease him.

"We know you're the team's man whore, no need to brag. You can have all the rights you want. I can't wait for the sonogram to see what we're having," he smiles. No offense is ever taken. He's a great guy, Callie is lucky to have him.

"What do you want?" Finn inquires.

"I don't care. I'm happy with a boy or girl. First one is going to be epic."

"I bet. I can't imagine. I enjoy being married. It's nice to know Rachel has my back and supports me. It's weird to think how much my life changed when we met."

"You're not having a kid, are you?" I panic, thinking maybe it's in the water if two of them are preggers at the same time.

"Oh, hell no, not yet. I'm still young. We have plenty of time."

"That's what I'm talking about. We're young," I reply as our food is delivered.

"Yeah, that was some trip to St. Bart's," Finn adds. "I had a great summer. Why does it feel like it's been a year since I had a month off?"

Finn is our center who covers the ice as a great offensive player. He isn't shy about taking a whack if the puck rebounds. He doesn't mess around over passing.

"Because we're rarely off," I reply. "Besides, if we are in the playoffs this year, our season is longer. Can you imagine the toll of that? I mean, we only got a taste of it last season, and we crapped out in the first round," I add. "We don't know how it will feel until we make it to the end!"

It's still early in the season, the team is starting to jive. I'm optimistic this season will end better. "I hope we win tonight," Sean murmurs, swallowing his last tot and slurping down some soda.

He was at the Celebrity Skate event last year to help bail Wyatt out of deep shit. His face is plastered on billboards, and his reputation isn't... mine. As a right winger, he's young, only twenty-one, and fast as shit. He carries no extra weight and has a dimple in his cheek I'm jealous of. Teams are becoming faster these days and ones with older players can't compete well against them.

There isn't enough booze to wash away bad memories of the past, I don't drown myself in alcohol. However, a win tonight is paramount to everything else, mainly to rebuild our confidence.

Hockey always comes first with me. Women come second, followed by the fun night life and destination vacations in the summer. What's the point of having money if I can't use it? Life is to be enjoyed. Why have money if I can't have the lifestyle?

Our food is placed in front of us. I'm in the middle of putting hot sauce on my burger when Blake spits out the first bite of his.

"Oh, no! Kal! You're an asshole!" He stands so fast his chair tips back and crashes to the floor. The few patrons here look our way, thinking we're assholes.

I stifle a snicker, acting like I don't know anything as he grabs his glass of water and chokes numerous times. His face turns as red as a radish.

"I would use milk instead of water," I caution.

He grabs what's left of the sour cream from the tots, licks the ramekin clean, and drops the empty container on the table.

"What the fuck did you put in there?" Sean chortles, lifts the bun on his burger, checking it carefully before replacing the lid.

"Fuck, what the hell, Kal?" Alexandre checks his food with a subtle glance. "I knew we should have dumped something in your tea," he grumbles at an opportunity missed.

"Just a Trinidad chili pepper. You'll live." I let my snicker express itself.

Blake wipes his face with the closest napkin he can find, and Sally delivers him the second burger, carrying away the one tainted with enough heat to dent my drum.

Blake checks his new burger, promising to get even with me. "Remember, paybacks are a bitch, Kal," he warns.

"Yeah, whatever," I reply with my cocky attitude. I'm lucky. I've been iced the least amount of any player. I always have my guard up and anticipate their next move. It's me, after all. I'm pretty awesome.

After it's all said and done, we have a hearty laugh, replaying Blake's tipping of his chair. I wish I got a picture to plaster on his locker at the training facility.

We throw money in the middle of the table to cover the bill before we leave, knowing we'll see each other later.

My phone dings softly.

I glance at it before I get in my car.

Dad.

He leads with an innocuous text, asking how I am in order to illicit a response from me. Not happening today, or ever.

2

Annie

I can't believe I left Massachusetts General in Boston for Sloane Barber Medical Center in Maine. Hanging out with mom over the summer was great. She set me up with Blake, one of the Maulers. He's a nice guy, but he isn't the one for me. I was relieved to be going back to Boston when I left, and I haven't had a date since. It's November, and I don't care if I have a one-night stand, I need to get laid. Bad. Like, so bad, especially since I had to order a new female appliance, and it hasn't arrived on my doorstep, yet.

By now I should be used to the solitude called my life. I work, eat, sleep, repeat. Mom wants me to meet a man and give her grandkids, and it's mostly why I indulge her when she sets me up on blind dates. It seems I'm the loneliest person on the planet, as everyone wants to set me up.

I just want to meet a nice guy, who is faithful, and hot sex would be incredible. I've heard about it, I've never found it, but I'm still looking. I want to find a man, even if it's only to prove to myself I'm worthy of a decent one. I need to get my itch scratched.

I'm ahead of the game in life, having settled into my career in my late twenties. But I want to be married by the time I'm thirty. That will give me a couple years to make sure the marriage works before we have kids. I love kids.

I must scare off all the eligible bachelors. Career women are often on the shelf. As a doctor, most men assume I'm engaged or married. I don't want to be exempt from love. I miss being in love. I miss the brain fog from the first glance, which leads to the obsession of him in my thoughts all day. The part where I'm crushing on someone to the point of being lighthearted.

I want someone who knocks my socks off and I want to know what it's like to experience the hot, sweaty sex I see in the movies. I want to be dizzy from desire with the 'I want to fuck you now' passion which will render me speechless. I want to abandon all rational thoughts and be carried away because I'm too serious to accomplish this on my own.

I've experienced my share of dates with handsome men as I work with them all day long. Most women swoon over esteemed doctors. I assume there's magic in the power they wield and the way in which they never show emotion. Maybe being unobtainable translates into women speak for a strong and capable man.

This describes my dad to a tee. However, he's only like that with me. He adores my younger sister, Carla, but somehow, I never seem to measure up in his eyes.

I think of myself as being overly practical. I tend to over-think everything and have my life planned out years in advance with a list of goals. Carla is more laid back, a dreamer. I imagine dad has to have some of the dreamer in him to pursue the cup year after year.

I admit I have a difficult time living in the moment. Being spontaneous scares me. I'm the goat climbing steadily up a rocky hillside. I'm too serious and find it hard to laugh at trivial jokes. My brain goes a mile a minute and I'm known by co-workers to perform well under pressure.

I'm a freak of nature, is what I'm thinking as I enter the hospital. My paper cup buckles under the scalding temperature of the dark coffee and burns my hand.

Shit. Thinking fast, I blow on the coffee before I take a few quick sips and toss the rest in a garbage can by the elevator in a heap. I press the button for the second floor and glance at my exercise watch as I wait. I'm early as usual. I slip my hand inside my coat pocket and pull out a tiny square of chocolate wrapped in tin foil. Breakfast.

My new friend, Suzy, greets me as I step onto the second floor. She is single, like me, and sweet. She gave me the inside critique of working here and the heads up on Dr. Fluentes. I've dubbed him Dr. Dick because he acts like one.

"Suzy, how was your night?" As two single women, we have to stick together. Every woman knows a gal has to have a best friend and we always go to the bathroom in twos if we're out together.

"Boring. However, I got caught up on all my series," she replies energetically as her ponytail bobs behind her head. She's into a suspense thriller series and the new season just dropped.

"You must be a happy camper," I reply, knowing full well she enjoyed binge watching the entire season without a distraction. Her roommate is out of town this week.

We stop near the nurses' station to grab our electronic

devices and I check the medical cart for supplies. "Suzy, where the hell are all the four by fours?" We both know they should be here.

"Supply closet," Suzy informs me and says something to a nurse passing by.

"Any plans for the weekend?" I inquire. I should get out of my home to decompress from work. I need a break from the monotony of my life.

"Probably not, unless we take in the new blockbuster movie in the theater," she suggests.

"Normally I would. Funny, I ran into an old face this week. In spite of my lackluster love life, I dated him, and now, he's married," I gasp, rolling my eyes. "Go figure. It's just the way it goes with me. I always date the guy before he meets 'The One,'" I emphasize with air quotes. The nurse returns with the needed supplies, and I place them where they belong.

Suzy leans against the wall in the corridor while I look over the next patient's case.

"You'll know when you meet 'The One,' you just haven't met him yet," she shoves her hands in to the pockets of her white coat.

"Right, well, this friend has me meeting someone tonight. I have no clue who the 'new guy' is, and it's probably a waste of my time. I hate blind dates and yet, I still go. Why?" I ask hypothetically. "I'm too busy for a boyfriend, maybe I should cancel. I have to work tomorrow," I complain because I don't want to play dress up for a date who will be a dud. I'm rambling with my words as I mull my options over in my brain. Being a doctor is easy, rejection and lack of emotions are the real kickers.

"Don't cancel, you want to be married by thirty. Besides,

you need to make friends. Who knows? He might become your best friend and break up your lonely nights spent watching TV reruns of medical shows and eating decadent dark chocolate from Poland."

She looks towards the elevator as it dings and the door slides open. A group piles out, their voices arrive a minute before them.

"I wouldn't tell your date who your dad is. You want to weed out opportunists and losers. Speaking of that, Dr. Dick is coming this way." She stops talking and grabs her portable device from the top of the cart, so she looks busy.

"Fuck me," I groan. How do I get so lucky? Landing in the rotation of the doctor who gets handsy with his underlings is not my idea of fun. How can anyone be so unprofessional?

"Ah, Dr. Susneck, how are you?"

Dr. Fluentes is decent looking, I don't know why he has to be such a perve. He has a way of making innocuous words sound dirty, and he makes my skin crawl. I guess I should be thankful he doesn't work with kids.

"Fine, thank you. Just checking in on our patient who appears to be recovering nicely," I reply, hoping he goes away, the sooner the better.

"Great," he beams, managing to dust my arm with his fingertips as he passes. His male lackeys hang on his every word and pretend not to notice.

"We should report him," Suzy murmurs as she glances down the hall, her eyes boring into his back.

"Right. And get labeled? It's a no-win situation. You said it yourself; we have to avoid getting cornered by him."

"It gets old, doesn't it? In the light of #metoo, don't you think we'd win?" Suzy asks.

"Where's the camera? That's number one. And he's a name, but not a household name. Do we really expect the trickle-down theory to work? In my opinion, it only works when men pee or treat women like door mats," I reply as I review the electronic chart in my hand.

Suzy giggles. "You're pretty funny."

"Hm. Ready for rounds?" I chuckle, remembering the road trips as a kid and peeing in the truck stop bathrooms along the Michigan countryside. Good memories of traveling from one hotel to another for dad's job on the weekends as a coach of a travel team as fun. Dad even coached my sister's team the one summer he had open.

I wish I loved to skate, but I don't. I took lessons, I'm good. I just don't think of broken bones and knocked out teeth as a good time. There might be a subliminal message there. Maybe it's why I love fixing people.

"After you," Suzy buzzes as she sweeps her arm out as if I'm royalty. Humor goes a long way in our world. I reward her with a grin.

It's six in the morning, I should have had a second coffee. Hell, it would have been nice to finish the first one.

Dad put the down payment on my house to entice me to move here. Not that I can be bought by him, however, I have a desire to get to know him again.

My teen years were filled with rebellion, and it spilled over into our relationship. Now, I'm at the age to second guess past events and work on being a better person. We're getting older and I don't want to have regrets I might be able to fix. It's a byproduct of adulting, I guess.

The house has a long list of items requiring attention. All houses are fixer uppers! I'm suffering from buyer's remorse and afraid I've gotten in over my head. Dad loves the house, so do I.

Dad made it to the playoffs last season, and I don't even know the players on his team. Our worlds are light-years apart. Maybe I'm a masochist, thinking things between us will change. How can I gain his attention when he lives, eats, and drinks his job twenty-four hours a day? There's no time left for me.

My sister is the apple of his eye and is checking out colleges for January's admission. She delayed it a semester to spend the summer in Europe with mom.

Living here will give me an opportunity to be around Dad even if it's doubtful he will be able to put work down. Even at family dinners, someone will call and the rest of us will have dinner staring at his empty chair. It's always something.

Is it too difficult for him to validate my existence? 'I'm sorry you feel that way?' or 'I love you?' A hug would be great. I like affection, but he's had me on auto pilot for years.

Any form of validation outside of graduation day is a win. And I want my win, just like Dad wants his.

As a teenager, we moved to Ann Arbor when Dad became the head coach of the University of Michigan's hockey team.

I never thought of myself as pretty. Dad's larger-than-life persona threatened any guy who came close to me. I was off-limits to them. This fueled insecurities about not being good enough, strong enough, or tough enough to win their attention or affection. I couldn't win at home, and I couldn't win when I left it, either.

On a positive note, it made me super independent. I channeled my hurt into focusing on classes and earned college credits before I graduated high school. I fell in love with science and set my sights on a career in the medical field.

I'd love Dad to be there for me, not with his paycheck, but in person, to show up for me. When I had my appendix removed in my junior year, he couldn't make it. He was on an away game, and it hurt. Trying to compete with his team for his attention became pointless. It was easier to disassociate from him rather than risk getting hurt again.

I've waited for a sign to show I matter in his life, only taking the down payment on the house as a sign he wants me to live here and spend time with me. I'm making an effort. Only time will tell if I made the right call.

I know he's going to push hard to win the Stanley Cup again. It's been his dream, like every coach. I swear they have wet dreams over that Cup more than they do their wives who make sacrifices for their dream. Maybe I'm being un-fair. Mom seems happy, she loves the country club and the young players who pay homage to her.

In my defense, I save lives, and I don't need awards. My scoreboard is made up of the patients I heal and who get to return to productive lives. Being a geeky kid with nerd books didn't put me on the cool list getting here. Today, everyone thinks I'm so cool, and yet, I'm still untouchable. I long to be touched, to feel, to be loved.

Suzy and I exit the room after consulting with a patient and push the cart to the next patient's doorway.

"Where is Dr. Dick?" I ask Suzy.

"He got on the elevator with his new team of testosterone.

"Good, I'd say we have an hour or so before he pops up again."

"Just don't get caught alone with him," she reminds me.

"Okay. So, this date tonight, what the hell do I wear?"

"Dressy, not too easy, not too conservative."

"I'm not Goldilocks," I quip.

"Still, to land the right guy, don't be easy. Make him work for you."

"I doubt he'll be someone I want to go home with on a first date."

"No expectations, good," she says nodding her head as we walk.

3

Kal

The game against Boston, is all I can think about. If our opponent gets in our head, we'll be off our game. Every athlete has strong will power as most of our game is that and the fortitude needed to get the job done. Tonight, the Boston Sharks being in our arena is psyching us out.

We aren't ourselves. The locker room is too quiet. Normally, we're joking or getting pumped for the game. I think of it as us, getting in our zone. Tonight, the dark cloud from the past hangs over us like a plague of locusts.

I take it upon myself as alternate captain to talk to the guys and convince them they can win this in an indirect manner because Viktor is the team captain who normally covers the locker room. He took the loss last year hard. He blamed himself for a month. Even though coach preaches to us how every man has to do their job out there, Viktor still blamed himself. We didn't do our jobs well enough, even though we qualified for the semifinals.

Tonight, our state of mind is in the past. It needs to be in the present. I walk around the fancy pregame room, it's pretty with our logo on the ceiling. Our equipment manager puts out our jerseys and equipment, making sure our teammates' gear is where it needs to be as we all have quirks. This room has hooks and not much room to sit. Like I said, it's the showroom for the multi-million-dollar franchise.

"Luc, you can do this, you're the best goalie in the league," I encourage him. Even if he's fine, it can't hurt. To be honest, he's the second best in the league, behind the Shark's goalie.

Luc's no slouch. His wins are just under our opponents, and he wins just as many games by standing on his head when the team under performs. It happens. Everyone has those nights. In those situations, we hope our goalie can save our ass.

"I got you. You just let it rip out there." Luc smiles and knocks his helmet three times for good luck.

Fucking superstitions. But hey, we all have them. I can't judge anyone, it's the same for all athletes, no matter what sport. One of my favorite scenes in the old movie *Major League* is the part where fried chicken is used at the altar instead of sacrificing a live one.

My superstition is drinking a Red Bull with coffee with Alexandre. It's gross, but we do it anyway. I also nap. If I don't sleep, we'll probably lose. Plus, I'm going to be exhausted at the end of the game and that means I won't be going out afterwards. I'm not in a good mood after a loss, so I go home.

I'm always eating. After a game I'm starving so I'll grab take out since everything will be closed except for fast food windows and bars. It doesn't have to be fancy, I'm not picky. However, I'll try to make a healthy choice so I'm not dragging my ass the next day from fried food. I'm not twenty anymore.

"Blake, how's it going, man?" I breeze by my newest friend. He's not been with the team very long, but I like him.

"Good to see ya man," he turns to me as he chugs a water. "By the way, I have someone for you to go out with tomorrow night. It's our day off, so you don't have an excuse."

"I don't need a date," I dead pan. Like, who does he think he is setting me up without asking first? That's a chick thing, a mother thing. I don't need anyone's help.

"Yes, you do. It's painfully obvious your taste in women is deplorable." He gives me his look, the one he uses to call me on my flippant bullshit. "Look, your taste in women is so bad, you need all the help you can get."

"Ha," I puff my chest out, and put my hands go to my hips. "I take offense to that," I reply, suppressing a grin. I love to fuck with him.

"I doubt anyone could offend you," he shoots back, to which I feign a shocked face. "However, she's a nice girl, so you need to leave hockey talk and what you do for a living out of it. Take her somewhere nice. I had a date with her, she's a nice girl."

"You mean, ugly," I scoff. Nice girls aren't front page material if you get my drift.

"No man, seriously," Blake exclaims as he continues to wrap tape on his stick's handle for a better grip.

"Why would I agree to this?" The guys try to prank me because I currently hold the best record for not getting iced in the locker room, or any other shit they pull for that matter.

I'm constantly on guard around the team because of how far we'll go just to get someone, whether it's for a laugh, or to just fuck with someone. I happen to be the most impervious person on the team.

Few of our pranks ever leave our close-knit family. It stays in the locker room, even though we've been known to use eateries, or hotels, as they are places one might not suspect, and we tend to use the same places over and over again. I remain vigilant, knowing the guys are gunning for me.

"You have a woman who's trying to blackmail you with dick pictures, and a video of the night you were at the strip club before our playoff game last season. I would think it's in your best interest to get ahead of it in case it ends up on the GM's desk. Hockey Scoop has feed going to fans 24/7. In fact, I bet they're stalking you as we speak," he half chuckles as a way of saying, 'I told you so,' without actually saying it.

"Oh, that's a good point." He's brilliant. "Okay. We'll talk later." I tap him on the back and head to my peg to put my skates on. I hate Hockey Scoop. They love to get free publicity from publicizing my social life. I have a life; they need to get their own. A date with a wholesome woman might not be the worst idea in the world.

Viktor, our captain, delivers a short pep talk. Coach Susneck enters the room. We freeze, I can feel the air from the overhead vents. No one talks. It's not common for coaches to come in the locker room. The captain handles the team most of the time, but there are no hard and fast rules.

Coach? The man is a God. We love him. We didn't believe we'd make it to the playoffs last year. There was some locker room drama. We lost a player, but we gained a few new ones who filled the necessary gaps in my opinion. The gaps we had were more like chasms! We're bound to do better this year with a stronger defense and if Viktor remains healthy.

Max, our assistant coach, is a good man, rarely raises his voice, and is super positive. He's dedicated. He worked to get the best defensive coach for us and one of our trainers, Nicol, is incredible at helping with strength and conditioning and even helps with rehabbing our battered bodies.

Every year we have injuries and by the end of the year, it's kind of like, who won't be able to play when we get to the next game? The next round? Every team has a list of injuries, some guys can play with theirs, and others have the misfortune of getting sidelined during the final run. It's life in the big leagues.

"Listen up guys," Coach speaks softly. "I know last season is on your mind. I'm here to tell you to forget it. Don't look behind you, move forward. We learned from the losses. Every loss teaches us something. Now, go out there and show them who we are today. Have a good game. And have fun," he finishes, flashing us a smile as he turns to leave the room with our assistant and defensive coach's.

It takes a second for the team to regroup after he speaks, he has a presence about him. We respect him. We don't have to worry about bullshit with him, we know where we stand. He has one rule we never discount; every player has to wear their helmet on our two-minute warm-up on the ice. As coach puts it, I'm not going to be in the hot seat with the GM before a big game to explain why a multimillion-dollar player is not playing due to a concussion protocol from an errant puck.

The room's temperature changes like a thermometer left in the desert. Guys throw some zingers, someone laughs, and before we know it, we're no longer thinking about having our asses handed to us the last time we played Boston.

When I'm in the game, I always know where my teammates are when we have sticks in our hands. I like to analyze things even though my personality is more of an overgrown teenager with money and grown-up toys.

I like to figure out who the puck will most likely boomerang to and get a crack at a rebound if we're in the opponent's zone. Of course, a million other options can happen to the puck, a deflection off the opponent's skate, a tip by a stick. If the ice is super cold, the puck bounces and rolls like a fucking rubber tire flying off an axle while the car is traveling down the road.

I should know, that was me as a teenager. It's what happened when I was too lazy to take my car in for a new tire before shit happened. Luckily, the tire jumped the median and hit the windshield of an elderly couple, but they weren't hurt. Now, I have my pick of sports cars, and the dealer keeps it in pristine condition.

More often than not, a chippy game without good refereeing gets dicey. It's to be expected. I've been at this for many, many years. And momentum changes the entire game. One goal can tip the scale to the scoring team. Being up a few goals can easily come undone in those situations. We struggle in over time.

Those are the oh shit games where the momentum swings to our opponent who just scored, and the next thing we know, we are the ones coming from behind. Drawing penalties off the other team is strategic at times, a power play is an opportunity to score. Last year, we couldn't make them work for us. We aren't perfect. Every team has a weakness. If we can recover where we know we are deficient, we could become the winningest team in our division this year.

I can dream, we all have hope at the beginning of the season we'll end up in the top five by the end of it.

It's time for me to throw my number five jersey over my head. I tug it around my shoulder pads and grab my stick as I walk out the door. We all tap Viktor's gloved hand for good luck as we made our way to the tunnel where we stand, waiting to skate out for our two-minute warm-up.

Our entrance to the ice is only monumental to the fans who stand at glass level and bang on the plexiglass. They yell, I get pumped up even though the stadium only has five hundred people in it. I can't look at the fans as I have to have my head up and my eyes on the ice as we make concentric circles around our one-hundred feet of ice.

Boston skates close to the blue line. It's a line that's never crossed at this juncture. It's an indication the Sharks are going to get chirpy. I could be wrong, if we get in the lead, they might settle for hitting us hard and not gaining penalties.

I make contact with the puck in front of my stick and lob it in the net as Luc is fielding shot after shot. I can tell by his eyes if he's on his game. When he's super focused, he has crazy eyes. They look buggy, wide apart, he isn't looking at the fans. If he moves like a robot in front of the net as soon as the game starts, even better. It's a classic move goalies make in the pros.

If his eyes look in the stands, we're screwed. I wonder if he has ADHD, but on the other hand, goalies are a different breed. And why not? Who wants a puck spinning at 97 miles per hour at your head for sixty minutes? He goal tends most of the games with little rest. Last year, he played in approximately seventy of the eighty-two games.

That's crazy right there. The buzzer makes a sound reminding me of old schoolhouse bells used for fire drills.

We clear the ice. I wonder what fucker is going to screw with our goalie tonight. Every team has players you love on your team but hate to play against. And the Boston Sharks have some of those players on their team.

We constantly move our feet as we stand in the tunnel to keep them from getting tired and to keep blood circulating. It's important we do it as we wait for our mascot, represented by a moose head, painted in our team colors, to be lowered to the ice. The hissing sound of dry ice fills the hallway as it produces fog pouring out of our mascot's mouth and we skate through it, materializing in front of the fans who have suddenly filled the previously empty seats. The crowd goes wild.

Being booed by our fans last year was like pouring salt in an open cut. We were emotionally scarred in that game. We all needed the summer off to recover from our failed attempt to clinch our division.

The sold-out arena tonight sends a message to us, and the energy I feel conveys the fact that bygones are where they should be, forgotten and in the past. We have a clean slate with the new season, but the fans and owner will be waiting to see what we can accomplish this year. We have to prove ourselves, and we have to do it before we reach the halfway mark.

One game at a time is how I roll. No use looking too far ahead, too many variables. I'm not one to stress. We have rivalries where we know every game will become heated due to our history. We have some players who just like to get in another player's face every time we meet. It's part of the sport, and human nature.

I get my share of ice time in the first period. However, I get my elbows under the defenseman guarding me as he chirps, intent on pissing me off. Things get physical.

It's evident they want to rub our face in the past, and we're ready to tell them to go pound sand only I use more colorful words. We're hitting players like we should, we're hustling to be where we're supposed to, and still, this asshole is running his mouth and chopping my stick. It's dangerous and highly illegal.

I'm peeved the refs never call the penalty. I don't want my hand hurt by his bullshit. When the refs aren't looking, I give him a good face washing. The little fucker can smell that the rest of the period.

The game heats up when shoving and chirping on the ice becomes a bone of contention. When bodies start slamming against the boards, it's like a long game of Whacka-Mole, only it's not always our head getting banged, but our hips, knees, and backs.

We're called on high sticking and are a man down when I intercept a pass off of Boston's clumsy line change, leaving three of us in front of their goalie.

I pass to Alexandre and he chucks it back to me and I hit the puck from the crease and watch it slide behind the goalie who is drawn too far to the other side. I know to make it a short-sided attempt without thinking. No one has time to think out here, we've been doing this since we were tykes, we operate on experience, and opportunities. Boston is stacked with young players who are fast.

The light goes off after the puck leaves my stick. The crowd goes wild. The goal puts us up one, with under two minutes to go in regulation time. We haven't done well in overtime wins this year, so we work harder and dig deeper, ending the game 2-1.

The team is pumped coming off the bench. I'm the last to leave the ice because my teammates go before me. One captain runs the locker room, the others, if there is more than one, find a spot to make themselves useful. As much as I talk shit and prank my friends, I have no problem making everyone feel good about our win tonight. If we lost, it's words of encouragement and in the locker room, I'll cheer everyone up with my banter.

Viktor, who makes the first goal, remains by the bench after the game. He's mic'd up to answer the stupid questions the female reporters have to ask. I can only assume they make them ask shit like, "How did you feel when you got the puck in the net?" It irks me. Who the hell is going to say it was terrible?

It also makes women look stupid, asking these questions. I'm sure it's needed for a sound bite for something, but what the fuck? I for one am not a fan of women announcers, but I get it. We knew this day was inevitable years ago when the first female reporter showed in the NFL's locker room. It was before my time, but historical none the less.

For me, questions need merit. Come on, already! We have to be polite and act like we enjoy talking to reporters and all we want to do is sit down, take our skates off and decompress. Instead, we have to stand with our dicks in our hand, huffing and puffing after the game to be interviewed as we get delayed by a commercial break. I picture the fans when I have to do this to make it palpable. I understand I wouldn't have the job I love without fans.

4

Kal

All I can say for Blake, setting me up on this date, might be his undoing. I arrive at the steak house early to check out my alleged blind date. I don't wait at the front, that's for amateurs. Left to my own devices, I'd probably be trouble on a day off, I might as well be here. Thursday nights are for resting as we normally play on Wednesdays.

I'm curious as to what beers are on tap at the bar. I peruse the bottles on the mirrored shelves behind the bustling barbacks, keeping one eye on the door.

It never hurts to be anonymous and check out your date first. I should write a book on how to date. I know all the angles. There is a whirl of motion at the door and turn when the hair on the back of my neck rises, catching me off-guard as I'm in mid-sentence with the bartender.

Curious as to where the cool breeze came from, I notice a tall woman bypassing the maître d'. She has legs that won't quit, and a soft expression on her face as she glances around the immediate area near the bar while small groups stand around like apples on a tree.

'Please let it be her,' is the mantra I'm mumbling in my head.

My first glimpse, aside from her shapely legs, is her hair resembles clover honey, and in a messy bun, a few strands have escaped and fall to her shoulders, curling to frame her face perfectly. It's not a professional hairdo, but she gives me the sexy teacher vibe without the need for glasses.

She stands tall in her heels, and the fact that she doesn't have an hour glass figure doesn't faze me. I'm a boob man. It doesn't hurt she's loaded in that department. She's only two inches shorter than me, but then again, I'm used to models and tall strippers.

She looks around, scanning the room filled with hungry couples and single men perched at the bar, becoming inebriated, and looking at my watch, it's exactly seven.

Instinctively, I know it's Annie. She reminds me of the girl next door, the one you have a crush on knowing you're not good enough, so you keep your feelings a secret, not wanting to risk rejection, or jeopardizing your friendship. Her fall dress fits her to a tee, and from Blake's description, he understated her beauty.

She moves tentatively towards the bar. This is my cue, I move, sleek as a cat, to intercept her. I introduce myself and am able to pull her out of the bustling path of the servers carrying trays. I enjoyed rescuing her and smile.

I'm sure she's able to rescue herself, she's a doctor, after all. She knows a shit ton more than my four-year degree, and I hope I can keep up with her intellect at dinner. Being an athlete, I appreciate doctors, we have one for the team who can stitch us up between periods, and let's not underestimate the concussion protocols.

I don't have to ask her what her name is, but I do, to be polite. I arrived early for a reason. If she was a no go, I planned to slip away unnoticed. It's a terrible thing to do. I rationalize my busy schedule doesn't allow me time to waste on a pointless date, but I'd be lying.

The point is, I never should have agreed to this. I can't believe blind dates still happen, and yet, here I am, feeling the pressure of risqué video tapes from a stripper. And who knows what else I've done when I've been wasted on alcohol.

The evening can go either way. I like working the angles, on and off the ice. I'm running scenarios of the evening in my head, I'm a bit of an aficionado with numbers. It's a skill set I was taught by my father, and I learned it to figure out point spreads in my head at the age of five.

I remain optimistic Annie might be different from my standard fare. I'm willing to find out what she's about. I realize the women in my past loved my lifestyle of debauchery. I'm a jerk only dating women who resemble runway models, adore circling in my world under the media's spotlight, and at times, they exhibit a possessive nature. I like a little crazy, but some are over the top.

However, I am right. Blake under sold Annie, much to my surprise. Maybe he didn't have a connection with her. He ended up marrying Rachel. Supposedly, he only had one date with Annie, which ended with a chaste kiss on the cheek, and no physical contact. It's a bit of a bro's code. We don't poach another man's girl. Blake is now married; nothing stands in my way.

Annie is elegantly dressed in a dark blue dress with a floral pattern. When Blake said she would be carrying a designer purse and wearing matching, red bottom shoes, he got that right. I recognize Louboutin's because I've taken them off plenty of women. I've bought plenty as gifts for girls over the years. It makes them happy, and I don't have to put much thought into holiday gift giving.

I wouldn't be me if I didn't know these things. I have a knack for storing information and reciting lines from movies word by word. I also love to read thriller novels, something I wouldn't be caught doing on a plane with the guys. No, life with the guys is all about sports, babes, boozing, and fucking around with each other.

We're in the warmup phase as we order drinks. She's cute, her round cheeks glow, she seems happy as opposed to the slightly psychotic women I usually date.

"How do you like your wine?" I take charge of the evening. I'm a professional dater. Some might think I'm not that bright because I have large muscles. I don't try to impress her with my body. I want her to get a read on me and decide for herself if she likes me, and if we have anything in common.

"Red, not too sweet," she informs me.

I lean into the bartender within earshot. Wines happen to be in my wheelhouse. It's the latest trend with my teammates, going to wine tastings and ordering cases we love. I'm not a fan of sweet wines either. I order and turn back to my date, offering her a glass of red.

I sniff the wine, and swirl it, before I take a sip. I study the flavors as they linger on my tongue.

She takes a small sip. "Mm. It's perfect," she purrs with a quizzical look, wondering how I got it right out of the gate. God, if wine makes her purr, I wonder what she's like when she's excited by the sight of my hard cock. A jock always thinks with his dick.

The hostess calls for Kal and we follow her to our table where we take our seat and menus are placed before us. The woman who led us here disappears. We flip them open at the same time. It occurs to me this isn't her first blind date, and I don't understand why she needs to be set up unless she's too busy to meet men.

"Do you know what you want to eat?" I glance over the menu and catch her checking me out. I tap my fingers on the menu before I grin to put her at ease.

It's a standard first date. The guys told me to behave myself. If they wanted me to do that, they should be here to babysit me. This babe is smoking. And here I thought they'd fix me up with a stripper as a gag.

"Oh, I love steaks, Caesar salads, and loaded baked potatoes. I must be hungry, because everything on the menu looks amazing."

"Don't hold back, I love to eat. I'm like a cartoon character who thrives on food, and I'm known to raid the fridge. I love leftovers. Basically, I eat constantly."

"So, what do you do?"

"I'm a businessman, I'm on the road a lot." The guys told me to be a normal guy, not a jock, and to avoid the hockey talk. Sounds weird if you ask me, but they have my best interest in mind. My reputation is in the gutter, maybe I get called on it by the GM, maybe not. "How do you like it here?"

"So far, fine. I can't believe I moved further north. My folks are getting older. It's a bit of nostalgia on my part. My mother on the other hand, loves setting me up on dates. She's the definition of a social director."

"It sounds like she loves you very much."

The waitress returns and after conferring with Annie, I order the escargot.

"How do you know Blake?"

"We cross paths a lot."

"He's nice. I heard he got married."

"Yes, Rachel. She's very nice."

The appetizer arrives. I let Annie get first dibs.

I place the starched napkin in my lap and take a bite of the appetizer.

I eat another snail and notice Annie's swallowed one. I like a woman who eats. I'm tired of the models who survive on ice water and Keto bars. "Do you like spicy food?" I'm curious.

"What kind of heat are you talking?" she leans over the table as if she is sharing a secret.

"Hot, like Trinidad hot," I reply.

This girl is something, and it's not just the Double D-cup boobs conservatively put on display as they touch the starched tablecloth. My cock twitches as I keep the conversation on mutual topics, ones worthy of a second date if this goes well.

"Oh, those are enough to send someone to the emergency room. I'll go as high as a ghost pepper. They are good with Bistecca on bread. It's a Brazilian thing."

"Brazilian, huh? How did you discover that?" My interest just went up a few bars. She likes spicy, that's right up my alley.

"Worked with a woman from Brazil. They do amazing things with peppers. Have you ever had them in spaghetti sauce?"

"No, however, I'm willing to try it right after I learn how to boil water," I joke.

She chuckles. I wonder if she'll still laugh when she finds out it's the truth.

The guys mentioned Annie's dad is a bigwig, and she doesn't like to talk about him. They warned me to not to screw this up. Plus, I have a bet with Blake to not talk hockey, and I hate to lose at anything.

The small plates are cleared away and we order dinner. Sure as shit, she orders a steak medium rare, just like me.

"Would you like more wine with dinner?"

"That would be nice. It has a hint of chocolate in it." I detect her voice softening as the conversations takes a natural course. "I love dark chocolate," she informs me.

It's a comfortable first meeting. I've never met a woman who didn't grill me about my dating past and ask me how much I make, and where this is going to go within the first hour.

"Great, then I'll know what to bring you when I piss you off," I jest before I ask the passing waitress to bring a bottle of wine. The night is young and full of possibilities.

"Do you piss women off on a regular basis?"

"At times. It comes with the," I pause, I can't fill her in exactly, "fact I have money and this city has plenty of single women."

Fuck. I sound like a first-class douchebag.

The bottle of wine arrives.

"I didn't mean it to sound so harsh," I continue without putting my foot in my mouth.

"Never thought that about you, Kal," her voice is sweet, not overstated, just the right amount of...well, normal.

Annie and I banter back and forth, and she tells me she loved being on the fast track in high school, slated for medical school.

"Do you have a brother or sister?" I inquire, figuring it's safe to talk about family. "Who would beat my ass for being out with you?" I tease her.

I normally never ask these questions, but I can read her mind, and this question is probably one she would expect.

This is just a blind date, no expectations. And if I keep my career a secret, I win money from Blake. I can't wait for that because I don't make bets I can't win.

"That depends. Have you killed anyone?" she teases, fiddling with her fork. Is she doing that to cope with the sexual tension between us? "I have a younger sister; she's toured colleges this summer, but she's in Europe with my mom, now."

My cock is straining against the zipper in my pants. Thank God there's a napkin in my lap. I'm anxious for the food to arrive before my blue balls explode. Fuck, I never anticipated this blind date going so well.

"I love your blue eyes," she volunteers before she props her elbow on the table and leans her head into the palm of her hand as she gently fucks me with her eyes. Great, she's not a purist for table manners, or hiding our obvious attraction. Neither am I.

"Thank you, I have to say it was easy to pick you out. You have a presence about you when you walk into a room." Normally, I'd say I'm a horn dog and full of shit. However, Annie impresses me as a woman who won't put up with bullshit because my bullshit meter went into meltdown as soon as we said 'hello.'

She blushes. "That's sweet," she replies as she tucks a strand of fallen hair behind her ear. It only makes her look sexier, like a woman who baked all day and still wears lingerie when her man comes home from work, kind of sexy.

"What about you? Do you have family?"

"Yes, my parents are in Cleveland. I have a brother and a sister."

"That's nice. Are you close?"

"Yes. Where did you grow up? I assume most of us in

Maine are transplants from somewhere else now that everything is booming."

"I'm from Michigan, we ended up in Ann Arbor."

"Home of the Wolverines! We hated your team as kids," I
exclaim. Anyone from the area will know of our rivalry for
decades. "I'm from a small town, we lived outside city
limits." I stop short of mentioning the proximity to the
skating rink.

Fuck Blake. Why did he manipulate me into a bet I
couldn't refuse? Even told me to keep my dick in my pants.
Kind of possessive in light of the fact he only had one date
with her and is happily married to a woman who has a best-
selling novel.

"Yes, I love sports, well I did. Then life got busy," she
pauses as if she's reflecting on the past.

Thank you, God. She loves sports! Wait, she's not up
with the times? I heard that. She's out of touch, that's why
she's not asking me a million questions about hockey or
myself, to see if I'm dateable. Maybe this is a good thing?

The truth is, I'm not a redeemable jock. Something
about her is familiar, the shape and color of her eyes.

Hm. I can't figure it out.

"Life does get busy," I chuckle.

Her manicured nails, albeit short, wrap around the wine
glass, creating a desire in me for them to hold my cock. I'm
smitten with the thought of her red nails, any nails, digging
into my back as I give her the best orgasm of their life. I make
sure my women come before I satisfy myself. I'm not a total ass.

She's a far cry from the empty-headed Barbies I typically
date who are getting Botox treatments in their mid-twenties.
Her face is perfect, and I peg her to be close to thirty if she
went to med school.

She's adorable when she states facts in our conversation regarding the need for better health care. Her chin lifts, her face glows. Her award-winning smile is so inviting I want to kiss her perfect lips covered with deep red lipstick. I wonder what Annie is like at a hockey game. The guys told me to not bring it up, it's what lands me in trouble with the crazy chicks.

"Are you settled in at the hospital? I heard you bought a house here."

"Oh, yes. It's a bit of a fix it upper! Old wallpaper to take down, fixtures need to be redone and the entire place needs painting inside and out," she dabs her lips with the white linen napkin and returns it to her lap.

"That's a big commitment, I prefer to write a check and pay someone else to do the work. Do you do it yourself?"

"Oh, painting is easy, but tough on my non-existent nails. They bit the dust the minute I moved in."

"So, you're a go getter," I muse.

She chuckles. "Guilty as charged. Goal oriented is what I call it."

Goal. Interesting play on words. I want to tell her what I really do, however, I bet Blake five-hundred dollars I could go the entire night without telling her who I really am. Now, I'm kicking myself because if she knew who I was, she'd be all over me.

Fuck me.

Our dinner arrives as does the side of fettuccine Alfredo I had to try.

"Oh, that looks so good," she drools over the pasta.

"Help me!" I chuckle, putting some on her plate.

"That smells amazing," her eyes light up indicating she also loves Italian food.

"It's incredible. I've eaten here many times, and it's never been sub-par," I comment.

"Oh," her voice pauses a second as if she's lost in thought.

Shit, did I fuck this up? She's thinking I've been here with other women, and something is wrong with me.

"I don't cook. I come with friends," I add hastily. On the other hand, a jealous woman is a red flag.

"I can't imagine you'd come without a date. We all have a past, Kal, it's fine." Our eyes meet in a knowing stare, and I realize she's genuine. A woman who is secure with herself, imagine that.

Whew. I didn't blow it. Why am I worried about what she thinks?

I love hockey and women, one keeps my feet cold, the other keeps them warm. I sip my wine and watch Annie tip her head back in a pre-orgasmic fashion when she swallows her first bite of the pasta. I almost feel guilty over the fact I'm not into commitment. Why else would one go on a date with a stranger? Is she hoping to find a husband?

Dumb question, what woman under forty isn't looking for a one would be easier to answer.

I'm in a quandary. This first date won't be our last. I'm smitten with her as she twirls her pasta like a professional, savors it and comments on how the cream sauce is sheer perfection.

5

Annie

Leon's Steak House for a seven o'clock dinner sounds fancy for a weeknight. I rushed to get home, shower, and change. I'm famished and pray to God this man doesn't expect to get laid just because he pays for a steak dinner. Been there, and no way am I going to be pressured into anything. It only happened once, and it was because he was strung out on coke. I was afraid of what the alternative would be had I argued. I shake my head. I haven't thought of my freshman year in a long time. I learned the hard way to never let a man I don't know give me a ride home.

Horribly, some men still act entitled in today's world. I slip into my favorite dress, quickly adding a bronzer to my face before I step into heels, making me four inches taller. I hope this man is over six feet. Most men find themselves dwarfed by my height. I glance at my phone, I'll arrive on time, at seven o'clock.

I walk past the busy maître d' at the steakhouse and

survey the room. I have no clue who I'm looking for, Blake told me this guy is ruggedly handsome, in so many words, and has a college education. Rugged as in a lumberjack? What's rugged? Scruff on the face?

It can't be that hard to find a single man my age in this establishment reeking of wealth and old money. I've never been here, but Suzy looked it up online, and it's impeccable with five-star ratings on the foodie's website. As long as he doesn't get handsy, I won't bite.

The aroma of grilled lobster and steaks greets me as I saunter to the bar. A handsome man intercepts me, flashing me a smile full of teeth. His chiseled chin and thick black hair are nice features, but his eyes suck me in. For whatever reason, I find myself returning his smile.

"You must be Annie." He slides his hand into mine. "Kal."

"Kal," the word leaves my lips like droplets in a damp fog. Was that the man's name? I should be better with blind dates by now. With zero expectations, I find I brush off details I should have remembered.

"Annie," I reply as I force my hand not to go limp as I lose myself in his dreamy blue eyes with flecks of yellow. Subtle, and sexy, with a twinkle of mischief. His hair is straight, slicked back as it accentuates his angular cheek bones.

He gently places a hand under my elbow and steers me out of the way of incoming servers with heavy food trays.

"Thanks," I murmur, wondering how he's so quick to surmise a situation.

"Drinks? Our table will be ready in a few minutes," he informs me.

"Sure, dry red wine, please."

I don't object when his hand remains on my elbow, and I walk with him to the bar made of mahogany.

He orders drinks, hands over a credit card, and turns around, handing me a red. I lift it to my nose, breathing in the tannins with a hint of chocolate. Perfect.

"Nice to meet you, by the way," he taps his wine glass to mine, "To new acquaintances."

"To new acquaintances." I sip the flavorful wine. It's very tasty... perfect, actually. I need to find out the brand before we leave. This place is upscale, I bet the wine is limited to select restaurants, and can only be purchased through a wine rep.

"So, tell me something about yourself," Kal states.

I'm used to men asking how I like being a doctor, so this is refreshing. Excitedly, I meet his look halfway through my long eyelashes and saucer shaped eyes, a gift from my dad.

"Mm. Let me think. It's been so long since a man asked me anything about myself." I sip the wine, and enjoy the lingering taste on my parched lips.

"That's a shame." His eyes make me uncomfortable in a good way. He's pushing all the right buttons. The smooth moves, the suave first impression, and the wine on an empty stomach all go straight to my head.

"Thanks, well. Maybe it's my fault, I'm pre-occupied with work."

"I heard you recently moved to Maine. You have family here?"

"Yes, I came from Boston."

"Yikes, that's a very reputable city for doctors," the half smile on his lips tells me it's a compliment when most would assume I've traded down in my medical career.

"Really?" How does he know this? "Did Blake give you a cheat sheet?"

"No, but I wish he had," his insinuation warms my heart. "You look familiar, have we met before?" I veer my eyes from his, he's incredibly observant. So much so, it scares me and excites me at the same time. I press my lips together with apprehension.

"No, I would have remembered." I deflect him with my reply. How many times have I been told I have my dad's eyes? He's on TV all the time. Kal is probably a Mauler fan. Everyone in Maine is a fan, it's always cold and hockey is king.

Shit, I just want to be me tonight. Is that too much to ask? One night of freedom and debauchery, a get out of jail free card.

The bar is crowded, we've stepped aside at the same time, to let others order. Alcohol flows from the tap and bottles, voices mingle with casual conversation and pickup lines.

We've moved, and yet, we're still standing in each other's space. I'm rattled, deciding to swill the wine and stare into the mini ocean of red inside my wine glass.

We're called to our table, and a wave of relief engulfs me. I'm no longer under his acute scrutiny. How am I getting through a two-hour dinner with this man who could be on the cover of a man's fashion magazine?

I've been around handsome men before, but having met Kal, I decide he is the one man who would give me a reason to get out of bed in the morning. Or remain in it, if I'm being truthful.

Suzy was right, I don't need to advertise the fact my dad is the Maine Maulers head coach. I have to ensure the man who wants me, wants me for me, not access to my dad and free games. It's the safest move.

Meanwhile, I don't know if I'm getting tipsy on the wine,

or Kal's cologne. It's my first date as a new resident of Maine, with an eligible man, who has potential. I need to slow down on the wine as my stomach is empty, there is no need to do a face plant in the appetizers. How trite can I be? That would go down in the books as the worst date ever. I move my shoulders back, no longer being conscience about my height walking next to him and we converge on our table.

His blue eyes grow darker as the evening progresses past the initial small talk. Why am I a sucker for blue eyes? Are his eyes turning my insides to goo? Or the thought of what he's packing under his tailored shirt and jacket?

The warmth of the alcohol mixes with first date jitters. My heart is thumping faster than normal. I might need to have it checked, there is no way I'm so lame, losing my shit over a man's handsome face. Although I find his charming disposition contagious.

He puts me at ease with his poised, relaxed temperament. I like him leading the conversation. Maybe that's the trick with dating, make it fun. I've been looking at it as a hardship. A chore to cross off my list, as I'm always rushed.

His white shirt looks expensive, and I note the blue stretchy material of his jacket emphasizes his strapping torso and bulging biceps. I don't want to pry into his life; however, he must make good money to afford his wardrobe and the hours spent at the gym.

This is probably a one and done date, most blind dates are. I refuse to get my hopes up, choosing instead to enjoy the ambiance, sipping my wine as he refills my glass.

A quick glance around the room reveals women checking him out, and a few men, too. Sure, he's gorgeous, and sitting across from me, I can tell he's not fazed by the spectators he's ignoring.

What would a relationship with him be like, I wonder?

Blake has a plethora of friends and business associates; I'm not complaining about the eye candy aspect. It beats spending another night staring at cartons of leftover Mexican food and moldy salsa in my fridge.

Our waitress comes and goes without much fanfare, a pro who knows we're lost in bantering as we discuss the menu before we order our entrees. The appetizer soaked up some alcohol, and before I know it, dinner arrives.

I'm happy he shared his Alfredo with me, not only is it amazing, it added a level of intimacy to our date. He's not selfish with his food, another plus. I love to sample new recipes even if I don't have time to cook, I like the methodical nature of cooking. I cut into my steak, to find the succulent first taste is sex on a stick.

Our eyes catch over the meat, we're both carnivores judging from his smirk. I nibble at my baked potato, I was so hungry. Now, I'm stuffing myself, not wanting the night to end. And, holy moly, some of this food is going home with me.

Kal hasn't raised any red flags. When we finish eating, I excuse myself to use the restroom and check in with Suzy. In today's world, it pays to be safe, one never knows with all the posers out there. Blake is a man of stature in the community, I assume he knows the man he set me up with tonight.

I didn't tell mom about the date. She can be a real nudge when it comes to my love life. She drops comments like rain drops regarding her desire for grandchildren.

"Suzy, he's great. I'm obsessing over him. My hormones are going nuts. I don't know if I'm making good conversation or if I'm gushing because he's awesome. Is this a panic attack?"

"No, it will pass. Take a deep breath."

I suck in air and blow it out slowly. I know this, why can't

I apply this knowledge myself? I've never had an issue before. Maybe it's too much change at one time. I wasn't planning on meeting someone who is dating material, maybe even husband material. I can't fuck this up and tell myself to calm the fuck down.

"Better?" Suzy asks with a nonchalant voice. Of course, she can be calm, she's not in the hot seat.

"I think so. This place is amazing. Incredible food, wine. He's probably married," I mumble, pacing the chic gray and white tiled bathroom floor.

"Blake wouldn't do that to you," she counters, "he's a nice guy from what you told me. He didn't expect anything from you on your date."

"You're right. He knew I was the coach's daughter and was breaking the rules to date me. He was just accommodating my mother," I interject.

An older woman washing her hands hears me and is trying to suppress a grin. She's petite, dressed in a matching suit—old enough to be my grandmother. Lucky duck, she doesn't have to go through this anymore. She's in the safe zone, married or widowed, she can sail off into the sunset and no one will pressure her for anything.

"Pee and go back to him. See you in the morning."

"Okay, bye."

I pee quickly, not wanting to be away too long and alarm him. If I'm being honest, he's drop dead gorgeous, and it's doubtful he's into a girl like me. I noticed how the women in the room checked him out. He may be too good to be true. I should have grilled him with more questions. Suzy told me dating is a dance, and to curb my inquisitive nature. She reminded me to just have fun.

It's not easy for me to be carefree and go with the flow.

The journey doesn't lead me, I lead it. I need to know where I'm headed at all times.

I smile as I look at myself in the mirror, not bad. My dress is amazing and fits perfectly. Tonight wasn't as nerve wracking as I made it out to be. We're two professionals doing normal things. It's just food and polite conversation. He listened to me. For a first date, the evening went well. Did Blake put thought into this to fix me up? How would he? He doesn't really know me.

Suzy accused me of scaring guys off because they like the game, or dance, as she refers to it, and I tend to rush to the ending. I'm an efficient person and I want to know everything about someone on the first pass.

I hate playing games, and besides prom, never have I ever danced slow. Playing games should be reserved for Monopoly or Risk. I hate waiting and never fail to rush the games to find out who wins.

Fuck risk, on both accounts, I snicker as I dry my hands and proceed back to the table. My heels click over the tiled floors, my eyes search for the blue ones I can't wait to see again. Kal's sitting at the table, swirling remnants of wine in his glass, a pensive look on his face. He flips open the leather folder containing the bill, then closes it as he waits. I notice a paper bag with handles sitting where my plate used to be. He saved my leftovers for me.

I melt. He's thoughtful. He read my mind.

My breath catches in my throat.

I hope there's a second date.

"There you are. I took the liberty of packing your leftovers," he smiles.

Fuck me, he's had a happy demeanor all night, and I'm smitten with him.

"Thank you," I reply as I sit. I catch the woodsy, citrus

smell of his cologne as I passed him. It's not overpowering and compliments his personality.

I smooth my dress under my butt and watch him swig the last two sips of wine, his smooth face and neck convey strength and brawn. I reach for my water. I need to put out the fire in my panties. They say hydration is always beneficial.

"Are you ready to go?" his eyes soften; his confident voice is easy to listen to as he patiently waits for my reply, another good quality in a man. My dad is calm too, a good balance for my personality.

I'm not one to wait for the right moment to say things, I blurt them out. Dad is more reserved, waiting for the right moment and coming at issues with thought and resolve. An admirable quality in a coach.

"Sure." I slide my purse over my shoulder. We stand at the same time; I wobble on my heels. His arms catch me with a half embrace. I find myself staring into the eyes of a woman at the next table who sends me a knowing look, she accepts us as an adoring couple.

I give her a half smile, enjoying the fact I have a date and she approves of us. Not that it matters, however, the feeling of validation isn't lost on me.

My face must be red judging by the heat I feel. Normally, I'd be embarrassed, but Kal isn't fazed. "I can't have you getting hurt on my watch," he teases, pulling me closer to him.

Our eyes meet. We have a moment. I sense our guards are down, and we understand the flicker of our mutual attraction passing between us like a HVAC electrical cord. My pussy clinches, I feel the wetness in my lacy panties. It's been so long between dates; I can't deny how horny I am.

The tension ebbs as his warm lips meet mine in a gentle

kiss. My knees buckle, I slide an arm up to rest on his meaty bicep where I use him to steady myself as our closeness leaves me trembling. He breaks away, ending our kiss. The fleeting seconds were too short.

His chest moves away.

No! I want more.

"That was nice," his deep voice murmurs close to my ear.

"Yes, it was." I mumble, stunned by the animal magnetism. I want to rip off his shirt and run my hands over his chest. I desire his solid arms around my body again, and wish to stroke his muscular back.

Like a bear out of hibernation, I'm awake and hungry. I retract my hand and stand on my own as he slides his arm through mine. It's as if we're back in the nineteen-forties when the man escorts his lady to tell the world she's mine.

I stand taller, gaining confidence in the possibility of the night not ending in the parking lot.

He opens the glass door for me, and we step into the crisp night air.

"Where are you parked?"

"This way," I point toward my vehicle and shiver from the damp, cold October air. I should have brought a coat.

"Can I call you again?" he asks with a debonair tone as we stand at my vehicle.

Buddy, call me anytime.

"Yes." My butt rests against the door to my Mercedes. It's dark, the ambiance of the lake we never noticed reflects the moonlight.

My heart pitter patters.

"I should..." I begin to speak. He silences my next word with his lips. This time, he's more insistent, and demanding and I meet his enthusiasm as he slides a hand behind my neck. His strong fingers holding me just right. No man has ever done this before. It's a bit scary. Possessive. But, I like it.

A groan full of simmering passion escapes my throat. I can't think. His hard cock presses against my abdomen. I love tall men. He's strength, virility, and protection all rolled into one plus, he's a great kisser, my lips will be swollen after this.

His tongue enters my mouth. I don't protest. I sense his unwillingness to touch my body, deciding to not risk it on a first date.

"Can I follow you home?" he asks casually.

"Yes!" I gasp, surprising myself. I'm not supposed to put out on a first date, but I can't help myself. I want this as much, if not more, than him.

6

Annie

He follows me home, I'm nervous. I become overly cautious at road signs. I chastise myself for being easy. Is it a hard and fast rule men won't call if I don't play hard to get?

It's too late. We park at the back of my house. He meets me at my car door.

"You're very pretty, Annie." He slides his arm around my waist. I'm nervous as I unlock the door and even though the porch light is on, I can't find the damn keyhole.

"Let me," he offers. I hand the keys to him, being careful to not touch his fingers. I need to pace myself.

The door swings open.

"Do you want a drink?" I walk in first and drop my blue purse on the couch. I only have two outfits with matching handbags and shoes, tonight's was one of them. I don't know why I knocked myself out for a stranger, but now, I'm glad I did.

He pulls me into his arms, not like a caveman, but definitely the man in charge. His lips find mine in the dim lighting.

"I want you," he proclaims, and I know I made the right decision. I can't deny our attraction. I don't want to, if this is wrong, fuck being right. If we never have a second date, so be it. I need this. I need him. My biggest concern is the fact my panties might slide down my leg before he pulls them off. My lady bits are so wet, my underwear is saturated to the point of no return.

Kal's hungry lips ravage mine, thrilling me to no end. His hand grabs the back of my neck to hold me where I stand as he slides his suit jacket off. It falls to the floor. My hand grabs his crotch over the material of his slacks and his cock is huge, but he's still pent up.

We're separated by the thin material and I'm growing impatient, caught up in the end game, the one where I come to high heaven. I'm impatient to have him in me.

His guttural groan confirms his arousal, he's digging this too. His kisses move down to my neck, he suckles my supple skin and gives me a nip, shocking and exhilarating me at the same time.

My pussy gushes.

I step back, towards the steps; he unzips my dress and the clunk I hear tells me his shoes were kicked off. He peels my dress off, letting it drop without a care. I should pick it up, it's expensive, but it would kill the mood. He unclasps my bra with one hand and my ample breasts tumble into his large hands.

I'm delirious, locked in a place where it's the two of us without my compulsion to over think the situation.

I relax, trusting him with my body as the soft light from the adjoining kitchen keeps us from stumbling over my boxes and sparse furniture. I unbutton his shirt and it slides off with ease, revealing his broad shoulders and a chest covered with the perfect amount of hair. I slide my fingers over his rigid abs, he has a line of hair leading to his cock. I rub my hand firmly over his bulge, maybe making him wait will push his buttons like he pushed mine.

"Ah," he sighs as I'm feeling his cock and wonder when we'll go upstairs to the bedroom.

I tease him with my hand, but make no move to release him of his need to free the stallion in there. His cock was huge, but now it's positively engorged. His teeth graze a nipple, his tongue flicks the other until it stands at attention. He rubs it between his finger and thumb until I gasp. Then he adds more pressure, making me rise on my toes.

He shifts on his feet, taking one breast into his mouth, suckling on it with enough vigor to constrict my uterine muscles. Holy, mother of God, this is so...

My head rolls back. I'm limp, a rag doll in his hands. He moves me to the futon and with one hand, he swipes the overstuffed pillows on it to the floor, making it evident this is the place we'll use. I stand, dressed only in my panties. He takes my shoes off, one at a time, caressing my foot before he runs his hand gently up my leg but stops short of touching my triangle.

Holy fuck.

This is cruel. He's making me wait!

I grab his hair. I want his lips on mine and his cock in me. I need him more than ever. I refuse to have another night with my vibrator.

I expect his hair to be stiff with the gel to keep it perfectly in place, but it gives way, becoming pliable under my fingers. My hands sink into the thickness of his dark locks. I run my fingertips through his hair and down his neck as he lowers his lips to claim mine.

"You make me so hard," he murmurs as I unbuckle his belt. He pulls his pelvis away from me and I wonder how we'll fuck on this shit furniture. I hear his zipper; he tugs his slacks until they are off. He's commando, and the notion of this excites me as my hands fly to his buttocks. The few nails I have dig into his flesh. He winces, then flashes me a smile.

"You like this, huh?" With a half grin on his face, he's a man I have to fuck, the anticipation is driving me insane.

"Mm." I purse my lips, not wanting to give him the satisfaction he craves.

He tugs my panties off. "I want you to sit on my face."

"What?"

"You heard me."

Oh, thank God I had a Brazilian wax job this week. It pays to keep the patch landscaped.

He lies on his back; the cushions sink under the weight. His hand gently tugs at mine and pulls me into a position whereby I'm straddling him.

"Incredible," he breathes as his hot tongue touches my inner sanctum. My hands fly to the side of the Futon couch, my fist clinching from the pleasure ripping through me. It's been so long, and I could pop at any second so I will myself to not come when I hear him murmur, "You taste so sweet."

His tongue moves around my labia and flicks my clit. As he licks and rubs my nub with his thumb, I gush over him; he laps it up. My body begs for more.

"Don't come," he orders.

"Well, stop making me," I argue.

He chuckles. "Fine, get on the floor."

My first inclination is to ask why, but he has a way of making me forget reason. I comply, move to the floor, and lay on my back. I've always been so convential.

"Doggie?"

I don't have one, oh, right.

I move to my hands and knees.

He runs his hand up my back, the palm pushes me a bit as he plays with my clit as he's situated behind me. Next, he's rubbing his dick over it causing my back to arch. God, I just want him to fuck me, to feel the release I need to let out, to scream, to yell, to get off on him.

I want to shout, 'fuck me,' but suppress it.

He enters me and I gasp. It's intense, taking him in. He's gentle. I can understand why. He pumps me from behind and my hands reach for the area rug for traction, my fists clench the fibers. I realize I might walk funny tomorrow. I've never had it this rough before, but fuck, it feels so awesome.

Pleasure runs up my spine and clit, and when I think I can't bear it, and I'm about to protest waiting, he flips me under him. Our eyes meet as he lays over me, one arm extended as if he's going to do push-ups, the other is gliding his thick cock into my opening whereby he teases my clit.

He runs himself over my opening. My body has a mind of its own. I squirm. He gives me pleasure and torture at the same time. I raise my hips to meet his, anxious to have him sink deeper into me.

"Hold on. Baby. Just enjoy."

I can't pull back, I want to, but I want him as much as I've ever wanted anyone in my life. Maybe more so. I pull his chest hair to bring him closer. He appeases me, gently entering me slowly. I hear myself letting out a long moan. He fills me completely. I'm so tight it would have been painful if I wasn't already lubricated.

He thrusts once more, entering me completely as I cry out in euphoria, suspended on the cusp of an orgasm. The chemistry between our bodies ignites into flames as we grope, grab, tug and lick each other. No skin within reach is left untouched.

Our eyes meet again and exchange something. I'm not sure what. His gaze makes me vulnerable.

His hand softly strokes the side of my face, and his eyes meet mine as he thrusts again and again. I swell with pre-orgasm quivers. He slides over me, prone, like a cadet, moving himself in me from different angles to rub my G-spot and I'm surprised to find I have others I never knew existed.

I wither beneath him. My arms have become noodles struggling to hang onto him as he thrusts into me faster and faster.

We're in sync, climbing to epic proportions, his hand grabs a breast, he tweaks my nipple just right, causing me to explode. I'm riding the wave as it takes me higher and higher. I'm panting, tears form in my eyes, it's so incredible.

He caresses the side of my face, watching me come all over him, he lays over me reaching his peak, but reaches down to rub my nub causing me to come again as he shudders, groans, and comes, dumping his seed in me. Drops of drool fall on my neck as he lifts his head.

"Sorry about that," he smiles.

Fuck me.. I came twice, is that normal?

He pauses, remaining still for a long minute. My palm feels the vibration of his heart before his chest stops heaving. He regains his breath and pulls out, sliding his swollen cock out of me, much to my disappointment. I want to stay in the cocoon of warmth filled with lust. I liked how he made love to me. It wasn't the hurried affair I expected. He's an expert lover.

"That was epic," he murmurs.

Now comes the real reason for regret. I should have held

off, made him work for me, made sure he's real, see if we have a future. How many other women has he been with? Does he have a ton of women he hooked up with in his phone waiting for him to call?

My thoughts disappear when he pulls me into his arms. I resist my impulse to fight him because I've already let him in. I lay my head on his chest.

He's fun, even exciting, and he makes me forget all the to-do lists circling in my head all the time. I spent the evening breaking my rules and oddly, I'm okay.

I smile, his cologne wafts over me as I close my eyes.

I WAKE, and it occurs to me I'm in my bed. A memory of him carrying me up the steps makes my eyes fly open. It's almost dawn.

His arm is draped over me. I remain motionless, not wanting to wake him, but it's Friday and I'm working so I can have Sunday off. Carefully, I turn my head to observe him. His chiseled chin and long lashes are a sight to behold. His tussled hair is long enough to tuck behind his ears.

My phone blares with the Marvel comics theme song.

Shit! It's downstairs in my purse.

Fuck, fuck, fuck.

Kal wakes. "Is that your phone?"

"Yes, sorry," I rollout from under his arm and leap from the bed. He looks puzzled but doesn't question me as I grab an oversized sweatshirt to pull over my nakedness. I bolt from the room to answer Suzy's call. I listen to her message checking in to make sure I'll be at work.

I text her I'm fine and will see her soon.

"Everything okay?" he yells.

"Yes, my friend is checking in with me," I reply.

"Come back to bed," he implores me. A male voice in my house is a welcomed addition. Maybe a serious relationship isn't out of the question, I like him here.

I return to my room and find him leaning back on his pillow. I pause, taking in the view of him in daylight. Splendid in all his glory, he turns his head, smiles at me and judging from the tent he makes with the sheet draped over his lower body, he's sporting morning wood.

"I have to work." I try to hide my smile by covering my mouth with my fingers.

"Surely, you don't have to be at work in the next fifteen minutes. A quickie? You see, I have this problem," he grins impishly.

"I see your problem, and it's a big one," I chuckle.

"You gonna help me? Or is it shower time?"

God, damn. He means business.

"When you put it like that," I drag out the words to tease him. Overnight, I've become a greedy woman with needs.

I never knew being naughty could be so much fun.

He rolls onto his stomach and reaches for me with his long arms. I walk to the bedside; he pulls me into him. My king-sized bed never looked so small.

I let out a squeal as I crash into him, he breaks my fall with his strong arms and pulls me back to bed, we're on our knees where we pretend to wrestle as our mouths and hands tease each other. We kiss, our tongues find each other, and I give him the upper hand. I imagine this is what I might have had in high school had I had a boyfriend.

He kisses my neck, sucking gently, and trailing kisses down to my breasts as my fingers entwine in his thick hair, and I tug on it gently as I lean back and close my eyes, giving into the explosive sexual tension between us. He cups a breast and gently gives it a nip, in which I let out a yelp.

"Sorry," he murmurs, as his hand makes its way down the side of my body, the other reenforces my back. He returns his hand to my breast and when he flicks his thumb over it numerous times, it becomes hard under his strong fingers, he gently squeezes the nipple tweaks and I giggle, pulling back as a defensive move and cover them with my hands. I've left my belly exposed and he rakes his fingers ever so lightly over my untanned skin. The sexual tension builds, but his touch on my abs makes me shiver.

He uses his fingertips expertly as he attacks my sides, tickling me like we're two kids playing, and he doesn't seem to care my waistline isn't a twig. I giggle like a toddler. He has me over a barrel before his soft, sexy mouth lets out a chuckle, his deep voice turns me on. "I got you," he exclaims.

I slap his muscular ass, surprising myself. He feigns a look of shock, then flashes me an approving smile.

He tackles me like a linebacker, and we both sink into the large bed.

He grabs the covers, tosses them in the air as if to make a tent, then quickly dives under them before they float over us. We're hidden from the world. His warm lips find my pink folds between my legs, his tongue giving me a refresher course in patience as he sucks on my wetness. I gush like a grape, squirting in his mouth as I hover in limbo, waiting for an intense orgasm to carry me over the bridge.

"I could eat you all day," he says before he flicks his skilled tongue over my clit until my back arches and I moan. It's sheer punishment.

"I want you in me," I squirm beneath him. I want him to fill me with himself. I need the release.

One morning rushing to work won't kill me. But the intense orgasms might.

Kal straddles me. "Are you sure?" He baits me.

"Yes!"

He grabs his hard cock and circles it in my opening, I spread my legs, wanting more of him, and preparing myself for his very large cock. I clutch the sheets, strangling them with my anticipation as pleasure builds like a forceful tide inside me.

"Ah," I gasp as he enters me. I grab his back as he begins with a slow methodical motion as he eases himself in me. I take all of him. My endorphins rush. I wonder if my clit will get enough friction to get off as his cock doesn't leave much room for movement.

He lays prone over me, moving faster and faster, I grasp his meaty upper arms to withstand him pumping into me as we both break the wall between us. As it crumbles, we connect, our eyes meet, an intense connection transpires before I explode over his cock, experiencing numerous orgasms and he releases himself in me, the warmth adding to my mine as we climax together. I let out a blood curdling yell as I soar to the stratosphere. My voice is loud enough to rattle the windows as I hear myself and realize no man has ever made love to me like him. I never knew my body would perform like this. That sex could be so addicting. I've discovered a new world.

His fluids slide down my leg.

"Shower?"

"Sure," I reply, grabbing a few tissues from my nightstand and dabbing between my legs. My God, he shot one hell of a load.

The communal shower was a first for me. He lathered my body and tweaked my nipples covered in bubbles. We

French kissed under the streaming water. It's as if we've always been this way with no awkward moments.

It's refreshing to not do everything by myself. He started the shower, grabbed the towels, bathed me. He even dried me off kissing my curvy body and makes me forget my thighs aren't those of a younger woman. He kneads the bottom of my feet sending shock waves to my pussy. I didn't know it could be such an erogenous zone, I sigh. Every time he touches me, desire wafts over my pussy, making me insatiable.

Once he's finished with me, he disappears downstairs, and I apply lotion to myself and begin to dress. I hear the pod go into my coffee machine. He returns with coffee and is dressed in last night's clothes.

"I'll let you get ready for work. I'll call you later," he drops a kiss on my lips. I sip my coffee as the sound of the back door clicks behind him. A super charged engine rattles his muffler. I walk to a window across the hall to catch a glimpse of him. I observe two red LED taillights as he breaks before entering the main road.

I lean against the windowpane and replay moments of us.

Will he call? Do I tell Suzy?

I glance at my Gucci watch, shit! I need to get going and snack on something.

It's only now I realize I forgot my leftovers on the table last night.

Crap.

7

Kal

I return home with the sun in my eyes. A normal night for me. However, this is the first time in which I am in my home and the emptiness of the house hits me. I like order and Annie's house is anything but orderly. The futon made sex a challenge, so I improvised, hoping I didn't scare the shit out of her.

Sitting at the counter in my kitchen, I drink a cup of coffee. It's a huge island in the center of the kitchen. I glance at the built-in shelf for my copper skillets, each with a slot to house them, and they mock me. They look pretty and perfect. Ironic, all that money spent for the housekeeper to dust them.

I check social media on my phone and the Mauler's site is advertising the huge annual fundraiser for the Make a Kid Smile, the non-profit organization this weekend. It's an event where we hob knob with donors, boosters, corporations, and teammates, complete with wives and girlfriends. I ponder the thought of asking Annie to go with me.

She's not my girlfriend, but I'll make points for taking her to a fancy gala with the team. She'll fit in and, more importantly, be impressed. It's short notice, but I'm sure she's resourceful enough to obtain a gown. If that's an issue, I have connections to help.

Why am I knocking myself out? I shrug it off without an answer and head to the gym, where I meet Nicol. I constantly work to improve on my game. Who doesn't want to skate faster? We know what to do, however, form is everything and not worth risking an injury, especially when we have staff to help. I use a trainer when I do Bulgarian Split Squats. They can be tricky, but they build my glutes.

We have a game tonight, and I hope stretching this morning will help my sore muscles. The Boston game got chippy, and when that happens, we all get banged up.

"Morning," I greet Nicol as I enter the gym.

"Hey, Kal, how are you?" Nicol is wearing the Mauler track suit and gives me the rundown of my workout this morning.

"Fine, thanks, ready to work." I hit the mats to warm-up my muscles. Afterwards, he spots me with the squats.

I pick twenty-pound weights, Nicol has the mat in place, and I stand the way I'm supposed to as he checks my form.

"Hips are aligned, that's good," he says as he feels both sides of my hips for placement. "Lunge. Do you feel it in your glutes?"

"Yeah," I reply as I dip, causing my muscles to quiver with fatigue. Fuck me, this is intense, and I'm not even at the extremely advanced level.

"Stick your hips back, feel the glute," he says. The man is methodical. After a few reps, he hands me thirty-pound dumbbells. This ramps things up considerably. Some guys do them holding weights and front loaded.

"Ugh," I groan. I'm not into this today. Why did I go out last night? Beef, alcohol. I should still be sleeping.

He chuckles, "Wait until we add more weights."

The things I do for my job. I wouldn't trade it for anything. 'I was born to do this,' I replay this phrase over and over in my head to psyche myself to get through the pain of fatigued leg muscles.

Kinda like the social functions in which attendance is mandatory. Sure, we get a night of dinner and dancing at the River Walk Hotel, the newest hotel overlooking Moose River. The black-tie event would mean Annie has to get an expensive dress on short notice. I only know this as I hear the guy's groan about their wives shopping for these situations on top of the other WAGS events such as bridal and baby showers. Yuck.

"Nicol, do you have to give a woman a long notice for the gala?"

"Ha, if you want her to go, probably. Why?"

"Met a cute girl, thought I'd invite her. I rarely bring girls to these required attendance events." I take another dip into a lunge and gasp for air to feed my new muscles.

"You are the revolving door alright," he agrees with a smirk. No doubt he's heard about my wild nights at clubs. "The sooner you invite her, the better. She would probably love the gala. Is she into hockey?"

"I'm not sure."

"Guess you'll find out," he changes his voice from being a friend to that of instructor. "Okay, time to take a rest and then one more set."

I put the weight down, take a few breaths, and walk around before returning to finish my last set. After a few leg presses on the machines and lunges, I'm ready to call it a day.

I text Annie before I leave, wanting to know if she made it to work on time.

Yes, busy day. She replies in ten seconds.

Hm, must not be a 'rules' girl, she's supposed to make me wait before she returns a text.

Me, too. Working out at the gym. I text back.

I don't know much about her. There is only one way for me to find out more.

Would you join me for a function I have to go to on Sunday?

I'd love to. But I have plans with my dad. Now I know she's seeing her dad, I assume they must be close.

Raincheck?

Sure.

Now I have my answer. Do I call a backup date or go stag? It's not like Annie and I are official.

I know the guys will be with their wives and even though we're not serious, I call Rebecka, Becka for short.

"What's up, Kal?" She answers on the third ring. It's what I expected. She likes making me wait. She's never on time to go out either. I think it's her way of being in control. The games people play. We do make a nice-looking couple, but relationships have to be more than skin deep.

The guys sent think I'm capable of anything more, they might be right. The part they miss about me is I'm smart and see through everyone, even if I go out with girls who are superficial, I know what I'm getting into.

"Not much," I reply. "I wanted to know if you are in town." She's a weather announcer on our local channel in Maine.

I never know what's up with weather, it's not on my radar. If there is a huge storm on the coast, or a blizzard, she travels to put herself in the middle of it. I respect her dedication to her profession and putting herself in danger like that even if it's for ratings.

She has to be careful with her reputation, and it's often the reason she breaks it off with me. I don't make it easy for her to hold her head high when I party all night with the guys, and it gets splashed across social media and reaches international news.

"Yes, why?"

I hate when she's coy with me. Maybe we're both into lip service and if so, we're never going to move forward in our complicated relationship. It's always on and off. She wants to settle down, I don't. She's not the one for me, I should tell her how it is. As crass as I can be, I hate to hurt a woman's feelings.

I'm remiss for not telling her I don't have chemistry with her. I did at some point and it has crossed my mind to settle and marry her. She's the first on the list of potentials. We have known each other two years.

When I think about marriage, reality kicks in and boils down to one fact. Forever is a long time, too long to spend in a relationship I'm not sure will withstand the test of time.

Regrets often last forever. What if I meet the woman of my dreams tomorrow? What if Annie and I become something? I'm reckless most of the time, however, dating is filled with trepidation. It's a tightrope I try to balance with a string of women I've dated, knowing I will probably crash under the weight of it one day. Women on my list are temporary placeholders.

And yes, even with all these women who circle in and out of my life, no one has occupied my mind as much as Annie. The fire between the sheets is commendable. I can't say she doesn't put a spring in my step and a spark in my eye every time I think of her or looked at her throughout the night.

I don't want to end up with a surprise like my mom. Married for years with my dad gambling, not knowing there was a huge cliff he hid from her. It got so bad house payments were late and she started paying attention to what he was doing, and it led to gambling debt whereby he made her use our college fund savings to pay it off. The betrayal almost drove her into a mental breakdown.

Needless to say, their nasty divorce left me caught in the middle as the oldest child. I was entering high school. Parents aren't supposed to drag their kids through their misery. It was hard for me to have them both in my life, and I am guilty of knowing things he hid from mom. I was a kid and didn't know it was a big deal until mom went ballistic, crying on the floor, all the equity in the house was gone. She was starting over in her forties.

Now I can help her out and make sure she doesn't go without. A new car last Christmas gave me a feeling I'm busting my ass for more than just myself and of course there were plenty of luxury gifts for my siblings.

I grew up in a nice house and spent summers at sleep away hockey camps in Minnesota. After the divorce, life wasn't easy. My siblings were shuffled back and forth between the two of them, and my mom was working her ass off to make sure my college was paid for when dad bounced alimony and child support payments.

I loved my dad; he was my best friend and came to every game. Now that I'm older, I wonder if he placed bets on my games with opposing teams. It's probably best I don't know the answer to that. It took years for me to face the fact of his addiction and there is no difference if it's from drugs or gambling. They all change a person and their need for money is never ending.

It's a terrible addiction, gambling. We were so close growing up, he was my idol, the man I wanted to impress. Then came the heartbreaking facts of how sick he was, thinking he never lost. He hit rock bottom and ended up with no home. He rents a room at an extended stay motel, bouncing from one tech job to another.

I feel bad for mom because she was the last person to learn how dire the situation had become. Dad became a shell of a man, someone I no longer recognized. My eyes filled with idyllic visions of how great he was curdled like milk.

The only time I hear from my old man is when he needs money. He weaves tales of how much trouble he's in and says bookies are going to break his legs. I'm not a fool. He's worth more to the bookies alive than dead. Mom pointed out to me the facts behind all the lies he told her when I left home. She did her best to warn me. I resented her for it and didn't talk to her for two years.

When I made it big, dad re-surfaced. I hoped he had changed, and he managed to hold the facade for three days. Then he hit me up for money and I haven't spoken to him since. He texts from time to time; I ignore them, as I don't want to get involved. No redeeming qualities are left in him. The only way I can make peace with the past is to separate the good memories from the bad.

I read in the paper he was arrested five years ago for embezzling money. Seems he set up his own business and used clients' money, paid upfront, and gambled it away. His clients sued, and the state prosecuted. He spent three years in the pen.

Mom is still single, working at my elementary school as

a teacher. She's my biggest fan. She could do without my name in the press and having the sordid details of my life played out for her girlfriends and students to see. I tell her it's not her reputation. I'm allowed to blow off stress.

Now that I think about it, it's probably not so cool the kids think there are no consequences for my behavior. I tell mom she needs to focus on my positive vices like how hard I work to develop the skill sets I need on the ice. It sucks that perception is reality today. It shouldn't matter what I do in my personal life as long as I'm not breaking the law. My private life should be off-limits. I'm at the top of my game, with or without the partying.

Besides, the press wouldn't be hated so much if they weren't whores for ratings. They should stick to being professional in their reporting. Hockey Scoop preys on all of us. Exploitive headlines sell more ads than the bylines. What is that all about?

I can't help it if I'm popular. I'm a moving target for the media and I'm not denying the fact that there are plenty of women who want to land a multimillionaire. I have them all figured out. Annie is different. She doesn't need notoriety or fame. She has a career without the public scrutinizing her daily.

We shared intense heat last night. A doctor is a demanding professional, she would understand me living on the road half the year. I'd have to understand her emergencies.

She's sweet and smart. I can't figure out why she's not married. Maybe she's not buying into the hype about getting married? I don't understand why it's a big deal. The married guys on the team make bribes to goad me into making it official with someone. Tons of people have a very good life, a long life, without taking a walk down the aisle. I view the 'aisle' as a plank.

I wonder what Annie's dad is like as a father. I never asked what he does for a living. I wonder if her parents are still together.

In my debate, I invite Becka to the event and explain we're going as friends, we're not getting back together. I'm not sure she paid attention to me, judging from the shrill scream she let outs, numbing my eardrums. I hope I can hear before we reach the stadium.

It's Nap30, as I have a date with a puck and a game to win.

8

Kal

I wake up refreshed after a nap. My superstition indicates we're going to win tonight.

"Kal, how'd that date go?" Blake asks me.

"Great, you owe me five-hundred." I grin as we bump fists.

"You're out of control," he snickers. "I'll bring a check Saturday night. I can't believe you pulled it off." He shakes his head.

"Thank you. Any more bets?" I ask with humor in my voice.

"Nope, I'm good," Sean says. Alexandre and Wyatt mumble "pass."

"See? I can control myself." I brag, and at this point, Blake snickers.

"I'll believe that when the sun sets in the east."

"To each their own, this is the world we live in," I scoff.

"On a happy note, Emily and I are expecting," Wyatt announces. "It's early, so we're only telling close friends."

"You think we're your friend?" Sean teases.

"Very funny, Old Timer," is Wyatt's retort, knowing full well Sean is only twenty-one.

"Congrats, man." I step over with the others to tap his back and half the room gives him a high five.

"It will change your life, but it's worth it," Alexandre adds.

"Yeah, I'm excited." His face is one gigantic smile. That will fade for the first six months with no sleep. Glad it's not me.

"And another one drops out of poker night," I grumble.

"Not completely, but I'd rather my kid takes care of me when I'm older, and not you," he shouts over his shoulder, causing a few men to chuckle.

"Ouch," I quip, acting like my hand was scalded by hot water. Let the kid bring it.

"Not everyone wants to be single forever, Kal," Nicol murmurs as he walks through the room, then leaves quietly. I wonder what's up with him. Did I say something wrong? Usually, someone will call me out right away if I'm out of line.

The game tonight is against the Toronto Twisters, the team who lost to the Stanley Cup champs, Boston. We need for our defense to kick it up a notch if we want to obtain a hot streak and shore up some wins. So, what do we do? We lose to Toronto in overtime. Go figure. We suck in overtime.

It's not like it's a life-or-death situation, yet. It's still early in the season, we just rolled into November, and no one can be sure who will be in the cup from the standings this early in the season.

However, it would be nice to get into the bracket with the top three teams in our conference. The teams we need to beat in our division are the champs, Toronto Twister, followed by the Boston Sharks and the Fort Myers Gators.

I TEXTED Annie to have fun with her dad tonight. She replied, and we flirted a bit before she had to go. I should have waited for her to be able to make our second date. I realize this when I take the elevator to Becka's condo Saturday night.

"Kal, how are you? Come in." She swings the heavy door open and if I know her, it's an invitation for more than just hanging out a few minutes where she perpetually runs late. At this juncture in time, I realize I've made a big mistake. The past is repeating itself already; and no matter what we do, we're not compatible enough to get along without one of us being miserable.

She usually doesn't see anyone when we are 'off', and in her defense, it's probably because she's waiting for us to be 'on' again.

"Hm." I purse my lips. Tricky situation. "You know, we're running late," I make this up knowing it's probably true as she's always late, which is annoying. I was trained to be punctual. Try showing up to a game late and see where it lands you!

"Oh, I'll be just a minute," she pines away as she gives me a quick kiss on the lips. Looks like she's starting where we left off with our last goodbye.

I watch her move in her slinky silver dress with a slit up the side. She's hot, she might move up the ranks with her TV gig as they like a pretty face. However, as I stand here looking at this very pretty woman, it's not the same as in the past. Something is off. Like off-off. Normally, my cock is standing at attention. So far, he's unmoved and sulks in my expensive trousers.

Fuck.

I wonder if it's something I ate. Will I be hard when I want to have sex? It can't be hormones, I'm too young for Christ's sake. Immediate panic ensues as I close the condo door behind me.

"Are you okay?" Becka is looking into the huge mirror in her dining room next to the door, observing my reflection.

I glance at the expensive watch on my wrist. "I have to be on time, Becka, Coach will be pissed."

"Right," she purrs, as if I'm making it up.

"No, I'm not kidding. We leave now or you'll have to meet me there."

"Fine," she huffs. She clasps her last earring before she gathers her purse in a huff.

Shit, the night is starting off badly. This is how she gets when she can't manipulate me. I'm not settling with a mate. I'm waiting for the right one. This is proof we're not meant to be. I'm done. The only problem is I have to suffer through this night as I can't bail on her. That would be rude, even if I'm doing us both a favor by ending it once and for all.

We make our way to the parking garage; I clinch my fists and take a deep breath as her voice irritates me. It's flooding back to me all the reasons why I've been ignoring her texts for months. I open the door for her, and she slides her hand around my back for a brief second before she gets in.

She's horny all right. Only I'm not the guy for her and I'm not hooking up with her later. I think I'll put her in a cab after the event and skate out, so there isn't an uncomfortable parting scene.

She leans in for a kiss and I give her my cheek, she pretends to not notice.

Drama for me happens on the ice, not in my personal life. It's an uncomfortable silence as I we make our way to the swanky hotel.

Everyone is arriving now. We are at the end of a long line waiting on valet service. "Maybe we should walk," I suggest as I glance around for a teammate in a neighboring car wondering if anyone else is stuck in the line.

"I'm not walking in my Dolce & Gabbana's that far," she exclaims like I'm a monster to even suggest it.

"Fine." We wait. I tap my fingers on the steering wheel and peer out the front window. I wish I could crawl out of the car and leave her here. We begin to creep along. I nervously glance at my watch and see valets in red vest running around working the line as quickly as possible.

"You could have come over earlier..." she reiterates.

That would have been a no-win situation for me. I'm in the hot seat as it is with her and need to arrive on time to the fundraiser because the team is a sponsor.

"There, we're next," she announces as she flips the visor down before she peers into the mirror making sure her hair and lipstick are in perfect order.

It makes me remember Annie and her long curls laying on my shoulder the other morning. The thought of her calms me. I wish she was here with me. I'm such a dolt at times. I called her today and left her a message to let her know I was thinking of her, but it went to voice-mail. I assume she was out running errands or with her dad.

I hand the keys to the attendant and take Becka's arm, we stand in line for pictures to be taken by team photographer. They have a red carpet with the charity name on a backdrop and after pictures, we'll make our way inside.

I force a smile on my lips for the pictures but fall short. I forgot about the red-carpet event. Now we're out there as a couple because the press will see these.

As we step off the carpet, I notice Hockey Scoop's van across the street with their long-range camera lenses. Shit. They will splash these pictures everywhere and with fresh rumors. I just opened a can of worms.

"I hope that picture turns out. I thought he should have taken a few more," Becka comments.

And I thought I had an ego.

"I hear music." I steer her towards the lights and music, hoping my teammates will serve as my human shield.

In this moment, I'm lamenting the fact I brought her, not Annie, even more. I had more fun on my blind date than I ever had with Becka.

"Introduce me to anyone who might be a good connection for me," Becka coos in my ear as she slips her arm through mine.

She played me; she's using me to propel her in her career. I didn't see it coming until now. I'm off my game. I normally don't miss things as obvious as this.

I survey the room filled with music being mixed from a DJ. It's cocktail hour, later it will switch to dinner music. There is a wood dance floor under the elegant chandeliers at one end of the room. The other end is set for dinner with table after table covered with white linens and outlandish centerpieces.

People are decked out in formal wear. The air is filled with perfume, I want to gag. Annie smelled like apples, her sheets, fabric softener. I use this as my happy thought as I pull the vest to my tux to make sure it's in place and decide we're going to circulate around the room.

I need to find a teammate, and fast. Becka surveys the room filled with people who can help her career, no doubt she's going to schmooze with them. If only I can find Mr. Barber, he's the one with the oil companies and is connected to the hospital where Annie works.

I'd love to pawn Becka off. It would be priceless if she found a contact to take her off my hands until we're forced to sit together at dinner. I chuckle, Barber's old enough to be her father, but I wouldn't put it past her to shop the candy store while she's here. Barber might love a pretty young thing on his arm, too boot.

"Kal." A familiar voice at last. I'm looking through the crowd gathered in front of the main bar and find Viktor, Sean, Luc, and Blake.

My smile expresses the relief I'm experiencing when I approach them. Becka heads to the bar to grab us drinks.

"Hey guys." We shake hands. "Becka is a pain tonight. What a disaster," I comment.

A couple stands next to us, a man with salt and pepper hair and a tall woman at his side. They turn around, slowly, and elegantly. My jaw drops in shock and then horror. No wonder those eyes look so familiar, it's Annie.

What? What is she doing here? She said she was going out with her dad.

"I don't think you've met my daughter, Kal," Coach says, "this is Annie."

Becka has impeccable timing as she stands with a drink in her hand, slipping the other through my arm possessively.

Annie is giving me a death stare. If looks could kill, I'd be a dead man twice over.

9

Kal

al, nice to meet you," she says as she shakes my hand and smiles. She's playing this off, giving me the look to play along.

Fuck.

I all but swallow my tonsils meeting Annie when I least expected it. Shocked doesn't come close to describing it. Seeing Coach next to her makes me nervous as hell. Petrified is a better description.

Fuck. I'm a dead man.

Surprise is written on her face as well. She didn't know I'm a hockey player. She is quick on her feet and rebounds from the awkward silence as we shake hands. The contact gives my arm the tingles. Apparently, we still have a connection. And it's not lost on the team. I'm hoping Coach is too busy being one of the most popular faces here tonight and misses the fireworks imploding between our looks.

I want to ask her questions. Why would she not mention

her father? He's popular in Maine and has nothing to be ashamed of, unlike my father.

Becka shows up and I'm caught red-handed with an attractive woman who hands me a drink. Her timing; impeccable.

Right, I can do this.

"Annie, nice to meet you, This is Becka." I played the dating game and now it includes my ex-girlfriend. Shit.

Becka barely shakes Annie's hand. I find it rude. She's picked up on the electricity between us and there will be hell to pay.

I causally glance at Annie's dad, hoping I covered the panic in my eyes. He can't find out we've met. Met, hell, we've seen each other naked and acted on it.

I can't wait to get Annie alone. I need to explain, my eyes roam the room nervously as I try to conceal my anticipation of a worst-case scenario.

Coach is called away. I breathe like I just skated suicide drills. Finally, we're left in our uncomfortable silence. Becka slurps the Cosmo in her hand, she's getting tipsy. How long before we're on our first course of dinner?

"Let's go find the others." Becka says slipping her arm possessively through mine to drag me off to find my teammates who scattered like a hill of fire ants making themselves the quickest disappearing act in the history of the world.

I turn my feet to leave. I don't want to leave Annie here by herself. My eyes meet hers as I try to convey an apology. I implore her to do something. I'll need her empathy to recover from what has transpired.

Annie's eyes are vibrant, her glare is hot. I'm sure she meant to turn me to stone. She moves past us mumbling

"Excuse us," as she swipes my arm from Becka, leaving a dazed look on her face. My Cosmo tips in the ensuing aftermath, spilling onto my hand. "Kal, a minute please," she smiles sweetly, but her mood is anything but sweet.

I shoot a quick glance to Blake, who has managed to escape the general area. I try to read his face, as I'm out of my element. He shrugs his shoulders as if to say he's sorry. I'm sure he isn't happy with the turn of events, either.

Coach Susneck has his back to me as he talks to the other patrons. The buzzing of numerous voices all talking at the same time goes in one ear and out the other because I've been snookered by Blake and Annie. Were they in on this together? She seems genuinely surprised. I'm not amused.

Coach turns his body to observe us briefly, his eyes give me a once over and my heart sinks. Does he know? Is it written on my face? I always know the play, and tonight, I'm utterly baffled.

Everyone wants to speak to Coach. Judging by the bright lights at the end of electrical equipment he's being filmed by the camera crew for tonight's evening news.

Annie stops in a corner of the room by another set of doors. There is no one to eavesdrop on us. As I wished it, at long last, Annie begins to talk.

I briefly turn my head to check the whereabouts of her dad, and he's still occupied. I'm beginning to feel like I'm in an alternate universe and my spy craft is severely lacking.

"What the hell? You're on the team?" Annie bombards me.

"Me? You!" I reply heatedly. "You," I point to her, "could have mentioned the fact your dad is the coach to the Maulers!" I huff.

"So, sue me for wanting to know if a man is into me for

me, and not to obtain access to my famous dad," she puts a hand on her hip as she jets the other one out mimicking a paper doll on a stand.

"Oh," I reply, wanting to go on ranting, but she has a point. I never thought of what her life was like, being the coach's daughter. "Well, likewise." I struggle to find my angle to argue. "Maybe, I wanted someone to get to know me for me, too." I'm full of shit. I won a bet and that will not help the situation. I make my excuse sound legit as I prepare to come up with a zinger.

"Not likely. Dad spoke about how the guys on the team are not husband material and I'm to avoid all of you. It appears most of you have some sort of reputation for Dad to even bring it up." Her smug voice hits a chord of truth and makes me uncomfortable.

I'm at a loss for words. She's managed to render me speechless in under three minutes. One, if I don't count the two minutes spent with the group.

"Truth be known, Blake set me up for payback on a prank," I roll the words slowly off my tongue and draw my eyebrows together like a furry caterpillar. It's beginning to make sense now.

"What? Blake?" Her eyes convey the betrayal I've seen in my mother's. It's the moment when it all starts to click together like a puzzle. She's been used as our fodder to have a good laugh. Only none of us are laughing.

"I'm sure Blake didn't mean for it to get out of control. He had no way of knowing we would ever run into each other. I'm sure he was going to tell me at practice tomorrow."

I glance towards Blake, who is sheepishly looking at me as he jesters with a shrug and turns to his wife. There is no way he could foresee this. I'm the one left holding the bag on this shitty situation, and my ass is on the line if Coach finds out.

"You even brought a date after we did the wild thing?" her voice is hurt combined with disdain. I should have known better than to put out on a first date. I broke my rules for you, Kal Kohlman."

"I'm sorry, really. Where is your dad?" I ask coyly.

She turns slightly, letting her arm drop to a normal position by her side. "He's talking to some couples who gave a ton of money and helped sponsor this event." She returns her attention to me. "I came here to be closer to my dad, to fix us, and if he finds out about you, it will be a wedge between us. You've ruined my ability to be honest with my father," she emphatically exclaims, trying hard to refrain from yelling, but her hands are moving as fast as a waterspout.

"I'm sorry, really, I had no idea," I begin, but she puts her palm towards my face. "We can't be seen together," I eek out in one rushed breath. "We have to keep this a secret."

"No, shit," she huffs. "And don't bother calling. I don't find this amusing." She shakes her head before she stomps off in her designer heels, leaving an apple orchard aroma in her wake.

"I don't find it funny, either." I make my plea, but I doubt she heard anything because her back is to me and the voices in the crowded room drown me out. I check on the team, then Coach, who still hasn't moved. It appears everyone, who is anyone, is here. A glass is used as a bell as it *tings,* so everyone knows it's time to take a seat. The long evening commences.

I watch in silence as Annie makes her way through the

crowd. Her hair is sleek and shiny showing her delicate neck I'd love to kiss. I hear compliments from women passing on how divine she looks in the black, strapless velvet dress. She's a hit tonight, coach's daughter, or not. I can't escape noticing how incredible the dress fits her every curve. Her red shoes and handbag are merely punctuation marks, giving her a sexy, classy look. She stands out amongst her peers.

My cock grows hard. Now, he wants to fuck around. Funny, that didn't happen with Becka.

Fuck me. What I want to do is have another night with Annie. A lot of nights and mornings, like the one we had after our date. I'm sure she'll cool down in time. We can talk reasonably–like adults, when the time is right.

On the other hand, she is pretty pissed. This is a colossal disaster. I've seen plenty in nineteen years of naked dudes in locker rooms and messy break-ups. Somehow, this event trumps everything else. We pushed our pranks too far.

Blake, Sean, Finn, Alexandre, and Viktor are hanging together looking for their name plate in order to sit. No doubt it's a minute to themselves before our time is required to partake in the social event because we're handsome faces and stars on the team. We play it by ear most of the time. Too many details for us to track in a day.

I search for Annie in the crowd. She's joined her dad and is sitting with a group of people. I wonder why she's so upset about being honest with her dad. What is going on between the two of them?

Let me rethink this. I'm glad she wasn't upfront with her dad because all hell is going to break loose if he finds out about us. There is no telling how he would punish us for bringing his eldest daughter into our world of debauchery.

Coach knows my wildness, and I've been told, as long as

I don't have run ins with the law, I've have carte blanche to do as I want because I do a good job for the organization. I'm a key player and I have five years on my contract. In theory, it's security, however, shit happens, players get traded, sent to the minors, or worse, like acquiring an injury. Management hasn't given me a difficult time over my private life, it's the media who stalks me.

I return to my date and the pout on Becka's face implies I'm neglecting her. I assume before the night is over, her cat claws will come out. I'm unsure if Annie is her target, or me. Possibly both of us. This is the first time I've been a part of girl drama where it could interfere with my job.

Blake and Wyatt are sitting with their wives. Bits of pieces of someone telling a story float on the formal air as I approach our table. Others are laughing and having a good time, impervious of my situation. I want them to join me in laughter but I'm left to wallow in regret over how badly I handled this situation.

Annie is special. Why did I bring Becka tonight? Could it be I got too close to Annie so quickly? I could have come by myself. This is the first time my antics have kicked me in the ass.

My cock grew hard just seeing Annie across the room. My heart feels like she drilled a screwdriver in it. The disappointment in her eyes brought me to my knees. I want a second chance, but will I get it?

I love my life. Being single is where it is. I love the high-flying weekends to anywhere I want to go, summer vacations overseas, and toys. Let's not forget the summers filled with boating and the Lobster festival. I can get into any sporting event I want because those who need to know who I am, do. It opens doors.

Only tonight, a door slammed shut. Annie was another

woman on my list. But, if that's the case, why do I feel sucker punched when the man sitting next to her begins to chat her up? And why am I jealous he's making her smile?

That should be me. I should be the only man who makes her smile.

10

Annie

I gulp my pride and hold back tears brimming on the edge of my eyelashes. I can't let my mascara run. I spent the morning getting my nails and hair fixed up to be daddy's little girl tonight. I've been played. Now I know why dad was so overly protective of me all these years.

These men are cruel. I foolishly assumed they would have grown up by now. Pranking the locker room in high school with frozen cans of shaving cream is one thing. Setting me up on a blind date to get back at someone is entirely unacceptable behavior. These men should have adulted years ago.

Kal is nothing more than a man-child with a vocabulary larger than a teen. The only things going on in his head are jokes, boozing, and fucking me over.

I stupidly fell for it. The one time I open up...bam.

Suzy is not going to believe this. I'm so angry I'm shaking as if I caught a chill. I don't want to see the team. If Kal comes near me, I'll deck him.

I leave the nice trainer who's talking to me at the table to swing by the bar, making a wide berth to avoid Kal and Blake's looks. If my mother finds out about this, Blake will catch hell for sure. If my dad finds out, he'll be disappointed in me, and it will jeopardize the progress we're making getting reacquainted. Effectively, this snafu could negate the only reason I moved here. I'm distraught as this blows on so many levels.

No telling what dad would do if he found out the team players were involved in disgracing his daughter. I doubt they know Kal stayed over, but how do I know?

I will myself to calm down as I clutch money in one hand, while my other hand gingerly affixes my fingers around the round bottom of a champagne flute. I'm afraid to touch the fragile stem, knowing it will break under my anger.

I tip the bartender and grab both flutes of champagne before re-joining my table. It galls me to have to fake being happy tonight. I'm covering up the situation for myself, so I don't see the disdain in dad's eyes. However, I'm also covering for Kal, which pisses me off even more.

Dad quizzical eyes question me briefly. I nod giving him a reassuring smile to put him at ease before he stands, and heads to the podium. I bat my eyelashes as if I'm having the time of my life and engage with Nicol, a trainer on the team who is conversing with me.

The woman next to him, however, is interesting, and she's married to the general manager of the team, John Price. Mary and I make small talk. Mom has mentioned her, I remember she said they were friends, and we can trust her. Something about an inner circle. She's a huge supporter of dad and John renewed daddy's contract last year.

Dad gets up and makes a speech, becoming more

animated the longer he talks about the Make a Kid Smile program. Dad loves the team, but also special organizations who help children.

It's now evident to me the extra hours he spends with work is partly related to these charity events. It dawns on me we might not be so different. I love my work and I'll be attending the fundraising event for the new children's wing.

Sure, I have to contend with chauvinistic jokes and make sure Dr. Dick never corners me. I haven't heard how far he goes with his hands and intimidating threats. I don't want to find out, either. Dad would say keep my head on a swivel, but it's hard to do when my hands are busy with gluing or stapling gaping holes together. How far will Dr. Dick go? Is he capable of rape?

Work should be free from these worries. I wonder why the hospital paid off a woman. If so, how many more are there? I assume preventing the lawsuit saved the Board of Director's from scandal. But why was he never fired?

Suzy texts me from work. I'm relieved to be on my phone as the man next to me is sweet, but I'm still obsessing over Kal.

The room is decked out with the Make a Kid Smile banner and a disco ball hangs over the elegant ball room, no doubt the couples here are going to dance tonight and the picture of it makes me smile. Too bad Kal isn't available. I would have loved for him to take me in his arms, hold me against his chest and wrap his arms around me as we sway to music. He has a way of making me embrace our time together, and work fades to the background. Our conversations aren't forced and I enjoyed how effortless it was to be alone in a room with him. Am I doomed to despise him for playing me?

The gala is a hit. Dad and I talked in-between his obligations and, for the first time in a long time, I enjoyed being a part of his world. We're peers now, along with our father-daughter relationship.

"You must be Annie." A handsome man introduces himself to me.

"Yes." I turn in my seat. He takes my hand in his.

"I'm Greg, I'm the owner of the team, it's so nice to meet you. Your dad thinks the world of you." He says flashing me a friendly smile.

He has really nice teeth, he's built like a fright train, and I wonder how many hours a week he works out.

I'm stunned. Did he say my dad talks highly of me? Come again?

"Does he?" I jest, but I want to make sure my ears aren't hearing things. Outlandish things. Dad doesn't praise me.

"Oh, yes, he's so proud of you," he continues as he politely drops my hand and excuses himself so I can eat my rabbit food.

Dad gets up and walks to speak to strangers three feet away. He's older now, his hair is thinning on top, and he looks tired. I hope he's alright. Mom will be home soon; she'll make sure he's taking care of himself.

I text Suzy who is working and tell her she would cream in her pants over the hotties here. I also inform her Kal and I won't be seeing each other.

Why? He was hot for you and even asked you out again.

He showed up at the event tonight with another woman.

No shit, she types.

The asshole. In his eyes, I'm daddy's little girl and he's worried over his job. Can you believe this shit? Now, we're all acting like nothing happened, so dad doesn't find out. I can't risk losing him when we're making progress.

Good point. Gottcha. Oh, well, you'll find someone. We'll look them up and run a background check the next time.

I let out a chuckle just as everyone is clapping as entrees are being delivered to our table.

Damn right we will.

I'm off tomorrow, which will be nice. I can get some painting done. I chuckle, if daddy made all the guys come over to paint, it would be finished in a day.

Tonight is a night for dad and me to enjoy being together, and I intend to enjoy it. Greg Anderson is standing behind a podium. He thanks everyone who volunteers for the non-profit and announces the silent auction going on down the hall. The players signed jerseys and sticks to raise money. Other affluent supporters donated trips and second houses as vacation packages.

Next, players rotate to speak of their experience with the program and I listen to Blake as he mentions his recent trip for the cause. I want his balls to shrink to the size of grapes, but seeing as how I can't make that happen, I stare blankly into the greenery decorating the stage and my eyes wander to Greg.

He's sitting in the front of the room without a date. He's handsome, mid-forties, and I wonder if he's single. The only way to move on from my debacle is to be more selective. Greg might be more my speed, and daddy would approve, too.

I know I have eyes boring into my back and I refuse to turn. I'm sure it's Becka or Kal. I hold my head high and pick at my food.

The room claps after every speaker as the entrees are still being delivered to tables. I'm thirsty, and I head to the bar to grab more champagne. The waiters are in the weeds and scurry around the room like bees around a hive.

I ask the bartender for a refill and Blake appears.

I put my hand up, my palm is facing him. "I don't want to hear it. I expected more from you."

"I didn't mean to hurt you, Annie. You're sweet, I just wanted to give Kal a lesson, turn the tables on him, so to speak. I'm sorry you got caught up in this."

His face is void of joy, a woman appears on his arm, asking him to get her another drink.

"Oh, by the way, this is Rachel," he says as a pretty woman pops her head around his large upper body. We shake hands amicably in front of his chest.

"Pleasure," I murmur. Rachel is enthusiastic and stunning in her vintage dress with beading I would kill for. I love the forties, I compliment her on her dress. "We met over the summer. I think you were having lunch together," I add.

"That's right. You have quite the collection of designer bags, I love the one you are carrying tonight," she smiles.

"Thanks." I can't tell her my dad bought it for me because Mom mentioned Rachel's book is a bestseller, so she probably has oodles of money. Everyone here tonight seems to be more successful than me. Why is it I'm running into all the couples on the team?

"I heard you're a doctor, that's so cool."

"Thanks," I reply with a weak smile. I'm sure she's being nice. I grab the drinks the bartender slides to me.

"Welcome to Maine, I heard you just moved here. I'll have Blake text you my number. We need to get together. If you need anything, give me a shout," she turns on her heel and I catch how her lovely hair bounces as she says goodbye and they return to their table, and Kal, only Kal isn't there.

There are two camps here tonight, his and mine.

I turn to go in the opposite direction and suddenly, Kal is in my face, blocking my getaway.

"Annie, it's not what you think, Becka is with me because you couldn't make it. She's here making contacts for work."

"As a stripper?" I'm still peeved.

He chuckles and tries to stifle it, knowing it's no laughing situation. "No, but with the way she works a room, I can understand your creative narrative."

"Good, me and my creative narrative are leaving." I move to make my way past him, but he places a hand on my bare shoulder.

It turns me inside out. I want to be cold and indifferent to him, but his touch and close proximity is turning me to into ice cream soup. I can't forget our night together or, how expertly he made love to me. I can't stand beside him with these memories, so I turn my thoughts to Becka and the anger returns as I'm forced to thoughts of the two of them, together, doing what we did, and I'm... jealous.

Would he have gone home with her tonight if I didn't show up? Maybe he will anyway. I can't trust him. He's smooth. How can I trust anything he says?

I look up to meet his eyes, and it's the wrong move. I'm sucked into them again; my knees grow weak. I wonder how long the hurt look in his gorgeous eyes will haunt me.

"I'm sorry, you got caught up in our prank wars. It won't happen again."

It takes all my will power to reply, "That's right, because we're done." I turn, leaving his hand to slide off my naked shoulder as he stands, a sad expression on his handsome face.

Take that, you arrogant jock. It might be the first time he's ever been rejected, but he's a big boy. He needs to understand actions have consequences.

I look for my table and Dad's eyes are on me. I wonder how long he's been watching. He has the look of a parent on his face. I hope he didn't witness us talking. I play it off as Dad starts on his bread and salad.

"Nice event Dad, thanks for inviting me." I place our drinks on the starched tablecloth and sit.

"Glad you could come. How is work going? Are they treating you okay?"

I want to discuss Dr. Dick with him, and I don't know how to approach it. He's not the warmest person in the room when it comes to me. I doubt he'll want to know the truth. "Fine." I lie. "I have a new friend, Suzy, she's nice. We are on the same team and work the same schedule, so it's nice to have another woman around."

He fiddles with his bread and a tiny floret of butter on the tiny plate. "I'm glad you moved here, Annie. I've missed you."

"You have?" My heart stops. Dad missed me?

"I hope we see more of you around the house and the rink. Will you come to a game?"

"Sure," gushes out of my mouth at the mere thought of seeing him in action. It's been years since I watched him coach and I always end up watching him more than the game. Only this time, I assume it will be different. I'm not little anymore and he's my dad, not my hero.

"Great, just let me know when you want to come. I'll leave tickets at the will call window."

"Great, I'd love that."

We eat our salads and talk about Mom and Carla before we're interrupted by a couple walking past Dad.

I smile to myself. Tonight, I don't mind the interruption. In fact, I welcome it. I hope he'll be distracted and forget the looks he witnessed between Kal and I when he introduced us. Dad is a man of few words, he mulls things over and presents a united, calm front, whereas Mom is emotional and will go off her rocker.

I understand both sides of their personalities as I have a bit of both. Carla is a mini of Mom, all emotion and overly dramatic. In my opinion it might be why Dad babies her, she's a bit fragile, they call it "young for her age." Whatever.

"So, what's up with Kal? I thought you two might know each other," Dad picks up where he left off.

Fuck. There it is.

"Oh, nothing. He seems nice." I lie, again. Double damn Kal and Blake. Now I'm lying to cover all three of us.

"Hm, I thought you knew each other. I must be mistaken."

"Oh, wow, look at the prime rib," I interject as I turn my eyes to the beef on my plate.

Dad chuckles. "Do you eat any regular food? Or do you live in a vending machine?"

We both share a chuckle.

He looks over to me and I meet his gaze, we share a laugh, and it's a perfect moment.

He knows I love vending machines from when we were on the road because Mom didn't let me eat things out of bags. She said the preservatives and coloring were bad for my health. Turns out, she was right. My love of cheese puffed corn substances and ice cream sandwiches will make sure none of these items will ever go begging for a taker if I'm around.

11

Kal

I t is obvious we both had reasons for the secrets we harbored the other night.

She is a spitfire when she's pissed. I can't blame her. Unlike her father, who is the voice of calm and reason, she articulates her words well, more vocally. Coach saves his explosions for important objections in the game. Sometimes, his public objections come with consequences.

I'm not even sure the game coach was tossed from last season was legit. He questioned a referee. I've gotten away with more, so much more. It's easy to get some sticks under skates when the refs aren't looking.

I return to my friends where Blake surprises me with a clap on my back. "Aren't you glad you behaved yourself?" he quips. Why he believes I didn't tap that, I'll never know, but I'm letting him keep his PG13 version intact.

"Mm, sure. I'm glad. Yep." I force a wry half smile, no longer proud of myself.

Instead of being glib, I'm thinking, *I'm so fucked*. Why

didn't I lock my cock up? Don't zippers get stuck? My eyes peruse the room, looking for the velvety, vulnerable, dark eyes I stared into two nights ago.

Her eyes, that's it! They are the same as Coach's. Fuck me. I should have known. I'm kicking myself. I'm always the prankster and I've been had. I can't tell anyone I slept with Annie. The coach's daughter is sacred. She's off-limits, everyone knows this. Besides, the guys will string me up by my nut sack if they find out we banged each other all night long.

"You knowingly set me up with Annie. Sometimes you can be an ass, Blake," I lower my voice so only he can hear me.

"Yeah, well, you always get off Scott free, so I wanted to give you a dose of your own medicine. I think it's funny as shit. Only now Annie is mad at me, too."

"You won't lose sleep over it like I will," I reply, keeping my anger bottled up. If he knows he got to me, this will never end. It will also give him new avenues to prank me. Any way I look at this situation, it's bad. Really bad.

Sean drinks champagne as he walks behind us sitting and finds his place seating. "She's hot, I'll say that," he replies before a low whistle passes through his lips to make his point.

"Let's not talk about how hot she is, some respect would be nice," I grumble. Everyone turns to focus on me. Great, now I'm the bad guy.

"What?" I ask. Like anyone should have a problem with me. I'm the victim here, me and Annie.

"That's a first for you, Kal," Viktor chimes in, grabbing the last finger food off a passing tray before dinner is announced. "Hm, respecting women," a sly grin adorns his face, and it appears he's the cat and I'm the mouse. He

caught me going into a melt down over my lack of convenient morals. Everyone thinks I'm a man whore. I just
happen to love women. I love making love to women, I just
haven't found the one I want to keep forever.

Our table is adjacent to Annie's. She's turned towards
the stage, her shapely body twists, her head held high as she
listens to the speakers and leans over to say something to
her father.

Blake cautioned me to behave myself, but my cock got in
the way of my better judgement. I should have given Annie a
few dates before making a move. I should have gotten to
know her before I fucked her.

In my defense, our tryst was mutual. How am I the bad
guy in this? It takes two, as they say.

Annie has a way of making me a better person. I don't
want to be her mistake. I don't want her free to date other
men. Then, the asshole side of me takes over my brain.

Why does it matter what she thinks of me?

I've never cared in the past.

Now, I've blown it. We both blew it. We could both walk
away and never see each other again. The room is large
enough and with over three hundred people here, I'm sure
we could avoid each other, no one would be the wiser.

The chemistry between us took over, and I was power-
less to stop it is my defense. The guys say I think with my
cock. What man doesn't? Annie and I had chemistry. I don't
know what I would do if I knew who her father was before
our date.

Maybe I should walk away, Annie deserves better.
However, my desire is to explain what happened. I don't
think she understands how it went down. I need to
explain. It's imperative I figure something out because
Coach is hovering. She and her dad look like they are

enjoying their evening, Annie and I exchange a look as their bread plates and salads are delivered. The fact her eyes meet mine is better than I could have hoped for all things considered.

Eventually Coach will find out, he always does. Fuck me, I'm screwed. There's no coming back from this. I wonder if I should start packing now.

"Um, using Annie to get to me isn't nice," I speak in a low voice to Blake, who sits beside me. His wife, Rachel, is on his left. The tables are circular to aid conversation. Just what I need, more talk about my date.

"Just had to get you once," he mumbles. "See, the mighty can fall. It might be good for you. This is the first time I've seen a woman give you the brush off."

"She's special," I emphatically argue and tuck the check he slid me into the pocket of my jacket.

It's dirty money. It wasn't from a bet over bedding the girl, however it feels dirty just the same.

No sooner are salads on cold plates set in front of us, I pull the check out of my pocket, and proceed to rip it up, dropping it on the table like confetti.

"What are you doing?" Becka asks.

"Nothing." I shrug, hoping she drops it.

"Oh, that's money, Kal," Becka exclaims, having eaten half of her salad by the time the main course is served. "I'm glad it was just a bet," she surmises as she raises a hand to her chest, "I was afraid you two were a thing while we were taking a break," her tart voice is an indication of jealousy.

As if the cold feet I had before we arrived isn't bad enough, she's capable of embarrassing rudeness. I don't answer and when she returns to mingle with the conversation going around the table, I'm relieved I don't have to pacify her.

"If I didn't know better, I'd say you like Annie," Blake whispers.

"I won't take the money," I argue.

"Suit yourself." He shrugs and turns as Rachel is speaking to him.

"Sean, where's your date tonight?" I ask.

"Stag man, I didn't want any drama tonight." He leans in closer to Blake so the others can't hear. "But it looks like you take the cake. Blake, you dog, I didn't know you had it in you. If Kal gets busted, you're going to pay." Sean shifts back in his seat, drains his rum and cola, and asks for another from the waiter who serves our entrees.

"What is going on?" Rachel's interest is piqued.

"The less you know, the better," Blake informs her.

"You guys are thicker than thieves, I swear," she replies in a playful tone. They haven't been married very long but they complement each other. I'm impressed she respects the bro code. There are nights, and afternoons, when we round up the team to hang out, play golf or just have a cookout. The camaraderie off the ice helps us to perform better when we're on it.

"Wyatt, what's new with you?" I change the subject again, hoping the guys will forget my blind date. The last thing I need is for Coach to find out from the gossip mill.

According to Annie, I'm the scorned man in the room. The sinking feeling in my gut when the puck is accidentally kicked into our own net and costs us the win.

"Nothing much. Emily is the one with news." He beams his toothy smile at me to rub salt in the room. For a youngster, he's pretty cocky.

"We've been busy." Emily is decked out in a fashionable red dress, one would find on an A-lister. She's a natural beauty who can wear a t-shirt and jeans and give any actress a run for her money.

"I heard congratulations are in order." I nod to them both and notice her face is particularly bright tonight, her smile is endless.

"Thank you," she replies, taking a sip of water as the server places her salad and breadbasket in front of her.

"Oh, congratulations on what?" Rachel gushes. "Are you..."

"Pregnant. Wyatt told the guys this week. We're only telling those closest to us until we're further along. For now, it's touch and go nausea." She picks up her fork and nibbles on her lettuce.

"Well, congrats, Emily!" Rachel touches her hand as a sign of support. "Shame on you for not saying anything." She taps Blake's arm as if she's upset, but I think she uses it as an excuse to touch him.

Emily is thin, I can't imagine her full term with a huge baby bump. I hope I'm still on the team to see it. Wyatt is young, and he's not fazed by it, judging from the huge smile of his face and the fact that he dotes on Emily and kisses her every time she looks adoringly to him. Still in the honeymoon phase, I assume. In fact, he's the same jovial kid who joined us earlier this year, only more mature.

Is it possible a couple can have a kid and not turn into cyborgs?

"Oh, by the way, Emily, congrats on the deal you got for Bella, I hear her record is doing well," Sean speaks glancing to her as he plays with his beer bottle, rolling it between his palms for lack of anything better to do. Salad plates are cleared to make room for the entrees as they are delivered to tables around us; we're still waiting. Sean is alone tonight; I wish I was, too.

"Yes, it is, thank you. It wasn't my connection. Alexandre had a hand in it. Bella and Troy are going to do a duet and it looks like she's off and running. She's in Vegas now as his opening act. My office has been flooded. I might have to go into entertainment repping and let my new attorney take over the sports contracts."

"Alexandre has a connection for everything," Rachel volunteers before continuing. "That's exciting, Vegas, huh? I've never been. Is Troy as nice as they say?"

"I don't know what they say, but yes, he's friendly. He hasn't forgotten his roots, and he gives to this charity as well as Bella's."

"That's awesome, I like feel good stories, the home boy who made it big," I add, trying not to be sardonic.

Simon is sitting at a table to our left with other players. He's smiling and texting on his phone. No doubt he's conversing with Bella because she isn't on stage yet, there is a three-hour time difference.

"I think anyone who makes it big has to have connections. I've been trying to move up to reporting the news for years, and so far, no luck," Becka complains.

"It can't hurt. Look how many people become a name from a video going viral," Blake adds. "I was raised in the techie world, and I still don't understand this social media thing and new apps come out every day. Kal, what about you?" He looks to me and it's like he's reminding me I have a bad rap outside of what I do on the ice.

I shrug. I'm not thrilled to be here or have Blake up in my grill rubbing in the fact he finally got one over on me.

"Food, great." I change the subject as my steak dinner is finally served.

The talks on the stage continue, people clap and Becka

fawns over me like we're love birds. I'm stuck in purgatory for another hour. I shift in my chair.

Irritated, I finally lean over, "Becka, stop it, we're not together. You had your fun for the night, but it's over."

"Kal, you don't mean that," she preens. "Everyone saw us together. We're back, baby," she runs her hand over my leg and grabs my cock.

I straighten in my chair, not wanting to create a scene as I move her hand onto her lap. I check on Annie again, she's the one I want by my side and Nicol is sitting next to her soaking up her attention. She even laughs at something he says.

I remember her laughing when I tickled her. She makes me feel younger than my years and I'm angry she didn't come with me tonight. Is it because I didn't get my way? Or the fact Blake got even with me? Or, is it Annie is unavailable and free to talk to any man she desires?

Probably all the above. I suffer in silence as the fantastic steak melts in my mouth. It could be shoe leather with as much as I care because I'm worrying over the fact Annie doesn't want to hear from me again.

My eyes continue to drift to Annie and coach all night. Coach is a professional and he wouldn't say anything to me here. For the first time in my life, I'm afraid I'll have to answer to our revered coach, and I don't want to be on his bad side. He could bench me, trade me, or just make my life miserable.

Watching Annie with her new admirer irks me. Coach is looking at Annie, and his lips curl into a smile as she turns to him and says something to which he nods his head. What are they talking about? This is the first time I'd like to have a second date with a woman, and I can't. Annie told me to leave her alone.

12

Annie

The night draws to a close. I leave after the first song plays. I have no inclination to dance with my father. That will be reserved for my wedding day —if I ever find the right man. Fat chance on that. I'm giving up after Kal. I'm not that desperate, am I?

I notice an elderly couple on the dance floor, moving to a song, and I know they've danced together for years. They have it all down pat, like professionals. I assume they've been together twenty to thirty years, and I wonder how they met. I'm amazed couples like them are still around and I long to have that special person in my life.

I have no wish to grow old alone. I have no viable candidates and wonder if I will find anyone to fertilize my eggs before they become empty shells.

Some days I'm tired of trying and I'll be damned if I will ever get excited over one date again. I'll bury myself in work and forget it.

Dad has the insight of his gender and has been coaching

for over two decades. He doesn't rule my life, but he knows men. Even if Kal and I worked through our current predicament, my dad would have a fit.

I can't discount the fact he called for a second date. We just didn't know we were going to the same one. No matter how much I wanted to say yes to a second date, I wouldn't dump my dad for him.

I'm conflicted. Where does my dad's life and mine separate? It was easier in another state, no one thought twice about us being related and I lived in relative anonymity.

I drive home, it's after ten. I put my car in the freestanding garage and walk under the moon light, stumbling on the uneven pavers. They are a makeshift sidewalk leading to my patio door. I text Suzy, who is working tonight, to call me on her break. As soon as I get in the house, my phone rings.

"Mom, where are you?" I can't remember her itinerary.

"I'm in Paris, it's lovely as usual. How did your night go?"

"It's like, three in the morning there," I protest.

"I don't sleep well without your father, never did. Something about the road I never got used to. We often fall asleep with video calls."

I can't fathom what that's like. For me, a relationship lasting more than a month is a big deal. Somehow, my parents knew who was perfect for them because they've been married forever, having met at college.

The other side of the coin is I'm jealous of what they have. I've never experienced the love they have for each other. Dad loves me, but he never says it. He may have been there for Mom, but I fell below the stature of his team. He mostly only talked to me if I was in trouble with a bad grade or got home late. He's says things like 'that'a girl, good job, glad you went to college.' I'm not one of his players. I'm his daughter. I want a dad who gives me bear hugs, shows up when he's supposed to and is emotionally available all the time, not when it's convenient for him.

"I had a nice time, so did Dad. Of course, I had to share him with the sponsors, and the media, and then hockey talk started." I speak to Mom and flip on a light as I enter the kitchen.

"That's how it goes. It's not just a job, it's part of who he is. You need to accept other people for who they are, one person isn't going to meet all your needs. You have a career, someone will have to understand what you do, as well. You're dedicated, like your dad."

"I don't think emotions make us weak, if that's what you mean."

"It's hard for people to apologize. If you looked at him as a normal person with faults like everyone else, it would be easier for you to see he loves you."

"I'll think about it," I reply, as I'm at a loss for words. How does our issues always revert back to me? Why is it the child's responsibility to make the parent happy? Granted, I'm not a child anymore, but the hurt feelings I racked up as one, are here for eternity. It's what defines us as adults. Every person has issues, we all deal with them differently.

"I gotta go, your father is calling. I love you, Annie."

"Love you, Mom."

I survey the building I call home, knowing it's a blank canvas. The walls are old, the paint is dirty and chipped. I don't own much. To say it's a mess is an understatement. Boxes are still unpacked because I want to paint the walls first.

I stumble to the steps, having kicked the corner of a suitcase on the floor. I need more lighting, another item to add to my growing list.

There wasn't any reason to move my old hand me down furniture from Boston. They were great for my first apartment, but no matter how much I had the couch cleaned, I never could get rid of the prior owners' beer pong parties.

Now that I'm getting settled, I will buy the things I like, and they will be new. I have no idea what color to put on the walls, or how to hang blinds. Maybe there is a nice neighborhood handy man looking for work.

I slip my heels off before I walk up the steps. Seems most of the homes in Maine are two stories. I unzip my dress on the landing. The zipper goes an inch but won't slide any further. I enter my bedroom and throw my purse on my bed that's still unmade. Who sees it?

Mom was a stickler for beds being made before the sheets grew cold. Who wants to do it first thing in the morning? Or ever? Mom had a status to uphold and obsessed over the fact someone might drop by. Our house had to be picture perfect.

My eyes take in the emptiness of my bed, particularly the side I don't use. It reminds me of Kal. A dull ache fills me. The hot sex, the many orgasms, his cute face. Damn it. It was a perfect night.

I choke on a sob forming in my throat. I repeat, "I will not cry," to myself, as I wonder how long it will be before I have another date. We just met, but I liked him. He was easy to talk to, he made me laugh.

Every part of my body was touched as if he loved me. How can he do that night after night with different women? It's a memory I'll cherish even though he turned out to be a poser. He never had feelings for me. I need to resign myself to the fact I was just another girl on his list.

How did I get to be so pathetic?

I argue with myself over the fact he stayed the night,

which is more than what most men would do. Did I mean anything to him?

I remind myself he wasted no time moving on after our hookup. I'm not available for one date and he moves on to someone else. I'm curious. What does Becka have that I don't? More importantly, why do I always feel like I'm on the outside looking in?

Meanwhile, I'm stuck in my dress. I rocked the event tonight and for once, it was nice being the coach's daughter. I never imagined I'd say that.

I bend my arm like a contortionist. I'm used to being single, I got this. I twist myself and my arm to reach the zipper on my back, only it's not budging.

Shit.

I pull the dress around until I'm in front of the cheap full-length mirror I hung myself. Granted, it doesn't hang straight, but why the hell do they have two tiny hooks on the back? Don't they know it's impossible to line it up correctly? Maybe the door isn't level.

I work with the velvety material. The zipper is stuck in the seam. I work the material back and forth until it breaks free. I step out of the dress and place it on a hanger where it will remain until I have another formal affair. I'm guessing it will probably be the hospital fundraiser, the Musical Gala for Harrow's Children's Hospital. Like Kal, it will help my career to show up when called upon. Mr. Harrow is a prominent name in elite circles. I assume the fundraiser will be a reoccurring event.

Great, I'll have to be in the same room as Dr. Dick at the Gala. I'm not looking forward to it.

I can't get my mind off Kal showing up with the young women who applies makeup like a mad genius. Are they together? What is their deal? My curiosity is driving me crazy as I compare myself to the woman on his arm. I wipe my makeup off in my tiny bathroom. What does he see in me? I'm tall, curvy hips, and my waistline isn't what I'd call slender. I skew my mouth to one side. Decidedly, my build is more of a hockey player than a model.

Why would Kal want me?

Athletes are all the same. Love you when it's convenient to them, then skate out the door. Only Kal didn't. I had a glimmer of hope with him, for us, only to have it smashed to hell two days later.

Go figure, people are always surprising me. But Becka? I overheard someone say she's a meteorologist on the local station in Maine. I glance at the elegant watch on my wrist, a present from Dad for my last birthday. It's eleven o'clock, the news is next.

I grab the remote off my nightstand and turn the TV on. I hate technology. If the clicker doesn't work, I want to be able to fix it. I don't want a talking bubble which can't be fixed with new batteries when it fails.

Commercials play as I open a dresser drawer to pull out my pink pajamas. I stand in front of the flat screen as I step into the comfy cotton bottoms before I pull the long-sleeved top over my head. Anxiously, I wait to see who pops up on the screen. There's no guarantee Becka will be on, I hold my breath, dying to know more about the competition.

Holy shit, it's a rerun of the earlier news. Becka! She looks better in person, judging from our first introduction. I wonder how she and Kal met. More importantly, what they are to each other? Every time I looked their way, she made suggestive moves on Kal and he didn't look happy about it. Good. Serves him right.

I secretly watched the two of them to see if Kal was affectionate towards his date. He sat stiffly in his chair and rarely smiled. Becka gave me weird vibes. I noticed her hand on Kal's arm, like he belonged to her, and she was making a point with every chance she had. Possessive. She was staking a claim because I was there!

Her eyes burn in my back as I sat through the speeches. I hope I don't have to see her again. Now, I understand when Mom talks about the wives and girlfriend drama. Money, power, and competing for status are not the types of endeavors to breed familiarity or contentment.

The strangest reaction, or lack of one, was dad. I was relieved to be in a room filled with people when Kal and I recognized each other, nothing could prepare for this exact moment. To add to my surprise, Dad remained silent.

His attention might have been diverted by the guests. My gut tells me he's too savvy to have missed the tension passing between us. I pray he leaves it alone.

Oddly, I'm satisfied seeing Becka Stamos on TV. I wonder if she and Kal are serious. His hockey buddies were rather quiet for the duration of the evening and trickled out shortly after dinner.

I pull my phone out and flip through the pictures from the evening. I smile at one of dad and me. It was nice having him to myself, for an instant. He's even more popular since he made it to the semifinals last year.

I click the TV off before I crawl into my cold bed. I curl myself into the shape of a crescent moon as I always sleep on my side. I can't fall asleep. I hope Suzy returns my call.

I don't know why I only use half my bed. Maybe secretly I'm an eternal optimist? Maybe one day a man will fill the spot next to me.

I search online with my phone for more information on Becka. She's twenty-six, a graduate of the local university, and dated Kal last year. The entertainment article says the two of them were on and off until a rumor surfaced that it was a mutual breakup. Tonight, however, puts her back on the active list.

Next, I search the Mauler site for my hockey player. I find out he plays center and is number five. His picture is old, his hair is longer now. I think he's cuter with it long. He's from Ohio, he didn't lie about that, and he happens to be the alternate captain of the team.

In my disappointment over our circumstances, I wonder how many broken hearts he's left in his wake.

My phone dings, startling me as the phone is still in my hand. I roll on my back and click the text box, expecting it to be Suzy.

I want to talk. Call me. I can explain.

Kal wants to talk.

Fat chance. It's late and I'm under no pressure. I wonder if he's still with her. I dismiss his text and continue clicking through articles as one blue link after another pop up. I learn he was one of the players who was at a strip club before the playoffs last year. Obviously, he lives his life to the fullest no matter what the public, or the General Manager, think of his behavior.

I can't risk falling for a man with his reputation. He loves to party, and so far, he's not been dealt any consequences by management. Does anything faze him? When will he ever grow up?

I stare at his text on my phone. I'm making him wait. It's time for the real rules of dating to commence. No matter how badly I want to type a reply, it will only complicate the situation further. I'm upset because I could be lighthearted with him. I can't forget how he tickled me in bed and the memory of it brings a smile to my face.

What if I give him an in, and he disappoints me again? I

don't need a broken heart. I had enough hurt experiencing Becka on his arm.

I've already processed my feelings of going from hope to devastation in a hot minute. My rose-colored glasses are off. I can't figure out why Blake didn't tell Kal who I was, clearly there is more at play here.

Thank goodness I had the foresight to not say a word to my mother. She would have asked a hundred questions, for which I wouldn't have any answers. I hate the inquisition she gives me. Sometimes, she forgets I want to be married, it's a tough world, dating.

Besides, I hated Dad traveling all the time, maybe it's best I don't date a hockey player. Kal's career is climbing, and it will come first in his life. I don't want to spend the rest of my life searching for validation from a man who's never home and wonder if he's screwing someone on the road. Kal has left a list of women in his wake.

Suzy calls.

"What's up? How was the event?"

"Great, and not so great."

"Daddy issues?" she guesses.

"Hm, kind of, but more importantly, it was a who's who of celebrities. You'll never guess who was there."

"No, I won't. Tell me." I know she's short on time, we're always short on staff.

"Kal showed up with a weather announcer on his arm."

"Shut the fuck up," she exclaims in disbelief. "You know how to pick them, that's for sure."

"Kal just texted, he wants to talk."

"In his dreams," she replies surly.

"I wasn't honest with Kal, in his defense. I kept my dad's name a secret. I'm screwed if I mention it, and this time it screwed me because I didn't put it out there. I hope my father doesn't find out."

"You had a reason to not say anything. People want access to your dad through you. You told me yourself that's all they talk about once they find out who you are. Can you trust him?"

"I don't know. I have never been out with a hockey player before. I don't think I could keep up with the scrutiny of the media and Mom rarely has anything nice to say about the hockey wives," I add, mulling it over. Do I trust Kal? How does one know? It takes more than a minute and one night to figure it out.

If I told Kal who my dad was, and he was a normal man, who liked sports, the evening would have been over as soon as it began. All our conversation would be on the Coach, and the team's record. It's not fair to me, but that's how it is.

"I'm ignoring him for now. I'm sure my dad wouldn't be impressed if I dated him," I continue. "Dad warned me about hockey players since I was a kid. He'd blow a gasket if he knew."

"You don't have to please your dad. What if Kal is the one?"

"He can't be. Dad and I are trying to get along, dating a player will put a wrench in it. How awkward would that be? He's Kal's boss, it's a conflict of interest."

"More like a crowbar," Suzy chuckles. "You sure know how to pick them. You're a magnet for lost causes," she laments.

"It seems moving changes the social scene for me. I'm to be seen, and not heard, or dated," I elaborate.

"That sucks. It's not your fault your dad is famous, and the players are so hot. I thought your dad's connections would put you in a position to land a good husband."

"One would think," I groan.

"I gotta go. You picked a good night to miss."

"Okay, hang in there."

I click my phone call off.

Shit. I didn't ask her what to do with Kal's text.

I can't pull my eyes away from the picture of him on the website. It's as if he's staring back at me. I want to know what happened to put us on a collision course. Is he a missed opportunity or a walking disaster?

I set my phone on the charger and roll over, turning off the light. I'm tired. Tonight was filled with mixed emotions. I close my eyes. Kal laying in my bed replays as a loop in my head. His smile, inviting abs, not to mention the best sex of my life. I loved digging my nails into his hard buttocks, it's not something a girl easily forgets. It only took one taste for me to be addicted to him.

I'll sleep on it. I can't let dad dictate my dating choices, on the other hand, coaches know everything about the guys, for better or worse. Dad has to hold in a ton of secrets and be careful with the press.

Dad used to play hockey, he has an eye for talent, but he's hard for me to read. However, he's pretty damn good at reading me.

I'm sure Kal has to be sweating this out, too. In the past players have been fired for referring to a coach's daughter as being fat. I can't imagine what he'd think of a player who had a sleep over with his daughter and went out with another woman two days later.

One way or another, Kal and I are in this together until it blows over.

13

Kal

Annie has yet to text me back. I normally don't sweat the small stuff, but it's sticking in my craw the way a tough piece from a rib bone will just lodge in a tooth and makes me run my tongue over it for hours until it's gone. That's the annoyance I find myself in tonight.

Damn. I thought she would text me back out of curiosity, if nothing else.

Breaking it off with Becka didn't go smoothly, not that I ever thought it would. There's a reason for breaks, they can last indefinitely, and I blew it by opening the door again. This break up was long overdue, and I regret not coming to terms with it sooner. I hate change. It's easier to go with the flow.

If I know women, Becka knew the final break was inevitable. She was jealous of Annie and made constant PDA's all night to stake her territory. I need a woman who isn't possessive.

"You made contacts tonight. Let's end this peacefully." I try to cajole her into being rational. I classified her as clinger before and I need to make my escape as soon as possible.

"Fuck you, Kal. I know you like her, the coach's daughter, of all the women to date! How did you two even find each other?"

Wanting to keep Annie and the coach out of this, "I never said it was Annie. You and I ran our course a long time ago. It was my mistake taking you tonight."

She gets out of my sports car, "You're an asshole," she yells and slams the door so hard I wonder if I need to have a mechanic look at it. Thankfully the window in the door didn't break. I take it as my cue to make a speedy exit. I push my foot on the gas pedal, my tires let out a squeal as I peel out on the road.

Once I'm home in my plush condo, I text Annie. I'm peeved Blake and the guys set me up. I'm a smart-ass. I prank everyone, but they got me good.

I thought Coach had a daughter in college and one younger. Not all families attend our events, and rumors aren't always true. In fact, rumors are the cause of bad blood between husbands and wives and sometimes teammates. I have to have a thick skin as the press loves to vilify me for being me. I'm not changing my world to please the press and fans who might condone what I do in my private life. A line has to be drawn. It's easier to be me, and remain me, from the time I turned eighteen.

I never expected Blake and the guys to be so bold. It's evident to me they didn't think this through. The only way anyone can prank me is to do the unexpected, and the guys hit it out of the park. Their only problem is they didn't think of how badly this could end for us.

I abhor secrets, but they can never find out I stayed

over at Annie's. It's what led to my mother's melt down when she found out about Dad. I covered for his gambling, I saw, I didn't know what to do; I was a kid. I figured Mom let him do it, it must be okay. I never want anyone to betray me like that, maybe that's why I don't allow myself to become attached. The pain on my mother's face as she cried on the kitchen floor, wailing when she saw the bank statements and tax returns, makes an impression.

I wasn't supposed to be home that day. Dad was out, and I came home earlier than expected from a hockey game. I stood there, dumbfounded. To make it worse, Mom was leaving. I adore my mother, and yet, we all stayed with dad. We still stayed with him even though he was a rolling stone, living with one girlfriend, then another, and unknown to us, he sweet talked them all out of their savings, using it to gamble.

I suppress the bad memories and remember only the good things about my time with Dad. The fun stuff like going to football or hockey games, and how he bought me autographed hockey jerseys for my birthday. Then the day came when he turned into a stranger, always asking my sister for money as she had a job after school.

Our needs were not being met. We grew tired of fast-food for dinner, and we were wearing clothing we had outgrown. We eventually scurried back to mom like children abandoning a sinking Titanic. I knew we'd be homeless soon.

Mom's house was not as grand as the one we had as kids, but we had a roof over our head, and food on the table.

I strip to my boxers as I sip on sherry oak scotch made in Scotland; aged eighteen years. I swill it around in the tulip shaped glass as I look down on the Moose River running under my window. It stretches from Canada to southern Maine, where it drains into the Atlantic Ocean.

It also runs between the Camden Arena and the new football stadium sponsored by the national bank, Eagle Trust & Investments. Rumor has it the new expansion football team will be called the Megalodons.

I walk over my floors, they would normally be chilled by the cold night air, but mine are heated. My sliding glass doors provide a city view of the nightscape. I'm just a heartbeat away from the arena and training facility. My building, River Run, has two elevators allowing me to use the override button to reach my penthouse.

The new tiles I used to renovate the place resemble natural wood. I picked a neutral color of beige with light brown. I love my condo life because everything is done for me. I have a cleaning person, and when I travel, I don't have to worry about maintenance issues. We have a building supervisor who takes care of repairs, accepts packages and other perks, for a monthly fee.

The building is secure. I enjoy limited contact with other residents, my job and social engagements are part of my job. My home is for me, and me only. I have no need to put down roots when life is unpredictable. I'm not letting anyone hurt me the way Dad hurt Mom.

PRACTICE IS eleven in the morning. I stroll in with my expensive coffee with a shot of espresso. Sean looks a bit rough; Colton Cermak definitely has a hangover. He's one of the newer players, a veteran, he's been to the playoffs, making it to round three. He's a fun guy, off the chain if you ask me, but we need a big boy on defense and he's the one to get chippy for us when we need the heavy hitting.

"Colton, you, okay?" I quip walking by him.

"I'll be fine," he chugs an eight-ounce water, before he gingerly raises one leg, then the other, as he steps into his butt pads.

I chuckle. He's a bit boozy, has long hair the press loves to rave about, and has a son from a previous relationship. Never married, thankfully we share the same opinion of marriage. Who needs it today?

Why do women need a ring? It's more of a status symbol. And yet, I watch as one guy after another go into the mist of wedded bliss. I'm afraid it won't be blissful for me. I suppose it's why I keep women at arm's length, afraid an idyllic night with a woman might lead to something permanent. I haven't thought about anything after that point, preferring to live day to day.

Our social media hockey pages are filled with adorable engagement pictures and wedding portraits, but we all know the women love the bling and size matters. Does it ever! If the ring isn't the one she wants, the men hear about it. They have this program at jewelry stores where the guys can go back and trade up the original ring into something bigger and better. The more a player makes, the bigger that diamond becomes for some unlucky bastard who has to pay for it.

I like my money in my savings account and traveling in the summer. I plan on retiring when I can no longer play. I have my life set up the way I want, no messy divorces, and no kids to support.

"Blake, everything go okay after I left last night?" I hate to ask, but I need to know if we're still in the clear.

"Yeah, why wouldn't it? Rachel wanted to dance, so we

left an hour after you. It was a nice affair, low key. How was Becka? She was seething all night."

"Between you and me, we're officially over. I'm glad it was only my car door she slammed," I speak softly as it's not something I want to broadcast. Nothing wrong with letting others think what they want. I don't comment to the press so all they can do is speculate and print lies.

He chuckles, "You got off easy. The tension between you and Annie was eleven on the richter scale, man. What is up with that?"

"I don't know what you're talking about. She's a nice girl." I chuck my empty coffee cup across the room and listen for the thud as it sinks into the old, circular container lined with a plastic bag. It's the ones I grew up with in every arena across the United States. Some things never change, and often, it's for the best.

Blake, Colton, and Finn are gearing up. I waste no time catching up, I'm usually waiting on them. The guys mill around with small talk, it's a lazy Friday as we have a game tomorrow night.

I grab my jersey, toss it on, and we head to the ice. I arrive first and skate out. I'm a quarter of the way around the rink when I realize no one is following me. Fuck, we did this to Blake when he was new to our team, I'm not new.

I turn to take in the guys laughing their asses off as they stand together on the ice, leaning on their sticks, not moving.

What the fuck?

I skate back, throwing snow as I stop.

"Dude, we got you," Colton crows.

"What?" I ask, letting my helmet sink to the ice as I paw at the back of my jersey. I get my grip and pull it off.

"This is priceless," Finn laughs as he doubles over, snapping a picture.

How can they possibly get me twice in a week? These bastards are unrelenting.

The back of my jersey says Kohlman-Susneck.

Fuck me.

"I give it to you for originality," I chuckle. "It ain't happening. No way do I want Coach as a father-in-law."

"Men," is heard above us. We freeze. Coach isn't supposed to be here today. It's our skate, and the captain is running today's practice. It's a down day to regroup and decompress. "Kal, in my office, the rest of you can do laps for an hour. Morning skate tomorrow is now six in the morning."

Coach turns towards the hallway without another word.

"You're so busted, Kal," Colton remarks so Coach can't hear.

"Fuck you," I reply. "Good luck getting up at five in the morning tomorrow. Nice going on the jersey, guys." My sarcastic retort doesn't come close to how peeved I am, as the guys pranked me twice in one week. I'm not a nervous man by nature, but I'm quaking in my skates.

I glare at Blake as I leave, the rest of the team hits the ice for an hour of skating. I'm sure I'll be joining them after Coach finishes reaming me a new asshole.

14

Annie

I don't have an artistic bone in my body. I take a swatch of colors off the rack at Jack O'Shea's, the local handyman store. I peruse the paint chips on the cards before I pick one with blue palettes and complementing accent colors. I lift the card to see the light on it, trying to decide if the house walls would look good with a pinch of blue on them. Maine, water, it seems to fit. I have five gallons of Worn Denim paint mixed and hope it gives my home a face lift.

The color is a mix of chic and rugged, fitting of the landscape. I can't stand the old eggshell color on the walls, it reminds me of scrambled eggs because the color has yellowed in spots. It's unclear if it's caused by sun damage or the age of the paint.

I toss plastic tarps in my cart, stirring sticks, and other miscellaneous items like rollers, brushes, and containers. I survey the cart and figure this should do it. There was a ladder left in the garage, so I chuck a step stool on my load and check myself out. Cooler fall weather rolled in when I wasn't paying attention this week. The sky is gray as I pile everything into the trunk of my SUV.

Kal is on my mind. I didn't return his text. I'm playing by the rules. No more missteps for me. I don't know why I can't get him out of my head. I turn the radio up to distract me and it's the Hillbilly weatherman. I listen to this man from New Hampshire and crack up with his colorful commentary. He's only on in winter as the weather is so horrendous. There's no telling when our first snowfall will come. I smile and chuckle, as the inbound weather isn't newsworthy. Looks like days in the sixties and nights in the forties for the week.

Getting the five-gallon container of paint in my house is not as easy as it was at the store with a rolling cart. In lieu of the fact I don't have a wagon to wheel it across the yard. I back up to the garage which was made to look like a barn with funky hinges.

I manage to lug the huge container out of the trunk and shimmy it across three feet of concrete and into the garage with a large cement apron. I lay the other bags filled with supplies next to it and head into the house. I text Suzy to tell her we can have a night of wine and painting one night this week. I even throw in the fact I will make homemade Bolognese sauce for dinner.

She calls me by the time I hit the coffee pot for a second time today.

"What's up? God, you're an early riser."

"Bad habit, I'm like my dad. Up with the sun."

"Ewe," she yawns.

"How was last night?"

"Good, busy, the flu is going around. Dr. Dick was off, so

I enjoyed work without having to keep my guard up. Why is it so exhausting when he's there?"

"Yeah, we're going to have to do something if this keeps up, I don't know what," I add, lamenting the fact one person can make our working environment intolerable.

"Any word from Kal?"

"Radio silence, I didn't text him back. I'm not breaking the dating rules ever again. It's so stressful, dating."

"Ah, the necessary evil."

"What about you? Aren't you on a dating app?"

"I have a fuck buddy, works for me. He's so much better than a vibrator. Did you know you have to lay off those things or you'll be desensitized when you have a man in you?"

"I know. But Kal's cock was so magnificent. It was even better than the vibrator, too, and I had multiple orgasms. I never knew I could do that."

"That's amazing, you're lucky. So, what are we doing today?"

"Oh, that new movie I want to see is out, we could do that."

"Sounds fun, I'll look for the one with the fighter jets in it and that aging hunk from the eighties, hold on, let me check the times on my phone." She pauses and I hear her *tapping* on her phone. "Yes. There is an early movie, two o'clock. Then I can follow you home and help you paint. We might be able to knock out a room."

"Great, I'll start the Bolognese sauce now and let it cook until I leave."

"Okay, and I'll meet you at the theater in Camden Bay, on Main Street."

"See ya there."

Great, I get to have some fun and get some work done

around here. I prep the ground beef, cooking it in an iron skillet I've had for years. I love the seasoned pan. I add old red wine from the fridge, letting it burn off, then add cream, stirring the contents together. I turn it down and quickly add cornstarch to more cream, adding a small can of tomato paste, diced tomatoes and Italian seasoning.

I stir and take a taste before adding a tablespoon of sugar. After stirring it again, I put the lid on and turn the burner to low so it will simmer and reduce the moisture.

Upstairs, I dressed in jeans, but want to look nicer, one never knows when they might run into a cute guy. Who am I fooling? All I can imagine are Kal's eyes staring into mine as he filled me up with his large . . . Mm, I sigh. The fit was as tight as a lug nut on an old tire.

Damn him.

I rummage through my closet and pull out sexy boots. I really need to organize my room. I chuck everything in my closet, and it's become the eighth wonder of the world. Finding a matching set of footwear in five minutes or less alludes me.

I decide on the short boots with a spiked heel to match my purse and apply a tinge of makeup. It's time to leave and I wobble over the pavers to my vehicle and if it wasn't for the narrow-spiked heels, I would be better off walking in the grass, or barefoot.

THE MOVIE WAS AMAZEBALLS. We talk excitedly as we walk to our cars. I turn my phone on and it lets off one ding after another. I'm not on call. What is going on?

"If it's telemarketers, I'm going to cuss them out," I mumble to Suzy.

"Sounds like it might be something important," she says as she gets into her car.

"I'll see you at the house," I reply as I walk four cars over and get in my vehicle.

Once I'm inside I listen to the voice mail from Kal. What could he possibly want now?

"Hey, just want to give you the head's up…"

Heads up on what? Where is the message? I check the battery bar and it's red, apparently it doesn't work when it's that low. In my frustration, I chuck it in my purse. He can't possibly have anything to tell me that's urgent. He's a hockey player, not immediate family, and definitely not my friend.

As much as I try to ignore the fact he called, I can't wait to charge my phone. My heart goes pitter patter every time I hear his voice.

I drive faster than normal to get home. My stomach is in knots as I push the gas pedal. What is going on? What is so urgent he's calling me?

15

Kal

Anxiety swells in my chest as I make the well-
known trek to Coach's office in the training facility. I stand inside the door as he moves past me,
slamming the door and moves behind his desk. He doesn't
sit down.

"What are you doing with my name on the back of your
jersey?"

I shift from one foot to the other as I teeter on my skates.
To stand on these mats is deplorable, I'd rather be on
the ice.

"It was just a silly prank, Coach."

"I have a feeling it's more than that. Are you seeing my
daughter? Because I have to tell you I'm not impressed. You
have the worst reputation on the team. No, strike that. The
entire NHL." He looms over his desk, forcing me to look into
his angry eyes.

"I know."

"Well, I don't want headlines of the two of you parading

around. I don't want you around my daughter, period. And if you are, you'd better be serious. And, you better clean up your act."

Coach's face softens a bit as he finishes the sentence. Maybe he's seeing the positive side of the situation. He'll be able to reign me in once and for all.

"Got it," I reply meekly. I'm in a no-win situation. The less I say, the better it is for all of us.

"Now get out there and skate your hour before practice," he dismisses me.

I open the door and retrace my steps to the ice, where I join the team.

"Nice going, Kal," Finn grumbles as he passes me on a corner.

"We're all in this together," I remind him, speaking more to myself.

We take our punishment as Coach, Nicol, and the assistant coach, Max Fortin, take their places behind us as we sit stoically on the bench.

Coach barks orders, still steaming over the revelation of me and his daughter seeing each other. I'm relieved he didn't ask for details. I'm not sure the situation is resolved. I've never seen him so pissed. The way he leaned over his desk was epic.

Methodically, we take turns showering after Coach drilled us at practice. The locker room is uncharacteristically quiet, like a bunny hopping across a yard.

I've never felt closer to my teammates than I do today. We prank each other, and it's only a matter of time before one goes sideways. It's a family tradition we have, and we all take our share of the fun, and the punishment. I figure this might make us all a team.

Blake's jovial demeanor is gone. In my defense, he

started this shit show.

We're in the doghouse. There isn't anything we can do to change the fact we're up early tomorrow and it will be a pain in the ass to play tomorrow night with an early alarm.

I find my real practice jersey is hanging in my locker when I open it.

Son of a bitch, they got me. They got me good. I don't know what to do with the extra jersey, so I carry it with me to my car.

Viktor is behind me, wearing a white baseball cap backwards, "See you tomorrow."

"See ya." I remote start my silver Porsche even though it's not cold enough to need it. I turn the stereo up to drown out the replay of Coach's voice.

I wonder what Annie is doing. She hasn't returned my text from last night and I'm sure she's seen it.

She has some of her father in her for sure. I wonder how long she'll be pissed. Normally, I don't give a shit about a woman blowing me off, it takes me by surprise as it's a rare occurrence. Puck bunnies know the rules of the game. Annie isn't that, however I find myself in new territory.

She's ignoring me on purpose, and it's driving me crazy. I'm annoyed. It's time she heard my side of the events. I have to make it right with her, this way, coach will be off my back. I'll end it once and for all, she'll get her closure and we can go our separate ways.

I stop into a local burger joint on the way home to eat and take the opportunity to look up Annie on a browser on my phone. I don't find much on her. How could I have been so blind to not know more about Coach? How am I so wrapped up in myself I don't even know his daughter moved to town? I was on a date with her for two hours and didn't put it together.

I finish my burger, remembering Annie's warmth on my skin, her soft hair, and full lips when she smiles. She's sweet, and not caught up in the media's spotlight, otherwise I would have seen her picture.

I can't get her out of my head. I need an in, something to make her call me.

I dial her number, fuck texting, it's too easy to ignore. She doesn't answer. I leave a short message. Time is moving as slow as an inch worm as I can't take waiting. I call again. I have to make it dramatic, then she'll have to call back.

"Annie, call me, it's about your dad," the second message might sound cryptic, but I'm pulling out all the stops. She should be warned her father is on the warpath. I have an obligation, don't I?

I let myself be guided by the system in my car. I travel out of Camden Bay. Normally, I don't vary from my set path in my daily routine. It's what I know and I'm comfortable with it. I turn on to an older road and look in my rear-view mirror, colorful fall leaves are stirred in my wake and blow effortlessly behind me.

I'm heading into uncharted territories on a few fronts and my hands turn sweaty on the steering wheel. I play with the air conditioning, setting it lower. Cold air jettisons out of the vents like a turbo engine.

I'm sweating bullets as I pull into her driveway and notice two cars.

I hope Coach isn't here. That would be awkward.

Annie and a woman with her are carting a five-gallon container into the side door of the house. I rethink my plan and am about to make a sharp U-turn, but it's too late. They've spotted my shiny car.

I inhale deeply as I prepare myself for another tongue lashing from another Susneck family member.

16

Annie

Kal parks his car and approaches us as we're trying to get the paint through the doorway. The five-gallon tub teeters precariously on the threshold.

"Hey, did you get my calls?" he inquires.

"The ones about Dad? I'm fine. What's the emergency?" Kal knows I'm a doctor. Crisis is my middle name; I thrive on it. Dad hasn't said anything to me and I'm content to let sleeping dogs lie."

"Hm." He shoves his key fob into the front pocket of his jeans and crosses his arms like Mr. Clean from the old TV commercials. I can't deny how dreamy he is in daylight.

"No emergency?" His voice is more pronounced and I'm shocked as I've never seen him this keyed up. "He's putting us together, and he's not a fan."

I suppress my chuckle. The irony of this is priceless.

He's a man who doesn't care about his reputation, or so

he professes. Why now? Is he concerned for himself, his career, or us?

"That sounds like a 'you' problem." I turn back to him as Suzy and I struggle with it once more.

"Let me," he says, moving us out of the way with his arms, gallantly lifts the container, and deposits it to the corner I point to.

"Thanks," I murmur.

He gives the paint a cursory glance before his attention shifts to me. "Are you okay?"

"I'm fine." I'm not making it easy on him. And I don't care.

"I have to explain about the date," he starts, only I interrupt him.

"Let me guess. Blake set you up on a blind date and didn't tell you who I am. Well, I'm not laughing at your childish antics. In my opinion, y'all need to adult." I put my hand on my hip, surveying the area we set up with the clear tarp, sticks, and painting trays, and ignore how handsome he is, especially when he pushes his aviator sunglasses over his head and our eyes meet, I'm in a trance.

My panties are damp even without his touch. I'm a doctor and some eyes change colors when the male become excited. It's strange to think of him in a clinical view, especially when I have flash backs to our hot night and how many times I orgasmed.

He glances around the room, then to his feet. Is this him not being arrogant? Is it possible he feels remorse over the situation? He shuffles his weight from one foot to the other, and remembers I haven't introduced him to my friend, and takes matters into his own hands.

"Hi, I'm Kal," he says, putting his hand out for Suzy to shake.

"Nice to meet you," she replies politely, shaking his outstretched hand.

"Pleasure to meet you." He gives her a polite smile before he turns back to me.

"I'm sorry for the way things went, but I'm not sorry we met. I kinda like you, and I was hoping we could go out again."

"I'm pretty busy, Kal," I mumble as I fiddle with my car keys hanging out of the waist band on my blue jeans.

"How about I leave you and Suzy tickets to the game tonight, think on it. It's the least I can do." He stretches his long arms out to imply he's harmless and making peace. I imagine his strong hands holding a stick and the thought of it excites me once more as my pussy gushes, making it painfully obvious this man is my kryptonite. "I'd love for us to have a do over."

My heart does a backflip in my chest, like riding my first rollercoaster. Can I give him another chance?

Wait. Did he just admit he wants to see me again? He likes me?

His eyelashes are long enough to frame his gorgeous eyes. I'd need professional extensions to make mine look that lush, and even with that, they would be nowhere near his. His voice is deep, but humble. I'm defenseless, trying to perform like I'm an ice queen and the 'no' I want to spit in his face gets stuck in my throat. I can't bring myself to say 'no'. I'm not an ice queen, even on my worst day.

I glance to Suzy, who I know would love to take in a Sunday night game. She can barely contain her excitement as her hands are at the ready, ready to clap if I say yes. She's my best friend, I can't disappoint her.

"We'll go to the game," I concede.

"Great, I'll leave tickets at will call," he replies with a jovial smile.

"Thanks, Kal." Suzy springs to life, giving him a hug, and claps her hands. She's elated. I hope she doesn't slip on my floor with her overpriced slip-on sneakers.

"Well, I have to go. I need my rest before the game," he informs me as he moves towards the door. "Can I call you later?"

"Sure," I reply. I've punished him enough for one day.

He hovers, at a loss of what to do. He makes a decision, steps close to me, and boldly leans in to kiss my lips. I swear he's smelling my neck at the same time. The lightest movement of air gives my nose a tickle. He must have used something with a citrus scent, it's airy, and calming. How does he make my heart race in anticipation before he touches me?

He's a walking contradiction where my body is concerned. I can't control the how or why my body turns into a slick mess, melting like butter in the desert, every time he's near me. It can be just a phone call, and the results are the same. Will I ever be able to concentrate with him around me?

"Talk to you later," he whispers in my ear. His lips leave me aching for more. "Nice meeting you Suzy," he throws over his shoulder as he makes a smooth exit and we both watch him sink into his sleek car.

"He's nice," Suzy adds breathlessly. She smiles, then turns to me when her eyes leave Kal's ass.

I give her a look, "Et tu Brute?" I'm not so amused observing the effect Kal has on women. Suzy is getting laid on an as needed basis and her jaw dropped a mile.

"What? A girl can look. Does he have friends?" she whines.

"I'm sure he does. Y'know, I can't say if they like him or tolerate him." I shrug.

"Good point. He couldn't keep his eyes off you," she replies as she bends over the paint and observes the color on the lid.

I glance at my fitness watch as we shuffle the tub of paint closer to the containers. "We have a few hours before the game, I guess we can get some painting done."

"We need to get to it before the paint settles," she agrees.

"Oh, I know I'll get smutzed up with paint before the game and my nails are perfect now. I'll start it later this week. How about we pre-game with some wine?"

"Sounds good to me," her voice conveys her relief, so we stack the paint with the supplies in the corner. "My, I'm out of shape, just getting that five-gallon container to the door kicked my ass." Suzy proceeds to the kitchen, making impromptu squats on the way as she slowly closes the distance between us.

"Are you alright? You're too young to be out of shape. Maybe this wine will loosen your muscles," I snicker as I grab a red from the counter and try to open it with a simple wine opener whereby, I manage to break the cork in two. "Damn it! This always happens when I really want a glass of alcohol." Anything I can find which will calm my nerves after that hunk of a man is going to be added to the kitchen. "It's like the universe is conspiring against me."

"Don't I know it!" She flips her wrists indicating she'll give it a try.

I wrestle with the wine gadget and I'm ready to break the damn bottle, it's so exasperating.

"Here, I'll do it," Suzy volunteers. I gladly hand her the opener and the bottle this time. I'm beyond help at this point.

"Good luck with that. Dry corks suck." I reach in a cabinet for two wine glasses, the good ones, compliments of my mother's great taste. The top is wide so the wine can breathe. These goblets aren't made with thin glass, and I love them.

I hear a tiny pop. "Eureka," she exclaims, "we have wine!"

"Yes, we do." I set the glasses on the counter with extra care.

She pours until the glasses are half full, and we sit on the black leather bar stools facing the open kitchen with a view of my backyard. I take a sip of the red liquid.

"You know," she glances around, "you need furniture."

"I know. I hate picking stuff out. I have deplorable taste and my mother and sister are in Paris."

"Lucky them." Suzy sips her wine for the fourth time, "This is good wine, I'm partial to ones with lighter body, but this is really good."

"Thanks, I'm a bit of a wine snob. Mom took me to Italy after high school."

"Wow, does your dad ever go?"

"Occasionally, the team will have a game overseas, Finland, or whatever. My parents take a big trip every summer, this year they went to Greece."

"Where would you go, if you were to go somewhere now?"

"Hm, any reason why?" I quip as I tilt my head to see her holding the glass to her lips again. The wine goes down smooth like sipping grape juice, catching me by surprise. I want to gobble more because each sip is as good as the last and the alcohol isn't hitting me, yet.

"Just curious, my fuck buddy wants me to go on a trip with him to Aruba, a cruise."

"Well, that sounds more like a boyfriend than a fuck buddy. Go, for heaven's sake. You get along okay in small places?"

"Um, my apartment is eight hundred square feet. We'll be on a huge boat, so yeah," she sips the wine, smacks her lips delicately, "I would call it a vacation even with a small cabin."

"Get on it, girl. You'll have a great time. Who is this mystery man, anyway?"

"Mitch, he's sweet, he owns a mechanic shop not far from the hospital."

"He sounds nice."

"I think so," she muses as she observes the afternoon sunlight on her glass.

"Is it serious?"

"I don't want to jinx it, so I'm just going with it," she replies.

"Well, eventually you have to have 'the talk'."

"I know." She twists her chair around to face me, using her feet on the bottom rung of my chair like a teenager.

"What's the downside?" I ask, curious as to how serious the relationship is, as things are never the same after your BFF gets officially hooked up, in my opinion.

"I haven't found one yet. We're very compatible."

"That's great. It's hard to find. Nothing is perfect. I mean, if he's supportive of your career and doesn't cheat on you, you are doing well in today's world."

"I know, right?" She grins, refilling her glass before it's empty.

∾

I PAY for parking and find my spot. I didn't tell Dad I'd be here, wishing to be a normal spectator with no pressure. If he knew I was here, his feelings might be hurt, but I can't be associated with Kal. I'm not ready to be bombarded with questions from Mom, I love her, but I don't need pressure. I'm going to enjoy being in this bubble with Kal and take life one day at a time.

I should be anxious, giving him a second chance, and not knowing what comes next. Normally, my compulsive behavior takes over and crushes the very thing I want with my overly zealous manner. Like those tiny orchids they sell in the grocery store, I kill every one of them as I over water them and yet, I pick up the challenge again. Maybe I'm a glutton for punishment.

Suzy and I enter the area with our tickets and the smell of candied pecans greets my nose, the air is energized as I see one Mauler jersey after another on fans as they walk the main corridor. We find our seats, then go back up top to grab expensive burgers and fries. We eat sitting in our chairs waiting for the guys to come out for their warmup on the ice.

I can't refrain from watching for player number five, and I'm excited when I see him zipping around. I wish we were standing with the small crowd on the glass to get an upfront view of him, but it would be too obvious. I'm sure the entire team knows my face after the event we attended. The cat is out of the bag on that.

I find I'm enthralled watching him skating in the game. I yelled so much I lose my voice by the third period. My ears ring from the noise as music is played at each stoppage of play but I have the time of my life. The Maulers beat the Detroit Brawlers 4-1.

17

Kal

It's Monday afternoon, Annie is off early, so I stop at the grocery store to see if there's anything I should bring with me. I notice a small planter of herbs, and I instinctively know she would love this. I can't remember what her kitchen looks like, but she can find a spot in any window. Winter is coming, so it has to remain indoors until spring.

I grab sandwiches. Since we're going to paint a few hours, we'll need food. I have a game later so my time is limited.

I'm decked out in older jeans as I don't do manual labor, however she needs help with painting. I need to help her fix her place up. Not that I'm perfect. Well, maybe I am a bit, which is why I find kids messy.

I knock, she's not here. Funny, she should be. Her car is here. I open the door and call her name. She's not answering. I put the planter in her windowsill to check the house, and finding it empty, I text her. Her phone dings in the kitchen.

Shit.

Worried, I walk outside to look around. I have no one to call and assume she might be at a neighbor's. The lots are one to two acres. That would take a few minutes, especially if she's chatting with someone.

I pace, where could she be? What do I do? My heart sinks to my stomach and it churns. See, having no attachments prevents me from having to worry and stress out. Only games should give me these ailments.

"There you are," she says, walking through the door with sunlight behind her, making a halo over her head. All my fear and dread fade away in an instant. I take her in my arms and squeeze her as if I'd never see her again.

"I was worried about you," I murmur into her ear as I take in a breath of her.

"I went over to help a neighbor with her new phone."

I pull away to kiss her lips, our time apart was too long. Her lips yield under mine as I apply more pressure, anxious to claim all of her.

"I want you, now."

"It's only afternoon, we have all night," she teases, running her hand up the side of my face. She pulls her head back, tilts it to one side and looks into my eyes. She's searching for something, and I have no clue what it might be. Does she trust me? Did she want me?

"Any time is a great time. Worry if I'm not chasing you around the house. It shouldn't be a complaint."

"You're right, I want you too, Kal. I've missed you."

"I missed you so much," I devour her lips, running my hands through her thick hair, move it off her shoulder to reveal her neck, and the sweet spots I know drive her crazy.

Her panties are wet, I can tell by her breathing. She's into me as much as I'm into her, and we have something special. I'm aching for her. My cock is hard, and the zipper is beginning to hurt.

"Hm," she moans, her hand feeling how hard I am before slipping her fingers under my balls covered by thin jeans.

"I saw you on TV the other night."

"The game?" I ask.

"Oh, I saw a few minutes of that, but you were on a talk show."

"That must have been taped a while ago or a rerun."

"Could be."

"Why, is there a problem?"

She pulls back, "Let's sit, it's been a long week."

My cock wanes, is this a blow off?

"What's up?" Panic in my chest. She can't be breaking this off, we're just getting started.

"I think we should get to know each other, instead of jumping into bed at the sight of one another."

"You're worried you're just another girl because of Becka and the media? That's in my past. We're here. Why are you putting the brakes on when we haven't even opened the engine to full throttle?"

"I don't even know what that is," she gives a tiny chuckle.

The situation is not 'chuckle' worthy.

"Did your dad say something to you?"

"No, but I'll be at the game tonight. I'm sitting behind him. So, behave," she warns.

"Thanks for the heads up. Why do I get the feeling there is something you're not telling me? What's up with you and your dad? He reamed me out a good one when the team put your name behind mine on the back of my jersey at a practice last week."

"What?"

She's not putting me on, her eyes are as wide as a Gerber Daisy's middle. Perfectly round, solid, and hers are bright with surprise.

"The team thought it was funny to let me skate out with the jersey by myself–with your last name added to it. I got halfway around the rink and knew something was up. It was funny for them, well, all of us, until your dad walked in."

"What? He knows?" she screeches and her breathing ramps up.

"Let's say he assumes something happened between us. He gave me shit, and it appears to have blown over."

"What did he say?"

"Well, we had to skate an hour, then we had a six a.m. practice the next day and he told me to not fuck around with you."

"Oh," she nods, suddenly calm. "He did?"

"Yeah, like that's never happened to you?"

"No player ever asked me out before. He intimidates everyone, I guess."

"What about you?"

Annie moves to the fridge and offers me lemonade. We both sit at the counter in the kitchen, our knees face each other.

"It's complicated. Dad was gone, he never seemed interested in me or what I was doing. I don't know him well, and I regret it. It's why I moved here to be near him. I'm trying to have a better relationship with him."

"Coach? He's great. I can't imagine him not being there for you. He's got our back with everything and he's always there to talk to."

"I know. That's part of my anger, I came last."

"Oh," I sip the homemade lemonade. Shit, I never thought we were taking away from coach's kids. Sure, we all have a demanding schedule. There's no way I could have known. "The team thought his kids were younger. We don't pry into his life." I set the drink on the counter and hear the glass meet the granite.

"Your dad is great. I don't have to tell you. Last year gave us a wake-up call and we're determined more than ever to make it to the playoffs. We're getting our stride."

"I can tell." She smiles emphatically and it makes me happy I'm sitting here, with her. "So, Dad will be more focused on the team than me as usual," she twists the glass between her fingers, wistfully.

"What's up Annie? I haven't known you long, but I'm here for you."

"Well, we have a handsy doctor at work who works over me and my friend Suzy."

"You shouldn't have to put up with a hostile work environment," I state, following her to the portion of the living room where the tub of paint sits.

"It's not a perfect world. We can't complain, we'll be putting our careers in the shitter. However, we can start painting."

"I had other things in mind," I reply as I pull her back into my arms and she lets out a shriek. "You're too serious, but I'll help you paint."

I sense she has something else on her mind, but I'll give her some time to share it with me. I'm not going anywhere. In fact, I think I'll ask her dad for permission to date her officially. I hate hiding us.

As much as I want to thrust my cock in her, there's a time and a place, this isn't the time to be selfish.

"What is your relationship with your dad?" she asks as I pop the lid off the paint, and she hands me a stir stick.

"He's not in my life anymore. He gave up that privilege."

"Why?"

"He gambled everything away, lied to mom, me. He has a record now, and he's never going to change. I have to distance myself from him."

I know she's thinking I have the money he wants access to.

"What's your main beef with your dad?"

"He says he never gave me advice, or overly fathered me like my sister because I didn't need him. He said I was independent; I knew what I wanted. I was an easy child to raise."

"Ouch. Yeah, even if you were, it doesn't mean you didn't need him. I get it." I'm done stirring and pour paint into the pan and from there I put some in her tiny pint with a handle to work the trim.

"So, can you paint?" she asks, "or are you just going through the motions to make it look good?" She has a thin paintbrush in her hand.

"Yes, on all accounts," I smile. She's radiant and adorable as she stands with short shorts on, even though it's cool in here. I can't wait to observe her bending over in them.

"You know... just to finish the dad issues. Mine is toxic. He's an addict. Yours works a demanding job with travel. Your job is demanding and stationary."

She raises her eyebrows. "Sure, you'll be on his side."

"There's no side, really. What I'm trying to say is, your dad did his best, and he's not perfect. What he's done isn't unforgivable. It's hurtful, sure, but so is betrayal. You dad is redeemable, mine isn't."

"Hm, good point. Are you going to become a lawyer

when you've retired?" She dips her paintbrush into the paint.

"Hell no, I'm going to be a sports announcer. That's what we all aim for when our knees give out and we're not so fast on the ice. Are you kidding me? It's in our blood." I act put out, and she lets out a hearty laugh.

"You're great. Thank you." She applies paint to the wall, and I'm mesmerized by the way she moves her paintbrush back and forth, as if she's lost in thought.

I kick my expensive sneakers off and bend over to pick up the roller and notice her feet are turned towards me. I lift my head.

"You're ogling my ass!"

"It's so cute," she coos. "A girl can't help but check out the goods."

"Oh, really?" I take a step towards her and put a streak of paint on her nose.

She inhales with surprise.

"Oh, you..." she runs her brush down my t-shirt.

I put my fingers in the paint and grab her tight ass, denim and flesh.

The look on her face is priceless. I laugh, a deep laugh, who knew painting could be fun?

She sets her container on the ladder behind her and we're all over each other. She's clawing at my shirt. I wipe my hand on her jeans and I hate to do it because I love them on her. The more pressing issue is I need my hands to not be wet and sticky, so I can undo her bra and strip her naked.

She bolts to the steps, kicking off her slip-on sneakers and shredding clothing as she flies up the staircase.

"I call interference, your clothes are obstacles," I yell as I take the steps three at a time with my long legs.

She giggles and I can't wait to kiss her all over and make

love to her in the day light. It's a beautiful day as I catch her leaping on her bed and let out a squeal.

I pull my shirt off and toss it. I unzip my pants and they slide off with my sneakers. Boxers, gone.

"Your turn." I give her a smirk before I pull her to me and reach my hands up to let her breasts tumble inside a t-shirt from her college years. I tug it over her head and my moist lips are on her nipple. I suck hard, making her moan as I grab her ass and dig my fingers in just enough to bring her towards me as I set her toes on the ground.

She runs her hand through my hair, our eyes meet. My insides warm, there is a twinge I've never experienced, and my cock is a flagpole.

Her hand slides over him, warming up the shaft. I lift her, laying her on top of the comforter as I hover over her.

"What am I to do with you, Annie?"

"Make love to me all day," she murmurs as she dips her fingers into her own wetness and places them in my mouth.

I groan because it's so hot, and she tastes so good.

"I could eat you all day, who needs food?"

"Mm." Her head tilts back, her eyelids close as her fingers lace through the hair on my chest and I experience a quick hurt as she gives a rough tug, drawing me closer to her. My cock is at the perfect angle to enter, I pause wondering if she wants more foreplay.

"So soon?"

"Fuck me Kal or I swear…"

I thrust into her causing her body to slide three inches over the bedsheets as she takes me in fully. I'm not small. She bites her bottom lip for an instant and her eyes finally open and she allows herself to stare into mine.

I'm on fire with desire as we grind into each other, harder and faster, until we explode together as she moans my name and her fingers cling to my shoulders as her back is arched like a gymnast.

"Damn, Annie, that was incredible." I roll off her, but not before I pull her into my chest and wrap my arms around her. I want to stay all day. Reality hits and I have to get home to prepare for a road trip.

I MISS Annie and order flowers to be delivered to her at work. It's a bit over the top. I can't stop thinking about her. I hope she likes spring flowers. I find roses are redundant. Yellow for friendship, red for love, and I'm not ready to commit to love, but we're more than friends. I'm afraid to get my hopes up out of fear something will befall us. I travel with her dad, and I'm on thin ice with the staff, so I can't have another fuck up. I also don't have years to make up my mind on what Annie is to me.

I call a landscaper to have her pavers fixed. It's an accident waiting to happen. I can't deny I'm preventing what could turn into a cautionary tale. Annie can't risk falling on those, the ground has shifted, and she needs to get in her house safely. She's a surgeon and needs her hands, just like I need mine for my job. What we do with them when we're together gives me plenty of thought at night as I replay our date in my head.

After talking with her more this past week, I can't deny how deep my attraction runs. I admire the fact she's smart and independent. If I knew the creep at work she mentioned gets handsy, we'd have an issue. It's sweet how she's protecting me, as she knows I'd have her back and put a stop to it.

She's calls me on my crap, and she can dish out one-liners, giving as good as she gets. If I'm honest with myself, I need someone like her to kick my ass. Our discussion on our dads was illuminating. I assumed she had a golden spoon in her mouth. I never thought of what might have been traded in the process for the career Coach has, and I wonder if he treats her sister differently.

Annie is tough, I'll give her credit for where she is, and maybe we went without nice things as kids, but Mom's love was evident every day. She hugged me well past being a kid, we're an affectionate bunch, and we all deliver one-liners to each other all the time. It's what kids do, and the tradition hasn't died.

I hated to see Mom struggle to make ends meet and lived in my hockey world to escape it. Annie went into a premed track in high school so we both are capable of overcoming obstacles. Adapting, I guess. There comes a point in every person's life whereby something good needs to come from the carnage we lived through. I prefer to leave mine in the past.

The hurt is always there, like a scar. I hope Annie can move on with a new understanding of her father. Families are complex, one's love language is giving gifts, another's affection. We can't read each other's minds and if we didn't have the low points of our lives, we wouldn't appreciate the days when everything in our world is amazing. We'd be static without change.

But having those scars, means we've survived. We loved, we lived, we may have lost, but we got back up. It's life. In my opinion, if a person doesn't have a past, they haven't lived. Annie has showed me if I don't put more into a relationship, I'll continue to repeat the past. Undoubtably, there will be more Becka's. I don't want someone who uses me to make a career. I don't want someone who is capable of being vindictive to manipulate me. I no longer want the status quo.

I want the fireworks I get with Annie. From misunderstandings we resolve, to working on her house, it's scary because it's new. When I enter my condo, it's sterile, and perfect. Annie has me walking on grass instead of the marble floors. Her house has character, and it's growing on me. We are opposites in some areas, but we fit, like puzzle pieces nestled together. I thought I left my country boy ways of the Midwest for the city here, but Annie brings me back to my roots.

The women I've dated have issues, but they let me get away without making me work on mine. Don't we all have issues? It's no wonder I lose interest quickly. I'm an athlete, I like a challenge. The fact that I jerk off and think of Annie's perfect breasts makes me miss her more after I've come and when she's not here to cuddle with me, I feel empty inside.

I can't believe I want cuddling to occur. I'm whipped. All thoughts outside of hockey are of her. Her lips meld with mine, and each kiss feeds my desire. She touches my heart and I know how she feels through her touch, no words are needed. However, I long to say them. I hold back because we haven't been together long enough for her to believe I'm capable of being serious and monogamous.

18

Annie

Kal called briefly after the following Sunday night game. I hear a room full of men eating and assume they aren't at the arena. After listening to him give me a play-by-play of the game, I can understand the rush my dad must experience after a win.

His voice seduces me over the phone as he walks to his hotel room. He mentions he would be so hard if I wore my come fuck me heels to bed.

I let out a chortle. "Seriously?"

"How the hell do you think those shoes earned that name?" he quips as if everyone in the world knows this.

"I'm not as worldly as you," I jest to cover my ignorance, then wonder if I need to get lingerie. Hell, I don't even know where it is since I moved. I doubt it's still in style, maybe I should add it to my list of errands.

"Are you banged up from the game?"

"Some, I had a rough check into the boards, my hip hurts."

I wince. Shit, this game is rough, I'm so glad I gave up skating.

"I've had worse. A day or two and it should be fine." Kal blows it off and I assume it comes with the territory.

"I can't wait to see you. I'm so horny."

"I know the feeling."

"We'll have to have phone sex one of these nights."

"Hm, I prefer it delivered in person," is my comment, and I can't believe it flew out of my mouth.

"I can make that happen, I wish I could be there now, kissing you all over..."

"This isn't fair," I exclaim.

"Are you wet?"

"What do you think?"

"Good, get your vibrator, I'll talk you through it."

TRUE TO HIS word I screamed with an intense orgasm by the time we hung up Sunday night. Kal called Monday morning. He was boarding a plane to Washington to play the Devils. I duck into a corridor to take his call.

"What do you guys do on the plane?" I'm inquire with the fortification I might not want to know.

I've heard stories over the years of players banging women, bathrooms with full-length mirrors, and private airports. Granted, these planes are not the everyday garden variety, but it would be nice to experience it once. I hate flying commercial. For a person close to six feet tall, I look like a giant in the chairs, and I have zero leg room.

"Fucking off, mostly," his jovial voice is flippant and honest.

I don't know what fucking off entails. I found our phone

sex exciting and hot. Kal seemed to like it. God, he's so good at everything. I'm waiting to find a flaw other than the fact he can't cook.

I'd love a destination vacation, like Mom and Dad. Once in five years is what I can afford. I'd love to pick up and go somewhere, anywhere, like the exotic locations I observe on the wedding proposal sites. I'm a softy at heart and I even follow a few hockey feeds of the WAGS since I've met Kal.

"Really? What constitutes fucking off?"

"Just a term, sweetie. I'm just nervous, waiting for Coach to board." He gives me the subtle hint, no doubt he needs to hide the fact we're talking to each other. For now, it's a good call. "Seriously," he continues, his voice is low, "we're boring, we sleep, eat, and play mini hockey on our tray tables."

"Send me a picture of you all dressed up on the plane."

"The guys will give me shit for that."

"Is that a no?" I challenge him.

"Fine. Hey, Blake, take a picture of me." I hear voices in the background, some laughs, and someone growls for him to get his prima donna fucking ass out of the aisle.

I chuckle as I take a second to picture the scene of these brawny men piling on a plane.

Kal's voice returns predominantly, "Hold on," he says.

A picture of Kal on the plane pops up in my texting app. He has a smirk on his face, as if it's an imposition, and he's doing me a favor. I can't imagine he's upset I asked for a picture. I'm sure the guys give each other crap all the time.

"Did you get it?" Kal asks. I can't help but smile that he's concerned about me getting the picture and I don't think it's about him showing off. He's sharing his world with me. I find it endearing.

"Yep, you're rocking that suit," I cajole him.

Kal might scorn the media and ignore them on his

personal time, but he plays the 'pretty' bad guy on the 'red' carpet of A-listers. He's a star who attends the NCAA tournaments, and Super Bowls, all while hobnobbing with comedic identities, B-list movie actors, and starlets.

I've seen enough of late-night talk shows and clips from watching these games over the years. Additionally, I may have scoured the internet this week as I compulsively searched for details of his erroneous affairs and debauchery. Dad wasn't kidding about jocks; they have a colorful life. Mine dulls in comparison.

I've seen the snippets of the bad boys of hockey played on social media mini movies. The pranks never end.

I save the picture he sent me to my phone. Judging from the background, it's a nice airplane with more leg room than normal commercial flights.

"Thanks, baby, gotta go. Someone is boarding and we're getting ready to take off. I'll text when I get to the hotel."

In the background, I hear someone tease him and the word "baby" is repeated by another voice. I assume the guys are giving him grief over his conversation with me, and doubt they are aware of the fact it's not Becka. Judging from the way we left the Make a Kid Smile charity event; I doubt anyone would place the two of us together.

Players respect the teammates' code on privacy. Hockey players never mention locker-room smack to the public. I can't be flippant about it either, we're in the first stages of getting to know each other. To tell my parents anything would be a nightmare. No, it has to remain a secret for now.

How long we can hide this? I have no clue. However, I need time to figure out if we're going to expand our relationship status. I'm not holding my breath. Sure, that's what I tell myself, but I like him. My body loves him. Then, my brain kicks in with the tough reality he's an athlete and will be on the road. It's not the ideal situation I wanted.

I hated Dad being away when I grew up. It's tough on kids. Cramming in minutes here and there is easy when I was young, but when I became a teen, it was a nightmare and I acted out. Something I'm not proud of, and I need to resolve the anger residing in me. To say it's not there is a lie. I harbor anger issues and I wouldn't be honest if I didn't acknowledge the small detail of how it spills over to my relationships with men.

Kal and I hang up before I fall asleep. At work I'm in dreamy la la land, thinking about how cute he is when my phone dings. I smile as I reach for it in as I'm walking down a hallway at work. Kal sends me a picture of Blake sitting beside him on the plane. Apparently, there are no hard feelings over the prank. I get a text.

Blake says he's really sorry.

Tell him I'll get even with him, eventually.

His flight is leaving, so I turn my attention to Suzy as she joins me. I decide the way Kal and I met is a great story. I wonder if he's the one. And will he be the father to my children? Does he want kids? It's an unknown question at this stage of the game.

"Hey, that was a great game last night," Suzy blows by me as I stand in line to get food at an eatery in the hospital, they have commissioned out all the food and drink venues so it's one line after another. Goodbye old school cafeterias.

"Where are you going?" I ask Suzy, as she ditches me.

"I have to go to another floor, maybe later?" She slides her card into a machine and grabs an apple and water as I stand in line adjacent to her.

"Sure," I reply with a shrug, not happy I have to wait to trade updates with her.

I forget how many patients I've seen today. I progress in the line, grab a sad sandwich and hate sitting at a table while others have friends they wave to, and those who have a filled table of four.

I'm new, and it sucks. I remind myself it's for the greater good, family comes first. I eat half my sandwich and find I'm full. I take one long drag on the paper straw as I stand and slurp the last remains of tea from my drink container. I dump everything in the first trash can I pass, and head upstairs.

The nurses ask me to pop in a room of an elderly woman with the flu. She was admitted due to dehydration. The nurses mentioned she is scared, and ask me to drop by her room to reassure her. She's not my patient, however, I make the effort to help. A wicked flu is going around this year.

I hope Kal doesn't catch it. God knows, if one on the bench gets sick, they will most likely pass it to a few of their teammates with the way they spit all over the place. Literally they are in each other's face between flights, buses, and their opponents with numerous games a week.

Professionally speaking, the surface ice becomes a bio-hazardous zone as soon as the puck is dropped. I cringe, it's unsanitary.

The ride in the elevator has the hospital smell to it. It's familiar, and yet, I can't describe it. My stomach lifts a bit as I come to a stop. The door opens and Dr. Dick is there with his entourage.

"Dr. Fluentes," I greet him.

"Dr. Susneck, I have a new admit I hope you can see. I have to head to another floor."

"I'll get on that." I breeze past him and make sure I'm out of his reach.

"Great, maybe we can go over cases later. I think 233B might need a different antibiotic, are you around?" His eyes quiz me.

Fuck.

"Sure, here till six." I force a smile and feign politeness.

I hope Suzy returns soon. A doctor called in sick and she's covering for him.

I round the corner on my way to the nurse's station and I'm off. I can't describe it, I'm just not right. I think I'm warm but when I feel my head with my fingers. I don't have a fever. A smell in the hallway catches me off guard. I'm woozy. I lean against a wall for a minute, waiting for it to pass. I can't be sick. It will ruin seeing Kal when he comes home.

I regain my balance and the episode passes. Whew. I speak to the charge nurse and get the name of Dr. Dick's patient.

I turn, feel my body shift inside and my watch pings with a message from the pharmacy, I have a medication past the refill date. I brush it off, I'll deal with later. It seems to me I've brushed it off once already.

19

Annie

Kal is still out of town, and I've become addicted to my phone. My heart surges with each *ping*. I'm infatuated with him. I walk with confidence of knowing I'm not alone in life. The time spent talking without physical touch gives us an opportunity to get to know each other. Even when he's away, I'm on his mind. We make the best of the road trip, knowing we'll make up for the time apart when we're together again.

I had two surgeries, returned phone calls, and visited patients. My day is over, I'm thirsty. I decide to grab a water out of the pantry before heading home. I'm in a cloud and I'm as satisfied as I would be wearing a hooded snuggy in the middle of the coldest winter. Kal awakes new emotions in me, and I've never fallen so fast, or so hard, for a man. I'm surprised and yet, I embrace it. It's nice having someone else in my house as I've lived alone most of my adult life.

I reach in the old fridge in the doctor's lounge, reaching for a water and I'm startled when I turn around to find Dr.

Dick in my face. Like, planted so close, I smell his sour breath as it wafts past my lips.

"Hello, Annie," his attempt at a smile is a muted grin. He has me isolated. And he knows it. Panic fills my chest. I have no room to move. He raises a hand and puts his palm on the freezer door behind me. He leans closer, his body scent—is in my nostrils. I'm suffocating in the smell of him. Life is moving in slow motion.

"Dr. Fluentes, I was just leaving," I gasp. I should scream. But with the carts going by for dinner, no one would hear me. These halls are long, and nurses are used to tuning out noise and, at times, patients, as we're understaffed.

"Great, I'm off. How about a drink somewhere? I know a place nearby. In fact, my apartment is within walking distance. I heard you're single," he purrs in a salacious manner.

He views himself as sexy, wanted. I know who he really is, and I need to get away. But how? My brain is frozen, I go over options as I attempt to keep him talking.

"I'm dating someone," I mutter, flipping the cap on my water loose with my thumb. My phone is in my pocket, but it's useless. I can't move my arms as his chest acts as human handcuffs. I wouldn't be able to see the keys on a phone either because we're looking into each other's eyes.

My blood pressure is rising, my chest expands. His eyes have a creeping lilt to them, hazel eyes, and I wonder where he is in there. It's as if he has two personalities. I'm dealing with the perverted one.

I experience the effects of jitters without shaking. This situation is surreal. My body is paralyzed. I'm an independent woman and this asshole is using his power over me to... what? Intimidate me? Get a piece of ass? Or is he venting his hatred of women toying with us like we're cat nip and he's the cat?

Dr. Dick moves his free hand. I'm certain he's going to grab a boob, and surprises me again as he lays it on my hip instead. I squint my eyes, repulsed by his touch. I want Kal. Where is he? I miss him. I need him.

Fluentes is the chief of surgery at the hospital. I've seen his face on billboards around town touting his praise and esteem. No wonder the hospital buys his victims off. To date, no women's lawsuit has made it to court. If it did, he wouldn't be here creating more victims. This is one of the hospital's dirty little secrets. And we're forced to live with it on a daily basis.

My shock has turned to anger with this revelation. Kneeing him in the balls would probably be considered assault. I know it's self-defense, but his word holds more merit than mine, that's the play he's banking on.

I give the bottle in my hands a hearty squeeze, and to my delight, water spays his entire face. The surprise catches him off guard, he steps back. He closes his eyes and yells, "You bitch!" as he moves to find napkins to dry his face and shirt.

Water drips from his menacing eyes and hits the floor.

It's my opening.

I will my legs to move, bolting past as I push his chest to give myself a solid exit route. I throw the heavy door open so fiercely it hits the wall with a bang. I run to the first Exit sign. I know he'll take the elevator, so I hit the button as if I'm going to the fourth floor to throw him off.

"Annie, hold up," Suzy shouts behind me.

"Hurry," I yell over my shoulder, making a B-line for the steps. Suzy is a few feet behind me and follows me as I continue my dissent, flight after flight. Suzy keeps asking me what's wrong.

"Did Kal do something?" She peers into my eyes as I stop on the last landing.

"No." I bend over to take a deep breath.

"You act like the devil is on your trail. What gives?"

"Dr. Dick, pantry, getting water," I gasp and cover my mouth with my hand. "I think I'm going to be sick."

I dry heave a few times and nothing comes up.

Suzy's hand is on my back and pulls my hair back.

"Jesus, what did he do? That fucker."

"He pinned me against the refrigerator. I accidentally squirted his face with my water." I raise my bottle and gulp down what's left. I straighten my back and stand next to her. She lets go of my hair.

"I'm so sorry Annie, I thought we could dodge him," she laments as she wraps her arms around me.

"I can't believe it. He put his hand on my hip." Chills run down my arms; I shake from shock. "I was lucky to get out of there. He wanted me to go out with him for drinks."

"Yeah, more like a date rape, I'm sure," she replies, annoyed with the situation. "I wonder if he gets drugs from the hospital or online. This is getting creepier by the minute."

"Oh, how could I have been so stupid?" I sob into her shoulder as my arms wrap around her.

"It could have been anyone, Annie. It could have been me. Or, a nurse, you don't have control in a situation like that. He's a perve, he takes advantage of women when they're alone. He's a coward."

"What would have happened if I didn't get out of there?" My nostrils come together as I sniffle. I raise a hand to wipe away the tears on my face and pull back, ready to leave the confined space we're in. "I'm fine."

"You're better, not fine," she reiterates. "Something needs to be done about this. We need to report it."

"Yeah, and I won't be assigned any more surgeries for the rest of my life."

"Let's get out of here. Can you come over?" I ask her, not wanting to be alone. Kal has been out of town a week. They flew to Fort Myers for a game and then the Midwest.

"Sure, let's swing by my place, I'll grab some clothes and stay with you tonight."

We walk the last flight of steps and as the cool evening air hits me, I breathe easier. Suzy glances over her shoulder to make sure we're not being followed and walks me to my car, she gets in. I drive her to where hers is parked. I let her back out before I pull up behind her green *Jurassic Park* looking jeep. My hands are weak on the steering wheel, and I force them to hang onto it as I focus and tighten my grip. I can do this.

I thought the shock would pass by now. I'm young and agile. I wonder what I would have done if the water didn't work so effectively. He's so sick he'll probably take this as a challenge.

Fuck. This isn't over. It won't be over until he's gone.

I follow Suzy to her apartment. My doors automatically lock when I drive, but it's not enough of an assurance. I can't resist the urge of looking over my shoulders, left, then right. I even glance up to check my rear-view mirror to make sure Dr. Dick didn't follow us.

I'm paranoid.

It's one thing to talk about Dr. Dick and what we've heard, it's another to live it. What can we do? Clearly, others have tried to sue him and get him out of here, so who does he know? He's a God in the operating room. Getting away with intimidating and molesting women sends the message it's okay.

Suzy follows me home. I take a shower while she whips up some eggs and bacon for dinner. I'm not able to think about anything, breakfast for dinner is all I could come up with, my brain is mush.

Suzy has the game playing on the living room TV and the one piece of furniture I've managed to have delivered to my door is a long cabinet with two shelves in the middle and a cubby on each end with a door. I have no clue how to drill brackets needed to hang the TV.

We sit on the futon to eat. I want to enjoy Kal playing as he made a great pass. I'm distracted by the evening's events and can't follow the puck and I don't know what pisses me off more. The fact Dr. Dick attacked me, or the fact his actions causes me to miss out on seeing Kal play. Thoughts of Kal are my happy place.

"I miss him," I sob. "I wish Kal was in town."

"He'll be back before you know it." Suzy tries to reassure me as any friend would, but it's not filling the hole in my heart tonight. Only Kal can do that.

The reality of my romance hits. I'm with an athlete who has to be on the road. Just like my dad. It's not what I would have picked. But we can't pick who we love. I love Kal and because of it, I'm ashamed to tell him I was so stupid to let Dr. Dick get the upper hand. It's probably for the best he isn't here to see me rattled.

"Thanks for cooking and for being here." I lay my head on Suzy's shoulder.

She swallows a mouth full of food. "This is actually a good omelet. You need to eat."

"It is good, I had a bite. I wish I could enjoy Kal's game."

I stare blankly at the TV. I can't concentrate on it. "I missed you all day," I mumble.

"I was all over and had three surgeries, textbook, thankfully. Did you hear from Kal?" Suzy wolfs down more eggs.

"Yes, he's sweet, texted me when he got on and off the plane, and from the hotel," I add, shifting my focus to my man crush as he flies across the ice and digs in the corner of our opponent's zone.

"Great. Are you going to tell him about Dr. Dick?"

"I don't know. It's embarrassing. I think I need Kal to show up at the hospital and Dickhead will see I'm not alone. It might be different if he knows I have a man who has my back." I take another bite of my food as the plate balances on my lap. I need energy.

"Right, Dr. Dick needs to know there's a name bigger than his in this town. Kal might have a reputation, but he's a household name in Maine. Plus, the team carries clout. You can't deny Kal has the media eating out of his hand."

I shoot her a look like 'really'?

"No, you misunderstand," she continues. "Any publicity can be good publicity. It's weird, I know. People believe what they want and most of them will believe the last tidbit of scandal they hear," she shrugs, "who knows? It might be a useful tool. The only problem is, it can be used for good or evil. How do we use it to our advantage?

"Are you saying we use Kal to throw shade on Dr. Dick?"

"Let me think on it. We're learning Dick's behavior pattern, maybe we will learn something useful. Cheer up. Your hunk will be home in no time." A moment of silence passes, and she screams when the Maulers score and jumps, scaring the shit out of me like a horror movie.

I chuckle over her enthusiasm and spit the half-chewed bacon out of my mouth to make sure it doesn't go down the wrong way. Laughing in light of the evening's situation is good. Normal.

"Yes," I agree, "I can't wait for him to be home." This is my life. Dr. Dick can well, bite his own dick. Fuck him for making me feel like a victim.

Suzy and I are both glued to the game in the final minutes. I struggle to keep my eyes open. Late night talks with Kal have left me light on sleeping hours. I'm sure it's nothing. I yawn and cover it with my hand.

"Hey, did I ever mention to you Mr. Barber's is a huge benefactor of the team? He owns some of the hospital. Hence, the name Barber, in case you missed it."

"Oh, I didn't put that together. Now it makes sense. He must own half this city. I grew up with the name, he has a son in college here, too," Suzy adds.

"Most cities have a few people who are wealthy and powerful," I add. It's the way of the world. "It's the world we live in," Kal would say.

"Barber might be a good guy to meet at one of the Mauler events. I'm just saying. Dr. Dick thinks he can get anything he wants," Suzy sighs as she gathers our plates and carries them to the sink. She returns with two glasses of juice.

"A water bottle... that was clever," she says as she hands me orange juice.

"It happened by accident. I wish I kicked him in the nuts." I down my juice, knowing it's good for me and will help me fight off the flu like symptoms I'm experiencing.

"He wouldn't be able to report the water incident, would he?" Suzy asks raising questions I didn't think were believable a day ago. I wonder if it's considered a battery under the law.

"Who knows. God, I hate the fact he got that far. I didn't even hear him come into the room."

"He's been at this a long time, men like him get very savvy. I'm sorry I wasn't there."

"It's not your fault. I know how he operates. Now, I just have to make sure he doesn't get another opening."

"Rise and shine," Suzy hails from the hall.

I rise from my pillow into a sitting position and a queasiness that could be passed off as nothing fills me with dread.

I take a breath, plant my feet on the floor and paddle to Suzy's room. wearing my sherpa lined pjs' with brown moose on them. I can't help but notice how adorable Suzy is in the morning, decked out in pink pajamas covered in multicolored dots.

I lean my back on the doorframe, raising a knee to put my foot on the sturdy wood.

"Suzy, I need a favor."

She twirls to observe me as she fluffs the comforter into place.

"Sure," she finishes and when she studies my face, she stops. "What is it?"

"Um, well… there's no easy way to say this so I'm just going to tell you, but don't judge, okay?" I wince.

"Sure," she slips in front of me takings my hand in hers. "What is it?"

"I got a call from the pharmacy wanting to know if I want to refill my birth control pills. I was so busy, I forgot to get them for weeks. But we know I can't go back on them until I get my period." I pause, feeling like an idiot. "And.. well, Maggie is late."

"That's crazy. You only hooked up a few times!"

"Well, a few all-nighters. Maybe it's the reason I was so horny," I lament. "I might have been dropping eggs coming off the pill."

"Ha, yeah right. I'm not buying that. I've seen that man and he's drop dead gorgeous, so you ride that horse as long as you have it," she chuckles.

I look at her, aghast.

"What? Don't shoot the messenger. There's a reason he's so popular with the ladies," she teases as she sashays away to grab her scrubs.

"I think we should do a blood test. It's quicker than the home test, they won't register this early, anyway."

"Agreed." She steps into cute lacy panties and a matching bra. Scrubs are great in that they end the morning debate over what to wear.

"So, you'll do it? Don't say anything. Kal and I are so new. This blows."

"You wanted to be a mom before thirty, so you might get your wish. It's off your bucket list, no more pressure."

"Only if I am, and chances are, I'm not," I reply. Surely it can't be that easy to get knocked up. I don't know how I could have been so stupid. I was busy and forgot. I tell myself I'm human, and I always put pressure on myself to be more than human. I have a compulsive need to be as close to perfect as I can so Dad will notice me for me. I want to live up to his expectations and get hugs like my sister. Nurses and surgeons aren't droids, I want affection, too.

"We'll see, now go get dressed because I'm starving, and you owe me food. Oh, and let's not be alone with Dr. Dick again," she reminds me like she's my mother.

"Got it!" I wave my hand in the air as I'm halfway to my room. Good thing I have a three-bedroom house. Mom is nagging me for grandkids to spoil. Maybe I'll give in and let them furnish my house.

Meanwhile, Kal texts, wanting to know what I'm up to.

Shit, the man has timing. I'll give him that. Is it great intuition or coincidence? Or both? How can I keep this from him?

I'm too embarrassed, and I don't have a definitive answer, so I wait. No need to get worked up over nothing. It could still be the flu.

20

Annie

I throw on my jacket to leave the house and text Kal. He wants to know what I'm doing.

I'm with a friend.

A friend?

Girlfriend. I clarify. It's sweet he is curious.

Oh, cool. I can't wait to see you.

I'm sure you're horny being on the road.

Horny for you. He texted.

Ditto. I type.

"Ugh," Suzy groans, "you two act like lovebirds."

"Mm." I smile, thinking about my boyfriend and counting the days until he's home.

I doubt his schedule has much room left in it between work and dating. I'm cautious of his reputation and hope I'm not making a mistake. I don't want to get hurt, but I have to take that risk to find love. It seems that most of what I do in life involves a tradeoff. Risk vs. Reward.

I call Kal on bluetooth as I drive. Suzy is in her car so I

have time to get him up to speed. I inform him of the incident at work.

"What? Why didn't say anything sooner?"

"It was yesterday evening, leaving work. I didn't know what to say," I reply. "How do I tell anyone I was felt up in the snack room at work?"

"You're right. Absolutely right. Let's take a breath. I wish I was there to punch him out. What's his name?" I jump into action, it's what I do best.

"I'm not telling you as I don't want you to do anything which could involve you landing in jail and off the team. I need to be more careful, that's all."

"Like hell," he shouts.

"I know, I'm fine. Suzy stayed over last night."

"Tell her thank you. I wish I was there."

"Me, too. I miss you."

"I miss you, too. Promise to be careful, if I find him..."

"I know..."

We ring off when I reach the cafe.

The bagels are baked daily on the premises. I order a full plate of home fries, eggs and sausage, and a bagel with nova. Shit. I'm eating more than enough for two.

I wish I knew if I were eating for two, the thought of a baby is exhilarating and overwhelming. What if I'm not? I'd be disappointed. To see a mini-me with Kal makes my heart lurch. I pace my breathing as I'm giving myself anxiety over something I can't control. Right now, Kal makes me deliriously happy.

"I phoned him on the way here and told him about the incident, but I didn't give him Dr. Dick's name."

"Good. Are you going to tell your dad about Dr. Dick?"

"I don't know what we can do. I'm documenting it, the time, place, just in case I need it."

"Good idea. I wish we could pour wax on his balls."

I choke on my laughter, imagining the prick and how much that would hurt. Hell, it's not a pleasant experience for women on their lady parts, but I imagine men would need to be knocked out first. Women are superhuman because we can push watermelons out of our vaginas.

"I have to make sure I'm not alone with him. He'll try again, it's a pattern. I wonder if I look like his other victims."

"I don't know. It was all hushed up. Only HR would know, and they can't tell us. People leave every day, we'd be looking for a needle in a haystack to find the one with the payout, and at that she'd have to sign a NDA. Otherwise, what's the point?"

"True. It sucks. I can't wait until Kal is back. I'd love to see Dr. Dick deal with him."

Our coffee is set in front of us, and we give our orders to the waitress.

"Miss him much?" she teases as she sips coffee. Her blond hair is in a ponytail as usual. I love her button nose and high cheekbones.

"Yeah." I smile. "He's my happy thought."

"Has your dad said anything?"

"No, so maybe he doesn't know. I can't say anything unless Kal and I are real."

My coffee has little taste. I pour sugar in it. Tasting it again, not much has changed, except for the calories. I switch to water.

"It's exciting though, isn't it? A pro hockey player. Can you imagine the media attention?"

"No, I can't."

Our food is delivered, the aroma of bacon arrives before the plate. I dive in with gusto.

"I looked it up, they have the WAGS site and PR for the

team. You'll be known if you see him. You don't have much time is what I'm saying, so you might want to rethink telling your dad."

I pause a second. What can I tell him? I can't risk Kal getting in trouble if he's on the fence. What of dad?

"I think it's better he doesn't know. Besides, the other issue is just as big."

"What will you do?"

"I can do it alone. Millions of women, and even men, do. I'm not rushing into anything if it's not for the right reasons."

"Okay," she replies and focuses on slathering her bagel in cream cheese. "I'll take your blood and slip it into the lab when we get to work. Let's make sure no one catches us."

"Great. I'm a new employee and might be a mom soon. That will go over well at work and give Dr. Dick a reason to screw me over. Why are mothers discriminated against behind closed doors? I mean, it was worse in our parents' age, but I still see it. Worse yet, I hear it. Women and men complain."

She replies as she casually sips her coffee. "Then, there are the parents who are good and have to be home more in those first few years. It's scientific. Kids need their parents, hence the word, care givers. Work has to adapt. They need more on-site daycare facilities."

"Yeah, like that will ever happen, we're in the real world, not the movies. I'm sure my mom will help. She's been nagging me to have kids," I let out a chuckle. "I bet she's never considered it would happen without a husband," I croak.

"Stuff happens, give yourself a break," she reassures me. "Your mom is the fashion boss. I can see your kid color coded in matching outfits and shoes as we speak."

"Oh, you have no idea!" Somehow, I don't think it will be bad, a cute kid all decked out like a GQ model. A boy, that would be cool. So would a girl. I never thought about having a tiny human in my hands. I want to be a mom. I never processed having a baby because my luck with men sucks and I didn't want to be disappointed if I never found the guy.

Is Kal my guy?

We finish, I pay the bill. "Thanks for last night."

"Don't sweat it. That's what friends are for," she replies.

We head to work. I'm filled with enough apprehension to rival a SEALS team heading into a high-risk mission as we enter the hospital. Between the attack yesterday and the pregnancy question, I'm a wreck. I'm torn in a million directions.

Dr. Dick weighs on my mind as we head to the lab. Suzy grabs a tube before we head to the second floor and enter an empty patient's room. We research how much blood we need for the test and I fill out a form with my information. Suzy preps my arm with an alcohol pad.

A whiff of it hits me, and in a flash, I understand how patients pass out thinking about the needle next. Suzy is efficient and after the tube is filled, she slips it into the batch to be sent out for processing behind the nurses' station.

"What do I do now?"

"You need to log into your application on your phone, that's where it will show up."

"Isn't it a few days?"

"Yes, urine is quicker, but you're not going to register on that for another month or two."

"Right." I wonder if I want to know the results, or if I should say fuck it, and ride it out.

Kal will be gone a few days, so that's a win for me. I'll

either know I'm having a baby or be on birth control before he returns.

I stand at the board of scheduled surgeries, and I have an eleven o'clock to remove a gallbladder and after it, I have an appendectomy. I wonder how women stand on their feet all day carrying an extra forty pounds for a baby.

I head to the room of the patients to confer with them before their surgery and I'm running on schedule.

Why am I obsessing over a baby? They are cute and give unconditional love. If Kal isn't in this with me, I can do it myself. Am I borrowing trouble or being pragmatic?

He's a celebrated bachelor. I found a video where he's kidded about being a dad and he didn't speak highly of it. People can change.

I tell myself to block out negativity as I'm anxious enough, and nothing good comes from it unless it's Christmas or a birthday. As a doctor, I believe in data. I've never missed a period in my life. These weird tummy things aren't in my head. Sure, it's early. However, I know my body and its quirks. What I'm experiencing isn't a quirk as much as I may desire it.

It's late in the afternoon. Kal calls as I'm walking to a floor with Suzy.

"Hey, how's it going?" I ask, keeping my voice as normal as possible. It's so hard to not blurt out information that may or may not be true, so I keep the secret to myself.

"Great, we're at a hotel in Seattle. The game will be late for you, so don't push yourself to stay up. I know how early your day starts."

"That's sweet of you. I might not be able to stay up to watch it," I agree. My phone beeps. "Kal, I gotta go, it's my Dad. Good luck tonight."

"Thanks, I'll be home in a few days, I'll see you then."

"Sounds great. See ya."

Dad is on the line.

"How's it going? I heard from Mom and Carla. They'll be home tomorrow. They can't wait to see you," his voice is calm. I wonder if he's really calm all the time, or if he bottles up his stress.

"Wow, that went fast," I remark, getting an iced tea from the eatery. "I can't wait to see them."

"Life goes fast, kid."

He's telling me. My childhood ended way too soon. I know how fast I lost the attention of my parents. Mom tried to guide me, I resisted. She was a flash in the pan as a model before she dedicated herself to Dad's career. I don't know if I could do what she did. I'm not sure Dad's job didn't leave her much of a choice.

"Can we get together for family dinner when I get back?" Dad asks. It's sweet coming from him.

"That would be great. Actually, I want to go to a game and see you in action again."

"Really?" He sounds surprised, even though I've told him I would go before.

"I wouldn't say it if I didn't want to, Dad. I've been out of the loop. I'm living here, the Maulers are my team. You're my dad."

He's quiet for a second, and I hope I didn't tip my hand, seeing as how I have another reason to take in games.

"You're coming to see me? I thought you hated my job."

"I do, but I'm adulting," I assure him. "I'll tap on the glass behind you," I tease.

"I bet you will. We'll catch up when I get back. I want to hear about your job. I gotta go," he says as I hear men in the background.

"Good luck tonight."

"Thanks." The phone clicks.

He's hung up faster than lightning. I stare at my phone. I remind myself it's baby steps. He's a man of brevity. Having a dad is a good thing, even if we agree to disagree. However, I'm hoping for a win. If only I can find a way to connect with him and have a heart to heart. After years of therapy, it's time. I want closure.

At the end of the day, I call in a to-go order from my favorite Italian restaurant and eat at home. The pasta is delicious. I take in the walls I've stared at for over a month now and they're haunting me. I have the paint and yet, I'm too tired to start. The walls are winning, there are so many of them and I'm alone, I'm tired. So tired.

I drag myself up to shower before I crawl into bed. I flip to rerun of a talk show and Kal is on there with some of the players. I can't tell how old it is, it looks recent. He's asked if he's dating anyone, and he says no one special. The announcer calls him the lone wolf of the team. It's not a compliment.

Kal shrugs. "When I find the right person, it will fall into place. My dating life and hockey are different."

Interesting. Am I lying to myself if I believe he's capable of change? Time will tell. And I might not have much time to get to know the man under the persona if the test is positive.

I fall asleep after the hockey game starts and wake up to my alarm. I have no idea how long it went off.

I'm still tired. Now, I'm worried I have a health issue. I've lost my nervous energy, as mom calls it. I'm sluggish and I don't want to overdo the caffeine.

Suzy and I run into each other in front of the employee's entrance.

"You look like you didn't sleep."

"Would you believe I fell asleep and had a difficult time waking up? I just wanted to hibernate. It's not like me. Do kids change your personality? Wait, forget I said anything," I add.

"Forgotten, check for your results, they are quicker today. I'm here if you need me."

"I'll be fine," I assure her. "Besides, it could be a new version of the flu going around."

"Right, and Santa Claus is real," she scoffs.

A positive will complicate things with Kal, especially if he doesn't want kids. Do I have to tell him if he's not into it? Is it fair to make the decision for him?

21

Kal

I enjoy my time with the guys. The upside of being on the road is the fact we're never alone and seeing as how I'm single, I have a built-in family. The down time when I'm alone makes me stir crazy. I don't want time to think about my past.

I'm relieved Annie is speaking to me again. It reminds me of the first crush I had as a teenager because I was a late bloomer. I've made up for lost time over the years, different girls, new experiences, and money went to my head. I went overboard on living the life, as many players before me have done. It's confusing when I experience my heart racing at the thought of seeing Annie again, and I picture her white voluptuous breasts in my hands as I bury my face in them.

I send her a text from a hallway at the hotel to say I've arrived safely. Short, simple. Nothing implied, even though I'd like to add I want to kiss her entire body and fuck her hard as my way to make up for being away.

I want to tell her I hate missing a night with her. I want

her sore between her legs so she will remember when I have to leave town again. These thoughts prompt me to text her from the arena later.

My phone dings. Annie wishes me good luck vibes and will be heading home soon. I need to get my head in the game and off Annie's incredible body. I replay our night together in my head; my cock stirs as I'm walking into our locker-room. My cock doesn't need life support, it needs Annie.

I let out a sigh. Fuck, this is going to hurt if I don't get him under control. He'll be bent and I won't be able to walk if he doesn't calm down.

I'm grateful I'm wearing a jacket and it's fucking cold in Washington, D.C.

We're close to game time, and I find myself yearning for a quick game.. Never in my life have I desired getting back to Maine as badly as I do now. I wonder if this is what the married guys go through on a daily basis. The pull to be in two different places at the same time is new to me.

I glance to Blake and Alexandre, who are texting on their phones, and I assume it's to their wives. I've never paid much attention to it before today. Sure, we give guys shit when they have a girlfriend, then get engaged, but after that, it's old news. Next, the kids pop out.

Today, I'm picturing Annie in my condo, and what it would be like to crawl into bed with her when I get home at two in the morning. Annie in my bed, there's a thought. I doubt she'd like my condo. It's picturesque, and close to everything. Single adults and couples with no kids love to live there. It's on the border of Camden Bay, and close to all the action.

I don't know Annie well enough to say she'd want to live

here, however, after seeing her house and yard, I think she's more of a country girl at heart.

Whoa. I'm getting ahead of myself. There is plenty of time before we discuss living together. This is new to me, and I can't blow it. Baby steps are enough. Especially with Coach around. He's never far from my mind. If Annie and I continue to see each other; it will lead to the issue of letting him know we're a thing and that means pressure at home and on the ice.

Okay. What's a thing? That won't go over well, I'm going to have to get my shit together. I don't know what my intentions are; we need time. Most athletes are engaged a minimum of a year, waiting for the season to be over, and even at that, they've dated for years. I'm not ready to decide my future right now.

The media reports what they want. They think I don't care what the world thinks of me and to a degree I don't. Annie is different. I can't have her name drug through the mud if I break up with her. She'll have regrets and everyone, including her father, will tell her 'I told you so' and I can't be responsible for the public humiliation to follow.

I'm shocked enough I'm falling for her. I consider the fact all my previous relationships had a shelf life of six months, to a year–tops. Some ended on good terms, others, not so good.

And yet, I remain curious, wondering if Annie and I will work. She's from a hockey family. It's a bit sticky, for sure. The way we met is one for the record books. I'm not concerned with my reputation; these blemishes have a way of disappearing with time. I say media attention is always good attention, even if it's not a positive spin, it generates buzz.

Anyone can reinvent themselves; all I need is a desire to

change my ways and until now, I've been fine being me. Change is like holding my stick in another hand if my dominate one is broken. It's a matter of putting one's mind and determination together for a goal and taking action.

I have action all right. I can't wait to relieve Annie of her clothes and let her know how much I missed her. I put the rest of my gear on without thinking, trying to listen to the vibe of the room.

Normally, I'm part of the locker room banter. Today, the jokes and innuendos fly around without me listening. I try to listen but focusing is difficult. For all I know, the guys could be making fun of me, and with that premise, I check the back of my jersey. I already checked my carry-on bag to make sure they didn't pop a shot of something disgusting in it. The pre-packaged shots are disgusting but easy to hide.

They aren't getting me again.

"You alright, Kal?" Viktor asks, pulling the Mauler jersey over his shoulder pads.

"Yeppers, why?"

"You're not yourself, man. Too quiet. You're freaking me out."

"I can't carry the room all the time," I jest to cover for the fact my mind isn't with the guys, it's in the clouds.

"Well, get it together," he mumbles, as his eyes narrow on my face. He gives me a double take.

Shit. He knows something is up. Of course, a deviation in behavior is a tip off. I can't talk to anyone about Annie. Blake is the only one who will understand, but can I risk it? I haven't committed a crime.

I pissed off my prior companion, who wants me so much she's on standby. In my eyes Becka's was a layaway plan and she's just been returned to the shelf. Permanently. I hope she won't be an issue.

I let the guys assume I'm still with Becka. As much as I regret taking her to the gala, I'm letting them think we might be back together as a few comments have been made about how hot she is, but a bit psycho.

I give myself a pass on deceiving them, I tell myself lying by omission is okay. I'm in a precarious position and stretching the truth will buy me the time.

I'm no angel. I get my digs on the ice and I'm hot off the ice. Honestly, I've enjoyed it for years. Annie makes me want to be a better person. I have boundaries with her, and I hope those stripper videos will burn. I have a few skeletons in my closet, and they are in my past. I see no reason to hire an expensive attorney until I need one.

Alexandre breezes by and hands me a cup with our pregame concoction. We tap them tighter before tossing the mixture of caffeine and energy drink down our throats. Our ritual continues.

"Ugh," I shake my head to clear the taste from my mouth, and to clear my mind of indecent thoughts of Annie laying under me. I need to focus on the game. It's imperative I play well.

One, it's my job, and two, I have to prove to myself I can play well with the brain fog I'm experiencing. Part of me is freaking out that my game will never be the same if I fall hard for someone. This is uncharted territory for me.

We storm out to the ice. I listen to the sound of my skates and fall into the routine of warming up. I drop, lean forward on the ice, and stretch my back and leg muscles. Afterwards, I glide behind Viktor, mimicking him as if we're doppelgängers as he skates around our side of the blue line.

He catches on when he circles to a stop and gives me a good punch in my back to push me away for fucking with him. I laugh, I so love being an instigator. If Annie were here, I'm sure she'd get a kick out of it.

It's all in good fun, Viktor knows this. My mood is lighter after a good chuckle, and in this moment, I fall into the head space needed to play. The fans in the stands are super charged, but not for us.

We clear the ice, and the festivities begin. The puck drops minutes later and I'm on the second string tonight. I'm a dog chasing a meaty bone, and I'm chasing the bone as it rolls and bounces over the ice.

The Washington Devils have a terrible line change and I intercept their pass. I skate with it, but their defensemen are all over me. I send the puck to Wyatt, who's further down the ice poised to take my pass. He skates fast and doesn't have enough room to deke the goalie, so he takes a shot. The goalie bobbles it and it falls to the right of the net where Colton, our D-man was waiting for a rebound shot and flips it over the goalie's leg.

The shot could have gone either way. But we scored first and that pumps us up. We gather, giving each other a high five before we fly by the bench, bumping fists.

"Nice job," Colton comments. We're in the game and we do best when we're in the lead. I hope to God, we keep it, and take a seat after my shift.

We win 3-2, The Devils are a tough team with a solid defense. That could have gone either way. We eat at the restaurant, in a room reserved for us as it's past dinner hours. We're in Polo shirts and jeans as we casually grab chairs and order.

My phone beeps, my pulse races. Annie.

When I look at the screen, I'm disappointed. It's Becka, trying to worm her way back into my life.

Crap. She's desperate. She's known to become unruly

after drinking hard liquor and when combined with her skills as a social climber, I have no idea what her angle is, or what she's planning. I ignore her message filled with graphic depictions of our sexual encounters. What is she trying to accomplish with these? Is it still called a dick pic if I'm wearing boxers?

22

Annie

"Did I tell you I saw Kal on a talk show this week? Are we out of Antarctica for Christ's sake? Lone wolf?" Suzy lets out a gasp as I rattle on, but like me, she is appalled by the reference as we leave work.

"A loner, I can see that," Suzy replies as she nods her head, contemplating my love life. I give her the look, the one where I tilt my head and stare down my nose at her; she knows she's overstepped. "Sorry, what do I know? I do think he's changing. His name hasn't been on social media since he met you." She shoves the strap on her oversized purse over her shoulder as we make our way to the parking lot.

"I didn't notice," I murmur. I haven't been checking up on his whereabouts either. I can't be bothered to keep tabs on anyone. Why the sudden change? Maybe he knows, if he fucks up, he's out.

"I think he really cares about you. How did your hot and heavy weekend go?"

"Amazing." I can't suppress the grin on my face. "I don't

know how he does it, making love to me the way he does. It's surreal."

"Did you get your results yet?" Suzy brings me back to the present and I have to give up my smutty thoughts of Kal. She's right, someone needs to push me for the test results. I've been lax.

"No," I sigh. "If I don't know, then I haven't lied to him. I'll do it soon, I promise." I have no clue how I'm going to break the news to him if the test is positive.

"Timing is everything, or so the saying goes."

"I'm just enjoying us right now."

"I get it. Mitch and I booked a cruise after the Musical Gala for the kids' wing. Did you invite Kal?"

"Oh, shit. I've mentioned it. I bet my parents will be there too. You know how they love their charities."

"Simon's on the Mauler's team, and his wife, Bella, is a singer and one of the headliners so you two will be out with that kind of visibility. Sometimes it sucks to be you," she sing-songs as she heads to her operating room.

Shit. I never thought of that. I'm new to Maine, I don't know all these details. I'm behind and I need to catch up. Do I really need to know the relationships of everyone? I assume I do if they become my peers.

I text Mom and she confirms they are going to the fundraiser. I text Kal informing him the parental units will be at the Musical Gala and he says he'll handle my father. Kal will figure it out. I can't worry over it as I have a long day ahead of me.

After work I arrive home with a meal I picked up at the grocery store and prepare myself to walk over the uneven pavers as the light on the garage flicks on with my movement. The only issue with the pavers is that they aren't where they used to be. I look behind me, and in front of me.

Shit, they are even, and in a straight line!

Who redid my walkway? This is amazing. I skip over the new pavers, happy with the improvement. Did Kal do this?

I open the porch door in the back of the house and find boxes left by a delivery service. That's weird, I didn't order anything. Curiosity grabs me and I look at the labels, and oddly, the name on it is addressed to me.

I drop my food inside and move the boxes inside. I open one. Security cameras. Good idea. I never thought of it.

I call Kal, of course he ordered them. "I hope you don't mind, I fixed your pavers. Worrying about you walking on those and falling was driving me crazy. Almost as crazy as you in lacy thongs."

I'm blushing. I never knew he took notes on everything Annie. I'm impressed. I can see why women fall for him, he's more than a nice package with dreamy eyes. He notices me.

"Do I need these cameras?"

"They're good to have, don't cost anything but batteries to run them and since you're with me, it might be a good idea. You can't go wrong with them."

"Okay. I'll leave it to you. By the way, I left a planter of herbs on the sink..." I'm in the kitchen and run my hand over the dainty green leaves of them as he speaks.

"Yeah, I thought of you at the store. Do you like them?"

"Love them. I don't have time to grow a garden, and it's too cold out. I'm sure the deer and bunnies would eat anything I plant, so this is perfect."

"Good."

"I gotta go–nap30."

"What is that?"

"I need a nap, like it's five o'clock somewhere, it's our nap time," he chuckles. "Maybe I'll see you after the game?"

"Sure."

"Good luck with Coach, I mean, your dad."

"Thanks."

I OBTAIN parking access near the players and can't contain my snicker as I walk past what I consider a convention for high-end cars. They are the ones millionaires drive and Dad has always had a nice two-seater to himself, leaving Mom the practical vehicle for kids. She has a Maserati now. It's not conducive for kids or transporting others if I'm being realistic.

A man named Max greets me inside the player's entrance. I assume he's important to the team and follow him down hallways to my dad.

"Annie, I'm so happy to see you. Thank you, Max." Dad nods and the quiet man leaves.

It's like I'm in the military, if movies are any indication. Dad ranks. As in, he's a God around this place.

I want to give him a hug, but he only does that with Mom. "So, this is your incredible office," I joke, as the room reminds of what I would find in a high school gym.

We're down the hall from the players, and my pussy tingles at the thought of Kal and his muscular chest. I need to stop these thoughts. I'm standing two feet away from my father.

"Sit. I have a minute. You look wonderful, Maine is great, isn't it?" His eyes are bright and even though he's calm on the outside, I gather he is keyed up for the game.

"Yes, I like it here more than I thought I would. But, then again, ask me when I have snow up to the second floor come winter," I jest. I cringe at the thought of winter. I haven't had a vacation in years and, ergo, no break from winter.

"I'm hoping you'll be by soon to see your mom. She misses you."

"Sure. How was her trip?" I sit, folding my hands in my lap. It's like I'm a little kid all over again. I'm afraid to talk to him. He's all business. What would it take for him to tell me he loves me, or give me a hug?

"I have to leave in a few minutes," he leans over his desk, the desk he's using to shield him from physical contact. "You're behind me like you wanted."

"Thanks, Dad." I take the ticket and fiddle with the paper. "How was the road trip?"

"Great, we're doing well. The team is coming together," he replies flashing me his perfect smile. He comes alive when he talks about them.

I stand, awkward with the silence making its presence between us. "I'll see you out there."

He walks me to the door. "Have a great time." He briefly touches me on the arm before he heads down the corridor. The voices of the players bounce off the walls.

I decide to check out the arena, it's been so long since I've been here. I grab a hamburger, fries, and a soda, and carry it to my seat. I have an unobstructed view of the players bench. I finish quickly, not thinking of much except for the fact I'm alone. I dump my garbage in the closest garbage receptacle and ask the attendant closest to me for the location where the guys warm-up.

"Behind the glass, down there." He points, giving me the section number. I had no idea I'd be allowed here and take pictures with my phone. Suzy will love this. Hell, I love this.

I stand next to the glass, observing the shiny two-hundred feet of frozen water in front of me. The calmness is refreshing, but I'm anxious for the game to begin. I make my way over to where the players will be warming up and my heart does a pitter-patter knowing Kal will come out soon. Two minutes are on the game clock.

A small group of fans are standing around, waiting for the players to rush out. They must be season ticket holders as they appear to know the drill.

Music starts, the blasts so loud I know my hearing will be affected before the night is over. I eagerly watch as the men rush out on the ice. They are so fast I can't make out who is who as I raise my phone to video tape them. Numbers flash like an action movie on speed. It's thrilling to think I'm so close to them and yet, I completely enjoy the sight of Kal as the players stretch, skate fast as they take shots on our goalie McDavid and breeze past me like an apparition.

The fans beside me are yelling and cheering them on. I shout, "Go Maulers." I doubt the players can hear me, but I scream anyway. It's amazing to be next to others like me, and without knowing anyone's name, occupation, or social status, we're bonding over our love for hockey and the impressive men skating in front of us.

It's as if I found a second family. I find Kal on the ice as he sends a puck to the goalie for warm-ups. The team appears relaxed, This is probably the fun they have before bodies start slamming into the boards.

It's an exciting sport, so physical and intense. I hope Kal isn't in a fight tonight. Sure, I look when it happens, fans get excited and involved in yelling and eggs them on. Yes, it gets my adrenaline going, but there's a part of me cringing inside, hoping the player isn't hurt. It's like a roller coaster, the thrill of going up and closing my eyes at the apex right before my stomach drops on the way down, hoping I'll arrive safely at the bottom.

Tonight, my guy is out there, and the two-minute buzzer

sounds. We disperse, the show is over, the main event is next.

The puck ricochets off the glass, and the clock stops for delay of the game. It was unintentional. I observe my dad, his stoic stance I know so well. His arms hang to the side of his body. He's thin, handsome. I know he won't turn around to acknowledge me. He's not one to deviate from his stoic stature, particularly in a game. He's all business.

Mom texts. Shit. I should have called her and my sister. Carla is Dad's favorite. Mom says you love each child differently, but maybe they are closer because she's more of a dreamer.

I text her I'm at the game and I don't know when I'm off yet. I wonder if Kal would come to a family dinner. I know I shouldn't expect him to come, but I can't help myself. I tell myself it's too soon to introduce him to everyone. We haven't defined ourselves with a label or come out on social media.

I lose myself in the game and people around me shouting Kal's name. It's surreal. That's my guy out there and my heart grows five sizes with pride.

Fans move around as the first period comes to a close. I decide now, of all times, to look up my test results. It's the responsible thing to do, I argue. I had to wrap my head around the possibility of becoming a mother. Then, I worry how I'll look in my parents' eyes, and I can't predict how Kal will react.

With trepidation I click on the button to reveal the results. Positive is the word leaping off the page.

I'm pregnant!

Holy fuck, it's real. I can't let go of my phone, staring at the screen dumbfounded.

People shuffle around me. I stand to let them pass. I'm oblivious to the fact the second period has started, but my eyes track Kal. Will he make a good father? What will he think of me? A baby?

I lean on my knees, elbow on one, and sink my chin into it, zeroing in on my dad. Will he be disappointed in me? He might enjoy being a grandfather, maybe he'll enjoy it more than being a father. They say grandkids are the best of both worlds.

Occasionally, Dad paces in the game. It's 1-1, it's his nervous pace, he chews on gum. He does that when he's nervous in a game. He confers with his assistant coach, Max Fortin, briefly.

My phone pings, Suzy.

I pull my phone up to check the scene as I straighten in my chair. She sent me a picture.

I click on the image and it's a post from Becka's personal media account where she states she and Kal are moving in together and posted a picture of them on her apartment balcony.

I text Suzy.

It has to be a lie.

Has to be, he's been with you.

Thanks for the heads up.

The game ends 4-2.

"The Maulers are on an upward trend beating the St. Louis Archers," the announcer on the radio continues with a recap of the game.

23

Kal

Annie is incredible. Try as I might to not fall in love, I discover I'm infatuated with her, possibly love her. My heart leaps at her voice. Tonight, I skate faster over the rink knowing she's here for her dad. I secretly hope I factor into her thoughts as she watches the game.

I throw my body into players, giving it my all, to make a good impression. The St. Louis Archers are on a winning streak, what could be better than a win tonight?

I horse around Viktor on the bench just to get a glimpse of Annie over his shoulder. I sneak a look as no one knows about us. I want to make us official with my friends and maybe she'll be able to meet my mom and siblings soon. If the paint fight that ended in hot sex is any indication of how it will be between until we're very, very old, I want to take a chance on it.

Annie makes me want to jump into the deep end of the pool and see what we'll find. She's not as adventuresome as me, however, we complement each other. Her structure is good for me, and she plans her life with more than the next day in mind.

We're both disciplined professionals, I only get in trouble in my private life. I'm sure it's me making up for my lost youth. Mom is a realtor and worked hard to support us. I don't doubt that watching my mom struggle for us kids is part of my aversion to kids. Kids take responsibility, and I'm still having fun fucking around with women who will never be a part of my future.

Annie's my future, and as such, the issue at the hospital is problematic. I understand her not telling me his name because I would annihilate him. Good call on her part. But if any man lays a hand on her around me, I'll make him regret it. No one should have to work in an environment where their safety is a concern. She's mine, and soon, everyone will know it.

The win at the end of the night puts us in a good place. The players are connecting and the magic of the team is happening. There is plenty of back slapping going around inside the locker room. November ushered in with our win, the games are stacking up. The deeper we get in the season we'll suffer some setbacks as players get injured. It's a fact for athletes. This will change the dynamics on the ice. Everyone else has to play up, and at times, we're too exhausted to skate anymore, but skate we must.

"Nice playing out there, Bagel," Blake snaps a towel and zings my butt cheeks.

"Thanks, I'm feeling good."

"Becka?" he asks with a wink.

I'm bug eyed. I can't fool him. "Something like that."

"I bet," he scoffs as we take our gear off. Someone is in

the jacuzzi, others shower before hitting the stationary bikes.

I have over an hour here, so I text Annie, informing her I saw her at the game. It wasn't difficult to glance over a team-mate's shoulder. Granted she wouldn't be able to see my entire face with the helmet. She appeared to be deep in thought when I caught a glimpse of her.

She's almost home, and she left me a message telling me I'm welcome to come over. Hot damn. I'm all in, baby.

I shower, ride the bike in my Mauler track suit, and file out with a few of the guys. Before I know it, my car is making a turn down her road. I haven't spent much time at my place of late. I should invite her to my condo. I'm lax on my social etiquette.

I arrive, and park next to her car. I walk across the lawn, crisp with the evening dew as the temperature falls. Her house is like a lighthouse, a warm glow to a man tired of traveling.

A bunny hops in front of me, then freezes. I stop, he makes his exit, unencumbered by my presence in the end. Tree frogs croak, crickets sing, and a slight wind causes leaves to tumble across the yard. I'm used to the silence of my condo, and the city view. I wonder if she'd even like my place.

"Hey, how are you?" Annie asks, greeting me at the tattered screen door.

"Better now." I pull her into my arms.

"Great win." She lets me kiss her as I slip her my tongue in her mouth. I'm hungry, but not for food.

My cock is hard, she excites the hell out of me. I've never had this with another woman. Only Annie can captivate me physically and mentally.

We're one person as we continue our lip lock as we move into the house as if we're in an awkward dance.

"Water?"

"Sure," I reply as she breaks away and notice she's wearing her cute pajamas and a tank top with her hard nipples straining against the cotton. I notice her breasts and can't wait to grab them. I judge how long it will take to get her naked.

"Hey, you didn't see it yet, but Becka," she annunciates her name louder than the other words, "has posted you two as a couple moving in together."

"Fuck, you're kidding." My heart falls sixteen stories. I move closer to her in the kitchen.

"Nope. It's out there. I know it's not true, of course," she explains.

Is she asking me to confirm? Deny? I'm dazed by the news and confused over how to handle this.

"I've been meaning to talk to your dad, it never seems to be the right time, I want to make us official." Truth wins out in the end, or so I desperately hope. "Becka is off her rocker, you know this. I don't know why I even went out with her. I wanted to be with you." I move beside Annie carrying two glasses of water, one in each hand. It occurs to me she doesn't intend to kick me out if she's still bringing me a drink.

I take this as a positive sign as I kick my lace less sneakers off.

"Let's sit, I think we should talk," she offers, setting the water on the trunk of a Maple tree which has been treated with a sealant, serving as a coffee table.

Fuck, talk is never a good word. Nothing good comes when the inevitable word is mentioned when all the person should do is just say what they have on their mind.

She appears restless as she sits, preoccupied by Becka, I assume.

Her silly futon gives the impression I'm an overgrown teenager as my arms and legs sprawl in awkward positions as the cushion sinks under my weight.

"When are you getting furniture for this place?"

"Soon. I'm sorry. My mother and sister will help. They just got back from Europe, and they want me over for a family dinner. Of course, Dad will be divided between us and his GM and whenever players call him."

She's not angry as she speaks, it's a resignation to the facts. I can deal with facts, I know most player's stats, I like knowing where I stand in general.

"So, when is this dinner?"

"I've been skirting it, not sure where we are," she pauses.

"We're together, Annie. We have something special." I lean back and take in her unique features. She gently moves the strands of hair which have fallen over her left eye, tucking it behind her small ear without a thought. Her eyes are her father's, and now I know why she looked familiar when we met. Her lips, thin on the top, full on the bottom, and swollen from our intense kissing a minute ago.

"I thought it might just be me." She looks to her hands as she places them in her lap. Our knees touch.

"No, not at all." I lift her chin and give her a kiss to seal the revelation. I've said it. I put myself out there.

"Okay, so let's make dinner with my parents for tomorrow night, you guys are off. I'm off at six, we can have dinner at seven."

"Sure." I wrap my fingers in her hair as she smiles at me. I can't wait to get her under me.

"There's one more thing, and it came as a surprise to me, but it's all my fault..."

"What's your fault?"

"There's no easy way to say this. I don't want you to think I'm careless or planned this. However, I've been so busy I forgot to take some medications when I moved here," her timid manner is scaring me.

"Are you okay?" I place my hand over hers. I can't believe the woman I want is sick. I never knew.

"I'm fine, Kal." Her beautiful round eyes meet mine. "I'm pregnant. I had a blood test done as it gives results before other tests. It's my fault."

"Yeah, right," I scoff. I'm amused but I'm not biting. "Did Blake put you up to this? Colton, or Finn?" I chuckle. "Blake and the guys just can't let me win."

"What?" She pulls back and my fingers are in thin air. Standing in a huff. "What the fuck, Kal? It's not easy to tell you this but I never thought for one minute you'd jump to me pranking you over something so serious."

I stand in response. "What? This is real? You're kidding, right? I swear I won't be pissed, but you have to tell me the truth."

"Pissed at not having a kid for real, or the guys getting one over on you?" Her hands fly to her hips, she's standing her ground. I realize I've fucked up, but it's too late.

"This is getting complicated. I don't need you to call me on my shit right now!" I run a hand over the top of my head. What can I say that doesn't make me an asshole?

"I can do it myself, seriously," she exclaims.

This is Annie, as independent as hell. She's trying to push me away, but I won't let her sabotage what we have.

I take her hands in mine. "Breathe, it's no biggie. I mean, it could come out to be ten pounds, which would suck for you, but we got this," I add, hoping I've calmed her down.

She laughs. "Ten pounds? It's a baby, not a watermelon,"

she argues.

"True, but it's gotta hurt coming out," I joke. Laughter is the cure for a tricky, sticky, situation.

"I'm surprised. It's my fault too, we never discussed birth control. I assumed. I always wear a condom, but I didn't with you," my voice fades. Why didn't I? It's my rule.

"You're not angry?" She quips.

"Angry over a little crib midget?" I shrug. "I just don't want your dad to beat the ever-loving shit out of me. Do they know?" I search her eyes, wide with...is it admiration?

"Oh, God no. I'm a bit embarrassed. I moved here, got so busy I forgot to pick up my birth control and didn't realize it until I suspected something was up. Then, I needed to make sure I wasn't pregnant before I could start the pill, and then, that wasn't an option," she explained as she tilts her head to see if I'm okay.

She's so damn cute talking a mile a minute. Little Annie, always planning her future and now she's got a surprise, a big surprise.

I pull her in my arms, reassuring her it will be fine. Her dad is my concern. Shit, he's gonna kick my ass.

"Look, it's late, I need some time to process. I'll meet you at your parents' tomorrow. Is that okay with you?"

"Sure." I know she wants to ask questions and do what women do at this point. Maybe think of the future and what names to put on a list? Hell, if I know.

I didn't plan on being a dad this early. I find kids noisy, and snotty, and I'm relieved to leave them so I can get away from their dirty hands which leave smudges on everything.

The responsibility my mother had providing for us and making ends meet when dad's child support didn't show up is tough to forget. I'm guilty of taking her hard-earned money just to remain in hockey. There were some scholarships, but we mostly fell between the cracks of assistance. I couldn't work. My days and nights were filled between hockey and making the grades needed to stay on the school team before I joined traveling leagues.

She found a way to keep me in hockey. I bought her a house in a better neighborhood in my third year of going pro. I'm glad I'm more stable to be bringing a kid into the world, but all the same, I'm shocked.

Annie walks me to the door, and I reach for the doorknob.

"We'll be okay," I drop a kiss on her lips, my boner fainted at the "p" word. I hope he'll get over the stage freight knowing a baby is coming out of 'the happy place' we've been parading in.

"You sure we're okay?"

She looks helpless standing in the shadow of the kitchen's overhead lights. I'm a schmuck to leave her after the news, but I need to process the information.

I have to get to Coach in the morning. I use the drive home to process the news. This isn't how I imagined the whole, "We're having a baby," would go. Not that I thought about it much, but this is a less than stellar situation. I always wear a condom for this reason. I don't leave this to chance, it's too big of a responsibility. I'm not prepared.

Is anyone?

Decidedly, Annie will make a good mother and it's the thought I cling to, and it brings me off the ledge of panic. She's a doctor, she'll know what to do. We don't have to get married in today's world, couples don't if it's not the right person. Plenty of players have baby mama's and they share custody and pay child support. The divorces and private situations are kept quiet. Guys on the team don't share these details outside of our group.

What do I want?

What does Annie want?

How do I know she's the one? The fact I risked my career to see her behind her dad's back is not what I envisioned, either. Then there are my exes, and the trail of bad media in my past.

My past. That's it, it's in my past. Annie is my future. But the past has a way of creeping up when I least expect it. Like this thing with Becka.

Posting what she did is odd even by my standards. What's her angle? She wants me, or she wants to get back with me. There's nothing she can do to hurt me, or Annie, except try to break us up. It's not the first time an ex has a grudge to grind with me.

How much do I care for Annie? I wrestle with the thought of the baby and wonder if it's a boy or girl and will they like cold winters? I don't even know if Annie loves winter, but she grew up in it just like me. We were in states next to each other, sharing a boarder as kids and never knew we'd meet one day. Our home football teams have rivaled each other since their existence and yet we've never talked much of anything but each other and our issues with our fathers.

I need some sleep. I'll have to reach coach tomorrow before the big dinner. I might have left Annie in a bit of a lurch, but she seemed fine when I left.

I change, flip on the TV and text her goodnight from my bed. It's late. I didn't anticipate not sleeping at Annie's tonight. I miss her, the smell of lilac in her hair, the way she cuddles up to me and I keep her warm.

I send a virtual hug and kiss. It seems too small of a gesture in light of the events. I'm the first to admit I'm not perfect. Life isn't perfect, either.

24

Annie

I throw a bagel in the toaster and chuckle, Kal's nickname, Bagel. I may never look at a one the same way again. He's Jewish. I wonder what we'll name the baby. It's too soon to think about it, I remind myself.

My eyes can't escape the living room Kal and I started to paint. It's not like it's going to get done anytime soon and I notice the boxes still sitting in corner where I left them.

I text him good morning and ask him about the cameras. Is forgetfulness part of pregnancy hormones? If so, I can do without it.

I nibble on the cream cheese I've spread on my hand-held breakfast. I walk over the even pavers and marvel at how thoughtful Kal was to think of fixing them. He must have hired a landscape company because it's not like either one of us can risk injuring our hands.

I'm happy he took it upon himself to do something thoughtful for me. Especially now. I smile as I walk, and text him a thank you. I've been so consumed with my run in with Dr. Dick and the pregnancy test I've forgotten my manners.

I like that he surprises me with the little things, like the flowers he sent to work. In my opinion, he'll be a good dad, he's attentive.

I have no experience with our situation, or his response to last night. Not that I envisioned it ending up in us saying "I love you" or "will you marry me?"

He was shell-shocked. I understand it's big news and coming from his years of being carefree, I don't want him to rush in for the wrong reasons.

I'm a bit of a hot mess myself. I have hormones going on, my body is different, and it's only the beginning. A baby is a life altering event and that's for couples who are planning a family.

To think the jocks would joke about a kid is crazy, but that's the type of shit they must do behind closed doors. I can't believe we'll have to re-tell the story of how we met to our children one day. It's evident one question in my life has been answered. I know who the father of my child is, so that's one mystery I can cross off my list.

What will the baby be? Where will we live? Shit, I got to get my head focused on work as I'm not present as I drive my car, arriving at work without much of a memory of how I got here. I have to operate in a few hours and I'm dreading the fact Dr. Dick works today.

Decidedly, I'll rely on Suzy for advice. She's knowledge-able with human behavior to get a bead on his reaction. She's not had the pampered youth I did. She's been around all walks of life outside of the hospital walls as she was raised by a single mom and government assistance until her mother finished her nursing degree.

We meet up at the coffee kiosk.

"Have you looked at your results yet?" she asks.

"Last night at the game."

"The game? Are you crazy? Who does that?" She makes a wide gesture with her arms like I'm more than my normal kind of crazy. She's not one to mince words. We're alike like that. Maybe it's why we get along so well.

"I don't know, Kal was on the bench, I saw his jersey and imagined his last name as mine. He has the right to know. I don't expect anything from him. I can do this on my own. To be married is a fantasy, I don't want it just because of the situation." I whisper the last word. There are eyes and ears everywhere. If the hospital filled with mostly female employees doesn't have enough rumor and innuendo floating around to make a great reality show, I don't know what does.

"Gee, Annie, I think he did well to not hurl. Most men are allergic to commitment, and even if they want kids, it's often left to the mom. They don't come with a manual or hockey stick," she quips without so much as a blink of an eye.

I snort the hot coffee in my mouth as I laugh and breathe at the same time. A hockey stick is a good idea, it would make it more relatable for him.

"That's great, I need a baby hockey stick, and everything will be fine. Seriously, I need to wing it with him, and I'm not good with improvising. I can't be too serious; he loves to have fun. If I'm not fun, he'll not want to be around me."

"He'll either step up or not," Suzy says. "What was his reaction?"

"He thought it was Blake playing a joke on him," I lament as I run my card in the kiosk for my coffee.

"You're kidding me. Who jokes about that?" She feigns being appalled.

"That's what I said," I take a sip of hot java as we make our way to the elevator.

"I would be more suspect if it was Becka," she says emphatically and punches the button to do a pre-surgery pep talk to our elderly patient.

"True, she's wacko, posting the two of them are moving in together. I want the drama to be over already."

"I hear yah, but every bad boy has a history. Why are they called bad boys?" We enter the elevator.

"I don't know, I've never been with one but given my issues with Dad, I'm surprised. I just focused on school and work."

"Me, too."

"Oh, how are you and Mitch? Are you both coming to the benefit this weekend?"

"Yes, actually. We're doing well. No pregnancies," she teases.

"You're a brat!"

The doors open and we're on the second floor.

"Do you think Kal's response was bad?"

"No. Everyone handles life differently, otherwise we'd all be clones. And what is the fun in that?"

"Exactly," I chuckle. "Let's wear blue dresses to the event. We need to get good pictures together and we'll look great with dresses in the same color palette."

"Couple pictures, too," she reminds me. "Blue it is."

"Yeah, I need to give Kal the details."

"Is he coming to the benefit?"

"He said yes. He's supposedly meeting my father today before our family dinner tonight. I've only brought one boyfriend home, and I knew the man wasn't going to work, he just didn't fit."

"That's a nice way to put it. So, he wasn't the love of your life, I take it?"

"Nope." Now that I've gotten to know Kal, I know why the others didn't stick. No pun intended." I raise a finger towards Suzy's face as a warning. "Kal turns me inside out every time I see him. I don't think I'll ever get tired of looking at him. I love to watch him play hockey, what he does on the ice is amazing. I can't imagine what it will be like to have a mini us running around and playing sports."

"Keep that thought, you'll need it for the first eighteen months, when the baby can walk and sleep through the night."

We turn down another hall, I instinctively look for Dr. Fluentes.

"Coast is clear," I murmur.

"Thanks, we're on the same case this morning."

Kal's name pops up in my message app. He just woke up. I guess he gets about eight more months of that. I call him.

"How's work?" He sounds sleepy.

"Normal. You?"

"Going to see your dad so he doesn't find out we're together from someone else."

"Good call," I admit.

"How are you?"

"Great, oh, the hospital benefit is a full house of who's who."

"Gotcha. What color suit do I wear?"

"A tux?"

"We can redo the botched gala where we officially met," he adds with a dash of his sarcasm.

"Nice. I like how you did that, just kind of slid that messy event under the radar."

"Why not have a happy event? We get to go together."

"Great, so we'll be 'out' officially," I muse. I have no clue what this entails. I have an inkling more press will be involved. They will think I'm his new flavor of the month, until we prove them wrong.

"Yes!"

"I like it," I reply.

We sign off and it occurs to me we haven't even listened to music together. I wonder when we'll obtain 'our' song. I've never had a relationship lasting longer than a year and now that I think about it, I believe we made more financial sense than emotional.

Kal is different. The chemistry was there from the minute we met. It's still there, and I don't foresee it changing. I love drinking him in as he enters a room. The cute ass, his deep voice, and his quirky humor cracks me up. I always need a good laugh.

I ARRIVE at my parents from work. I enter the large foyer and glance into the living room and am surprised to find Dad and Kal drinking beers. Carla rushes to me from my left, acting like a teenager as she squeals in joy and engulfs me with a bear hug, which lands hard enough to tackle a linebacker.

"Sis! Oh, my God, Europe was amazing. I missed you," her voice, filled with enthusiasm. I realize how young she is. We're opposites. She's carefree, throwing herself into each experience as if it's her last. I'm the over-thinker.

"Carla, you look amazing!" I gasp at how grown up she looks and wonder if the trip helped her to grow up. I can't for the life of me figure out where the cute kid who braided her hair and wore the hippest clothes went, but her nice sweater, albeit short, is an improvement over her tie-died t-shirts she used to wear daily.

"Annie," Mom gives me a hug and now the three of us all hug. Mom is the affectionate one.

"Mom, I'm so happy to see you." I send a 'save me' look to Kal.

"Annie, I'll take your jacket," Kal offers.

"Oh, yes, I forgot, we're smothering her, Carla," Mom adds as she backs up to take me in.

"You look great. Are you getting settled in the house? You know, I told your father it needs too much work. How is it coming?"

"Terrible. I don't have time."

"We've started painting," Kal interjects, and sends me a mischievous smile.

Like I could forget how that afternoon ended.

"Annie said you're the decorator, Mrs. Susneck," Kal compliments my mom.

"Oh, I just throw a few things together, but if you give me a list, I'll see what I can find."

"A couch would be great, that futon is deplorable," he chuckles.

"You moved that old thing? It was from your dorm!" Dad exclaims.

I'm shocked he remembers. There must be a photo book with me in it. Dad wasn't big on visits to Boston. We'd meet for dinner if he was in town for an overnight game.

"Something smells good," I distract everyone from talk of me, afraid the pregnancy is evident even though it's impossible. Just the same, I'd rather keep my mind occupied on topics other than myself.

"Moms made her famous baked ziti, of course," Carla croons. "And your guy is hot. Hooking up with a hockey hottie?" she whispers in my ear before she announces she's setting the table. "Really? You didn't even tell me?"

"It was new and happened so fast."

"Drink Annie?" Mom interrupts.

Shit, we always drink red wine.

"I'm fine. Just water."

Mom quizzes me, it's our thing. I'm baffled by her look. I shoot a look back to put her off.

"Kal, another beer?" she asks as she leaves for the kitchen.

"I'm fine, Mrs. Susneck."

"Oh, call me Julia," Mom remarks.

Kal nods. I don't know how comfortable he is now that the family is warming up to him. I expected a few fireworks. Mom wants me married with kids and hasn't made a secret of it, like with the blind date with Blake. Dad, I'm not so sure. He probably wants what makes Mom happy.

"So, Kal tells me you've been seeing each other," Dad starts.

Carla plops on the sofa and Mom materializes with a bottle and wine glasses. I'm sure they are all ears.

"Yes, well, it was new. We didn't want to say anything, until we got to know each other." I sit near where Kal and Dad are standing by his trophies. Some are from his days of playing and others are for leagues he coached.

"Hm, I suspected, but wanted to give you space to make your own decisions," Dad states. I guess that explains why he gave Kal shit and not me.

The timer on the oven dings and I'm out of the hot seat.

"Dinner," Mom announces as she turns on her heels.

"Best kept secret," Carla interjects as she flounces ahead of me. Dad leads us to the dining room and Kal slips his hand in mine.

"You, okay?" I ask Kal.

"Yeah, your dad probably isn't thrilled, but he's not interfering."

It's the best I could have hoped for, I imagine.

"Mom, can I help?"

"No, no, just sit, you're a guest." She carries a huge tray of pasta in a heavy wooden rack and places it on the table.

Carla pops up to grab the salad and bottles of dressing.

We all take our places at the table.

"Carla, I love the pictures you took in Italy," Dad states with admiration.

"Thanks, Dad. I'll make a book of our trip for you."

Dad nods.

"Kal, what do you do for fun?" Dad asks.

"I like to golf, like you. I take in sports and well, seeing Annie keeps me busy. She works hard." He squeezes my leg affectionately under the table.

"Annie, how is it going? You don't talk about work much," Dad scoops pasta on his plate and passes the spoon to Kal. Mom dishes up bowls of salad and Carla passes them around. Ziti is scooped on our plates and the smell of it reminds me I haven't eaten since morning.

"Not much going on, but the benefit this weekend. Mom says you'll both be there."

"Duty calls," Dad replies in-between bites.

Mom raves about the event and tells stories. Carla tells us about her trip and informs us she's applied to colleges. It's so nice to have a man with me for a family meal.

I notice Carla messing with her phone and she sends me a look, then glances back to her phone.

My eyes tell her to knock it off.

All through small talk, it's eating at me. What's so important?

Carla jumps as soon as we're finished and volunteers me to clear the table with her. Code for let's talk in the kitchen.

"What's up? You're being dramatic," I snap.

"Some stripper is selling a sex tape of her and Kal," she whispers.

"What?" I'm in disbelief.

She slips me her phone and Hockey Scoop is running with the rumor of a potential sale of the video.

"Shit. I gotta go. Let's clean up, and I'll say I have an early morning."

"Sorry sis, I thought you'd want to know."

"Sure, thanks."

Dad pops his head in. "Everything okay in here?" He moves to Carla and gives her a half hug, like they're the best of pals. And they are. I'm the odd man out.

"Yeah, only we're going to have to run. I have an early day tomorrow and I'm exhausted." I'm not fibbing, either. I'm very tired.

"Awe, no cards tonight? Like old times?"

"Sorry." I turn to see Kal talking to Mom and walk to them. I give Mom a hug, I lean my head into hers like I did as a child for comfort. I move away even though there is a perplexed look in her almond shaped eyes. We make our exit before Dad gets a call from the GM over the incident. This will go over like a lead pancake on my head.

We walk to our cars; Kal opens my door.

"Kal, were you with a stripper?"

"That was a long time ago," he comments, suddenly somber. "Why?"

"Carla showed me. Hockey Scoop has word a video of you is going to be sold. What is it?"

"Oh, shit. It's what has been dubbed as dick pics, it's

been floating out there for over a year. It's a video of me at a strip club."

"What? Do I even want to know what that is?"

"No, however, I need to call my attorney. I was taped dancing with a stripper, and it was without my consent."

"Please tell me you had a speedo on," I lament.

"Did have it on, until she pulled it off, with her teeth," his matter-of-fact acknowledgement makes me wonder if he worries over anything.

There are no words after this confession. I slip in my car, intent on not making a scene.

"I'll follow you," he says. "We need to talk about this."

I'm thinking, no I don't. The man is never phased by unexpected events. It's as if he's coated in flubber, everything bounces off him with his good-natured attitude.

I'm pissed and envious at the same time.

25

Kal

I call my sports manager from the car as I drive to Annie's. He's always available. He'll call an attorney. He informs me they'll handle it and for me to not do anything. I'm sure this will come with a hefty bill, but it's immaterial at this point. It needs to be cleaned up. Nothing but my game and Annie are important. I can't let her down. She's had to deal with my sordid past, one which I can't undo, but it needs to go away forever.

Logically, no media contact is good media. I have to lay low on this. Thankfully, the media can't get to me coming and going from games. They might stalk my condo.

I never want to see the devastating look on Annie's face again. I played it off but inside, I felt remorse over my risqué behavior. This is one of the worst incidents to happen to athletes and I'm relieved it is out in the open at last. This way, it can be put out to pasture.

I just hope Annie doesn't kick me out of her life.

Taping anyone against their knowledge usually gets shut down in court. It's fixable, it will come with a financial price tag, I just want to keep Annie calm. I'm not a man whore. I used to live in a self-destructing state of mind. A person can change.

Back then, nothing mattered. If it wasn't for hockey, I don't know where I would have ended up. I had a difficult time after we learned of Dad's betrayal. I'm guilty of not telling mom all the things he showed me as we sat at his computer and went to the horse track when we were supposed to be shopping for school clothes.

I was a kid, the shrink said, burdened by someone's addiction. I need to forgive myself. I thought the house for mom would have done that but there's a hole in me from the loss of a parent I had to cut loose. No dad in the stands cheering me on like old times. Now I understand why he had a beeper; it was coded with messages from his numerous bookies.

I have trained myself to remember only the good memories. I vow to be a better parent with my child. I'm having a kid. I marvel at this fact and for the first time, I'm excited. I wish I was married before I had kid because Mom will have my hide on that score. Annie deserves the best, and being an unwed mom isn't the future I want for her. We could wait until later, hockey players do it all the time. I'm not sure I agree with it.

Marriage without love isn't an option. It's why I've been single for so many years. Long-term commitment isn't my thing. Annie keeps my feet on the ground. The thought of her makes me happy. She might not be happy with me now, but overall, we are meant for each other. After all we've been through, saying I love you isn't enough.

I park and Annie stomps off leaving me in the dust.

"Annie," I call after her.

"Kal, I've had enough," she huffs as she bends over a clay flowerpot filled with dirt, no flowers, and lifts the key hidden there. "This is quicker than digging through my purse," she informs me. "My key fob is floating in my purse somewhere."

"We need to talk. I can explain," I plead as she unlocks the door. I follow her in.

"You want me and my dad to take you seriously, how can I? How can we?" she asks hysterically. She flings her arms out in frustration, and disappointment is written on her face.

"It's in my past, we all have one. I'm sure you did some things you weren't proud of at some point in your life."

"Nothing like this," she yells, her voice piercing my ears. "How many more Becka's are out there? How many strippers? Do you have kids you don't know of? What's next? I can't live waiting to see what drops on us, on me." She points to herself, and I get it, but I'm an ass to her just the same.

"So, it's about you?" I ask irritated with the situation. If I didn't have a girlfriend, it would be handled without all this drama.

"I'm the coach's daughter and Dad holds me to a higher standard than he does you! Here I am, hanging out with the bad boy of the team and your past is a reflection on me, my dad. Oh, for fuck's sake. My dad! He's going to call me, I know it. This is terrible. I can't bear to see how disappointed he will be. I need my parents Kal, what if you're not here? We're having a kid, I'll need help, lots of it."

"Well, I screwed up," I reply remorsefully. "Attorneys will

talk, and it will be blocked. Come'on, even Robert Downy, Jr. got a do-over, and I'm not even an alcoholic," I plead my case with my pragmatic view of the situation.

"No, maybe you're Charlie Sheen," she throws her insult before she chucks her purse and jacket on the kitchen counter and puts a hand on her head as if she has a headache. Maybe the arguing is making her overly warm.

"Are you, okay?" I tentative step towards her.

"Yes, no. Physically, yes, mentally, no."

"Please, take a second, sit. Let's sit." I motion to the terrible futon in the room.

She paces. It's ironic, she's just like her dad, pacing under duress. I wonder if our kid will have the same trait.

"Calm down, we'll get through this. I have a team of professionals who do this all day. It's not the first time this has happened. It won't be the last." When I catch her eye, and quickly add, "It's the last time for me." I stand tall, pulling my shoulders back to let her know I mean business.

"What of your job?"

"I'll be fine, it's not my first rodeo. Worst case scenario is they trade me."

She screams, "I don't need you to screw up my relationship with my father." She begins to sob. "I'll never be Carla in his eyes and you're not helping me earn his respect or affection."

"He respects you. Why don't you think so?"

"He never hugs me like my sister."

"You sister is young for her age, he might feel she needs him more."

"I'm sure, but it's not fair. I need him, too," she sobs and a few more tears trickle down her face.

"I think tonight is more than me. It's the fact your dad

doesn't validate your feelings, or his love for you. Those are deep issues, Annie."

"No, I mean," she stifles her sob. I grab a tissue from a box on the credenza by the door with a vase filled with my now dead bouquet. She snatches the Kleenex from my hand. "Thank you."

Her hands are busy and I seize the opportunity to hold her. She leans her head into my shoulder. I stroke her hair. Her breathing returns to normal.

"I think you needed that cry." I grin as she tilts her head back to see my face.

"I think you might be right."

"Your job is stress. This psycho doctor is stress. You read too much into your dad's attention to Carla. Some dynamics we can't change. Have you told him how you feel?"

"Not in a way he understands."

"I'll try to help you if you let me. Why don't we just go to bed and chill to a movie of prehistoric sharks getting loose and relax?"

I see her weighing her anger at me against her desire to be with me.

"Grab some water, I need to hydrate after all those tears," she adds as she grabs her purse and heads up the steps to the bedroom.

"Can I pay to have your house painted?" I call after her as I quickly fill a glass with cold tap water.

"Really?"

"Yeah, we don't have the time. And what do you want for the baby's room? I assume it won't be white?"

"I thought seafoam green. Is that weird?"

I place the water on her nightstand and undress, catching a glimpse of her naked before she slides under the sheets.

"I like it, works for a boy or girl."

"That's what I thought," she sighs. "Is it going to be alright, really?"

"No matter what, we're fine," I assure her as she turns the TV on and before I say another word, she's asleep.

26

Annie

Kal is in Los Angeles for a game, he text me when he was on his way to an interview with a popular late night show host. Blake and Viktor went as well. This one is live, so I tune the TV to it.

The hosts ask the guys about funny stories and play a silly game. Then, Kal is grilled about his personal life. I knew the video was what he wanted, the scumbag.

"You know, we live, we learn, but I have someone special who makes me complete."

The hosts digs for details. He's trying to be cute and make a joke, but I know what they are like. Gossip sells and drives up his ratings.

"We'll make it official soon, right now, I want to protect her privacy. She's new to the spotlight," he flashes his grin and the women in the crowd let out an "ooh".

"Someone who isn't used to the media, is that what you're inferring there, Kal?" the man with a clean-shaven face asks.

"Something like that," he replies ambiguously. If anyone can play his game, it's Kal.

"Another hockey player gets hitched, huh?" The interviewer pushes for a slip up.

"We'll see. Y'know, maybe Viktor will beat me to the punch, one never knows," Kal deflects the spotlight off of himself.

Good job, honey.

Luc comes up with a funny one-liner and after him, the show is on to the next guest, a movie starlet. I wonder if he got to meet her, she's promoting her new movie release and she's smoking hot.

I flip the TV off. The interview went better than I expected. He looked happy.

Tomorrow, I'm taking time off to see my baby doctor and buy a dress for the fundraiser. Suzy sent me a picture of hers last night. I can't wait to meet her guy, Mitch.

Kal calls me in the mid-morning as I'm in a dressing room trying on a dress.

"The judge gave us an injunction on the video. If they can't get money from it, we assume it will go away. I thought you'd want to know."

"Absolutely. I'm trying on dresses, and I just don't know if it's the right one," I reply with concern.

"Send me a picture," his warm voice makes me wet even though we're miles apart.

"Really?" I can't help but gush he's so attentive.

"You've never done some of the things we've done in the bedroom, and you liked those, trust me. Take a selfie and hit send."

I chuckle because he's right. I take a selfie and send the snapshot to him.

"Hum, try the one you have hanging behind you. There

is no reason you need to cover every inch of your body. Leave the dress and jacket for your mother. You're gorgeous, you need to show it off."

"I'm...afraid to."

"Oh, right," he replies pensively as he remembers my situation of being harassed at work. It's natural to assume the offending doctor will be at the event as well. "I'll be with you, Annie. He better not lay a hand on you. It's not right you are changing your life around him. Please tell me who it is. I want to protect you."

"Not now. I've put in a request for cameras to be put in the staff's pantry so I'm hoping they get him on camera."

"Great, it's a start but I'm not sure it's a deterrent. I wish there is something we could do, and not put your career in jeopardy."

"Me, too." I lay the phone on the chair as I change.

"You ready with that dress, yet?" he teases.

"Picture is coming."

"Wowzah, you are fantastic in that dress. Buy it."

"It's very expensive, Kal. I can't do that."

"You're not, I am. Call me from the register, no discussion on this. My treat."

"Fine," I consent to letting him buy the dress. The material is soft, it's navy blue and will look nice with his tuxedo. "I don't know if I'll ever fit in it again. It's very expensive," I murmur.

"Doesn't matter. By the way, is it okay to send my maintenance man's trusted people to your house to knock out some of the painting?"

"Sure, use the key under the mat. The paint's there."

"Alright. I have a short practice tomorrow; you'll be busy at work, but I'll text," he assures me.

I check out at a register where the saleswoman

comments on my good taste. She takes Kal's information over the phone. Clearly, she's a hockey fan as she's all smiles and a bit flirtatious with him as she takes his credit card information. I tell him my mother will go nuts over the dress before I hang up. The woman places my dress in a long plastic bag, knots it at the end and asks me what it's like to date a player.

"It's different," I assure her. "He's a great guy," I smile. However, it's time to head to my nail appointment.

I won't speak of personal details to anyone except my family and Suzy. I know all too well to be careful with what I share.

Having my nails done is relaxing. Before I leave, I book my salon to put my hair in a French braid for Saturday,.I have plenty of time to dress and finagle my makeup before the event. I briefly contemplate a professional makeup artist and quickly dismiss it. I'm not competing with any of Kal's exes.

Unlike my mother who looks like a model when she leaves her bedroom in the morning. I want to look like I belong in Kal's world but on my terms. It's important I network with the board members and get to know the powerful players in town. There is a board of directors like Suzy mentioned and Mr. Barber is on it. I hate networking, but it's a required attendance, and it is necessary for my future.

With the baby coming, I wonder about going into private practice and like Kal, I decide to push it off. We'll figure it out as we go. He might have the inside track on not stressing out over life events. I wonder what his thoughts are on the baby.

Is he ready? Will he flake out on me? Luckily there is time to figure out what our arrangement will be before the little one arrives. My goal is to stay clear of Dr. Dick until human resources catches him on tape.

I meet my mother after my nail appointment and we have an afternoon tea. By that, I mean a high tea, and I'm not donning a hat. I'm hungry and devour the tiny cucumber sandwiches as we play catch up with each other.

"Where is Carla going to college?"

"She might stay in Maine, she's not sure what she wants to major in," mom sips her hot tea. "She's not like you, with her future mapped out."

"I know. It would be nice to have her around." Especially now, she's good with kids. I wonder if I'll need a nanny and decide to save that thought for another day.

"Are you and Kal serious? He's so handsome and nice. I've heard he's... wild." She sets her teacup on the saucer, the scones arrive.

"You could say that. We're getting to know each other. He's sweet and thoughtful. I don't want to get too excited," I reply respectively.

"It's not a secret, he showed up at the house before dinner and I thought he was going to ask your dad to marry you," she replies aloofly.

"Really?" I'm befuddled. "What gives you the impression it was serious talk?"

"Well, men usually do that, well, some men still do. Besides, I saw the way you two look at each other. If that's not soulful eye fucking, I don't know what is."

"Mom!" I exclaim before I look around to see if anyone heard her. I had no idea she was capable of saying the word 'fuck' in public.

"What? It's true, the chemistry leaps between the two of you the second he enters the room. They say couples produce healthy babies if there's synergistic and hot chemistry. It's some scientific thing I read," she shrugs her shoulders as if to excuse how blunt she's behaving today.

"Oh, boy. I know you want me married and are ready for grandchildren, but it has to be on my timeline."

"Well, get on it," she pats my hand with an impish smile. "I'm getting older, and I want to see them grow up."

"You're young, Mom." I search her beautiful face. She's had some Botox here and there is my assumption. She covers the gray in her hair, but she's fit, goes to the gym a few times a week, and she has a trainer.

I can't tell her my news. I hope she and Dad won't mind an unwed mother in the family. She's going to freak out when I start to show. I have no idea when the right time is and trust it will organically unfold in the month ahead. I'm excited at the thought of the baby today, but it's best to not jinx it this early. She did enough surprise talk today for both of us with the eye fucking comment.

By the time I wrap up our luncheon, Kal is busy with the team.

"Kal's nice, I hope it works out, sweetie." Mom hugs me as we stand beside our vehicles.

"Thanks, Mom. No promises. You know my track record," I warn, so she doesn't get her hopes set on a wedding. I drive to my doctor's appointment. Oh, boy, fun stuff. I didn't want to push it off waiting for Kal, I want to know the due date as I assume the baby will come in August. My hope is he'll be home for the birth. I have no desire to go through it alone, but plenty of wives do.

Kal mentioned they might have an exhibition game overseas, and most women only get to have their husbands with them if the baby arrives when the team is playing in town, and he's granted the night off.

That's a lot of ifs.

After an embarrassing examination under a white paper sheet, the baby's heartbeat is strong, and fast. Fast, the doctor mentions, usually means a boy. Sure, it's anyone's guess, but a cute little boy would be great. Whether it's a boy or girl, I hope the baby has Kal's eyes.

The jury on the sex of the infant is unknown until later. So many decisions. I pull up on my house and find vans parked everywhere.

"What's wrong, what's up?" I ask a man in a white painter's outfit. He's wearing coveralls, and moves about with precision, taking his time.

"We're about done, are you Annie?" The man is short and is walking with a ladder.

"Yes, what's going on?" I survey the men and assume they are working on my house.

"We're almost done. It was a big job. You husband paid a ton of money to get it done today."

"What is done?" Did I hear husband? I'm not married.

"Maybe it's a surprise," he smiles and loads the ladder on his work vehicle.

"The walls are still drying; I'd keep a few windows open, but it's okay to breathe. He made sure of that," he replies before he disappears into my house and I'm on his trail like a novice stalker.

"Great." I go along with what he says, obviously I've been left out of the loop.

A few more men file past me and the head foreman hands me my key.

I thank them, wonder what I'll find after I walk through my back door. I hope Kal didn't install a stripper pole. He has a penchant for high heels in bed, and for all I know, there will be titty tassels under my pillowcase any day now.

The smell of paint greets me, but it's quickly forgotten

when I take in the incredible walls, all perfect, and the white ceiling. The house is now modern looking with the professional paint job and it's clean. Perfect for a newborn. I can't help the excitement I'm feeling and walk around carefully due to my eyes misting. I carry my dress upstairs so I can change and start dinner.

I smell paint on the second floor, but my room didn't need painting. I hang my dress over the top of my bedroom door. I lay my coat and purse on my bed before I gander down the hall to investigate. The room at the end of the hallway is—in seafoam!

My hand flies to my lips, goosebumps run up my arms and I'm bawling like a baby. He did this for me. He's the most romantic man I've ever met. No wonder he was asking me questions the other day.

I thought he was the king of pranks, but damn, he's good at surprises.

I love the room, it's perfect. And he listened to me when we discussed colors. I don't know how I'm going to keep up with him. He's got the jump on me at every turn.

I return to my room and reach for the phone. He doesn't pick up, but I leave him the sweetest message of how much I love what he did, and the baby's room is incredible. For the first time since we met, I allow myself to picture us here, as a family.

Surely, Kal loves me. Why else would he go out of his way to make all this happen for me? The flowers, the paint fight, the painters, and coming to Dad's family dinner. How do I know? He's never said he loves me, and I keep holding my words in as I wait. There is no way I'm saying those three words first.

27

Kal

The interview wasn't anything I couldn't handle. I've got skills. I receive a text from Annie, she's three hours ahead of me. She loved the fact the downstairs area was painted and the seafoam color for the baby's room is a hit as I stand in awe of it. I've never been able to plan for the future with a woman before. I'm a quick study and it reinforces the fact I don't totally suck at relationships. I conclude Annie is for me. I love her. They say you know when you've met the right woman, and I know. I've never been so intent on impressing anyone in my life, except for my mom.

Obviously, I hit the painting project out of the park. Will she always get what she wants? Probably. I can't wait to play the LA Thunder tomorrow night. I've never been so impatient to get home. I wish I heard the baby's heartbeat. It's incredible to imagine something so small and delicate. I can't wait for a sonogram.

"Blake," I pop him on the back and nod to Colton and Finn, who pass us in the hallway of our luxury hotel. "Are you and Rachel coming to the benefit this Saturday? I have the tickets, it's for a children's wing, and I'd love to have you at my table."

"If the Mrs. wants to go, we'll be there," he replies unmoved by my excitement. Maybe I'm always keyed up on the road. Or is it Annie who has me jazzed?

I never thought I'd have kids, period. Shit, Wyatt's wife is expecting and so is Alexandre's. Seems there is a baby boom going around and I drank the Babymaker Kool-Aid.

"I just want you to know there are no hard feelings over setting me up with Annie, turns out, she wasn't the one for you, my man."

He gives me a quizzical eye.

"She's amazing. We've been dating."

"No, shit." He slaps me on the back. "I thought you were with Becka."

"She was a red herring," I jest. "I didn't want anyone to know with Coach around. But he knows now, so it's all good," I beam as if I was handed a new sports car.

"Yeah, no more six a.m. practices man, that killed me. Like it really fucked up my day, and I played like shit that night."

"Tell me about it. So, come Saturday, you're my guest, and it's for a good cause. I'll ask a few of the guys, should be fun."

"Great, I'll text you," he replies as I scoot down the hall to pick Alexandre's brain for information, seeing as how his wife loves shiny objects housed in light blue boxes.

∾

WE WON the game in LA and the city is one of urban sprawl with no end, rocky hillsides, and colorful lights as we wind through traffic in the wee hours of the morning en route to the commercial airport. The flight home is bumpy. I hate east to west coast travel. The only trip that sucks more is flying into Denver because the Rockies are unpredictable. I've clutched my seat more often than not as the plane slices through head winds.

We all go our separate ways as the bus drops us off at the Camden Bay Arena.

I'm off my schedule with the time difference and fall asleep at four a.m. I'm up by ten, it's time to drink a shake and I shuffle to the kitchen to pick through old, shriveled blueberries in my fridge to find the edible ones. I make the shake, drink it as I shower and shave, knowing I have errands to run. It's Annie's big night and I have a fortunate opportunity to make up for the fiasco of the Gala.

I'm off to pick up my suit, making a few detours along the way. Annie's family, and her friend Suzy will be at the event tonight. Maybe Suzy will tell me who the offensive doctor is, and I can have a word or two with him. I might be able to trick Suzy into it if I pretend to know who the man is. She might assume Annie shared it with me and then, bingo!

I have to protect Annie. I'm surprised this doctor has skated out of lawsuits. Only a slime ball with a small dick would force themselves on women.

I have my tux in the car and a blue flower for it to match Annie's dress. I call her from the car on the Bluetooth. "Are we driving together tonight?"

"That would be nice."

"Great. I'll be there at six-fifteen, it will give us thirty minutes to get there, and we should be early."

"Are you always so methodical?"

I chuckle, "Let's just say I'm getting better with age. And if I fuck up, which I inevitably will, remember I learn from my mistakes, just give me time," I reply, easing her into the reality I'm human, and less than perfect.

"You're too sweet," she replies, however her sweet voice warms me and I'm on a deeper level with her. I have a desire to keep her safe and happy.

I'm not just blowing air up her ass. How can I find the right woman for me if I didn't make the mistakes in my past? I've heard it said that all the events of our lives bring us to where we are now. I happen to like where I am at the moment. I hope Annie is in the same frame of mind.

"I'd suggest I come over earlier, but I would mess up your hair, your makeup, and let's just agree you wouldn't want to spend an hour redoing everything."

"Hm, I like the sound of that. Pregnancy hormones are making me so horny. I miss you."

"I miss you, too."

"I'll see you tonight, I'm leaving for my hair appointment."

"Better you than me," I gleefully tease.

"Yeah, sitting in a chair for hours isn't my idea of fun."

"We'll have fun tonight," I assure her.

I hang up with Annie and have a light workout at home.

I'm on time as I leave the condo and toss a gift bag with a square box wrapped in silver paper into the back seat. I text Annie I'm on my way.

I have to go out of the city in my black Maserati and head towards Annie's. It's out of my way, but it's the right thing to do. I don't want her driving home late at night and seeing as how I'll be with her tonight, it makes sense to take one car.

I don't mind picking her up, even if I have to turn around

and head back to Camden Bay. The Musical Gala for Harrow's Children's Hospital is being held at the Hillot Hotel. I heard it's incredible with a botanical room to boot. I assume numerous teammates will be here as Simon's wife will be performing, I happened to put a bug in his ear she should be there. I've only heard good things about Troy Harrow, but he's out of town. Seeing as how our captain's wife is here, it makes sense for the team to support the benefit for kids.

This is an event I would have rolled my eyes at in the past, and would have come to for the guys, but now, I see it differently. It's a benefit to the growing community and makes a world of difference to the sick kids who would have to travel to Boston to get state-of-art care for life-threatening illnesses and special care for preemies.

I fidget with the radio and stop when I hear the Hillbilly Weatherman. I love the New England twang in his voice. He makes weather a sport in and of itself. I wonder if Annie listens to him.

I flip the station again as traffic slows to a standstill.

Shit.

I can't be late. It's an important night for Annie as it's her first event as a new doctor and I have to make a great impression in front of her friends and family.

I'm stuck, there aren't any other routes to take me to Annie. I passed the only turn off and at that, it's farm roads, tiny bridges over streams and it could take even longer if I deviate from my current situation.

Picking up my phone, the traffic app notifies me of a serious accident ahead. I hope everyone is okay, but I can't make a bad impression by being late. This is the world we live in, and at times, it's less than perfect.

Meanwhile, I text Annie I'm tied up in traffic and I won't get to her on time. If she leaves now, she'll be there on time. These events have a cocktail hour giving us a grace period in which to make our entrance. I wanted my entrance to be with Annie on my arm and glowing.

Dreading the thought of how this affects my evening, I hope I can make it before everyone is seated for the speeches and dinner. It's looking ominous. I think outside of the box. How else can I get to her?

I move into the right lane, drumming my fingers on the steering wheel. I've never been so anxious sitting in traffic. I should have left earlier.

I text Annie an apology, as she should be on the road by now. I creep along and thirty minutes later, I am able to take the exit off the interstate, go under the overpass and get back on, going in the opposite direction toward the hotel.

I give Annie an update and all the while I'm stewing over the fact the doctor who pinned her back against an appliance is on the loose in a room filled with unsuspecting women. I think of her sister Carla and wonder if Annie warned her.

I speed to make up for lost time, knowing most of the troopers are at the crash incident as a siren from an ambulance makes me check my mirror. They are riding the emergency lane to the accident. Thankfully, I never reached it as I was able to turn around before it.

I follow my car's GPS and make it to the luxury hotel where I joyfully toss my keys to the valet, pocketing the receipt. I check the event sign in the lobby and head towards the mentioned room. My direction is confirmed as music floats down the corridor. All the conference rooms are on the main floor. This is considered the 'in' place to have expensive weddings, and large conferences, if one wants a location outside of the Casino district. The upscale society has to have the newest and most expensive venues.

My shoes click on the marble flooring and the doors to the event in the Garden room are open. My first view focuses on the lavish centerpieces on each table in blue and silver. I glance to the right and finding numerous bars, all staffed with two bartenders. The alcohol is flowing as I scour the landscape for Annie or Coach. I'm sure she won't be far from her parents.

Light music is steaming, perfect for conversation and drinking. A stage sets in front of the dance floor and to the right is a podium with blue curtains as a backdrop.

I text Annie to meet me by the ice sculpture of swans with desserts around it. I make a note of how beautiful the two swans are as they face each other and relax when Annie's hand slides into mine as if we've known each other forever.

"Hello, you are gorgeous," I rave. Her hair is braided into a thick mane, it's elegant, but not overstated. She carries herself like a woman of the regency era, she stands out in the crowd in her Vera Wang dress.

"Thank you, you're handsome yourself," her voice is pure sweetness.

I lean towards her lips, hungry for her as my lips find hers and smear her lipstick. I stifle hot thoughts of her, as popping a boner now would be embarrassing. Thank God for tuxedo jackets, I'll keep mine buttoned until later. First impressions can't be redone.

"Sorry I couldn't pick you up," I apologize for my failed attempt at chivalry.

"No worries, it happens."

"I've missed you." I'm fucking her with my eyes as her breasts seem larger than normal, but it must be my imagination. "You were right, blue is your color, good job." I compliment her on her gorgeous full-length dress with a scoop neck, and long sleeves. Her cleavage is tastefully displayed and I'm pretty sure I'm the only man here who has dated her, and I enjoy the fact she's never had a boyfriend in this city. I'd like to tell myself she was waiting for the right guy. Maybe she was, she's never mentioned anything other than being new to town and working long hours.

We move to the table champagne fountain where we each pluck a filled flute.

"The doctor said a tiny bit is fine," she whispers to me to negate strangers having privy to our private conversation.

"Great, cheers," We clink our glasses and for a moment, time has stopped. I'm beholden to this incredible woman carrying my child.

"Kal," Simon gives me shout, and I turn to see Bella on his arm. She's dressed in a silver dress of sequins for her performance.

"Nice to see you, man. Bella, nice to see you, again." I nod in her direction.

"You too, Kal."

"This is my girlfriend, Annie, Coach's daughter."

"Yeah, we had to skate an hour over you," Simon jests.

"What?" Annie's eyes grow larger than normal when she hears this.

"Yeah, um, there was an incident at the rink and coach had to hand out a punishment," I cover for the fact it was over Annie not wanting her to think she was the reason we were punished.

Practical jokes under the nose of any coach is always

tricky, and best done in public to avoid repercussions. Everyone knows this, unless you have a rare coach who loves pranks, that is. Coach Susneck isn't one of those.

"When are you singing, Bella?" Annie inquires.

"After the dinner. I'll open the musical part of the evening with one song, then it will be turned over to the band. There is a DJ for the dinner music."

"I can't wait. I love your social media posts with Troy Harrow. Is he really nice?"

She flops her hand in front of her incredible formal gown, no doubt tailored by a designer for her to perform in Vegas. She's gorgeous, and I thought she'd be pretentious, but she's not.

"Yes, he really is," Simon answers for her. He gives Bella an adoring look, the kind that passes between Kal and me when words aren't needed because our eyes are filled with love and deep respect.

"Well, I love your songs," I reiterate my heart felt appreciation for her voice. "Where do you come up with your lyrics?"

"Personal experiences, a thought here, a word there. My mind is never far from creating music. And here I thought my manager would buy songs for me to sing, but no, I write them now."

"That's awesome, keep it up. And thank you for helping with the benefit. Kal didn't tell me asking you to sing was his idea," I reply, even though she doesn't need my stamp of approval.

"Thanks, I'm happy to help. I always want to use my talents to help others when I can. I hear you're a doctor. Congrats on the children's wing. Simon has a three-year-old, and she's adorable. It's nice to know the hospital will help so many kids. I'm thankful everyday we're healthy. I can't even imagine kids needing an oncology floor."

"It's a sad necessity. However, it will help kids get treated soon, and it's more affordable than going out of state."

She nods and we drift off to mingle with others.

28

Annie

I understand Kal getting tied up in traffic. Accidents happen, I see it when I'm called to assist the emergency room when it's bad weather and numerous cars collide, which happened when I was in Boston.

I spent the morning having my hair tugged and pulled. It wasn't the easiest part of my day. But as Mom says, being pretty isn't for the faint of heart. Far be it for me to question her, the once-in-a-lifetime model herself, knows all too well what the A-list lifestyle is about. I'm still learning, having shied away from it my entire life.

Mom is wearing an emerald green formal gown accentuating her slim waistline. She's in astonishingly great shape for a woman in her mid-fifties. Her dark brown hair is worn in a blunt cut, angled toward her chin and straight as a freshly minted one-hundred-dollar bill.

My hair is course, dense, it will frizz at the mere inkling of humidity. Living in Maine makes this more of an everyday occurrence than an anomaly.

I'm being introduced to one player after another. Emily and Wyatt are cozy and when Kal informs me they are expecting, I understand them being in the babymoon phase even though she's not showing.

Carla sneaks up behind us, giving us both a hug.

"What's new? I thought you hated big affairs," she teases. She's dressed in a red, form fitting elegant dress and the last minute I saw her she was bouncing around with mom meeting hockey studs and CEO's.

"This one is for kids," I reply.

She looks at me so suspiciously. "It's networking for you."

We both know I'd rather be home eating popcorn and binge-watching TV with no interruptions, like Suzy. She's a maven of society life; the cute button nose, the picture perfect hair and bubbly personality. It makes sense she's the belle of this ball.

Carla's cocktail dress compliments her skin tone. Her hair is wavy and rests above her shoulders with numerous hand-painted red highlights appropriately placed to show off her high cheekbones. It's a modified shag which has made a comeback. She's one to be up on current fashion. In fact, she wants to become an interior decorator if modeling falls through. I assume she gets her creativity from mom.

I take in her height, flawless skin and makeup. I have no doubt with her looks and Dad's last name she'd get hired to model and travel the world. Mom insists she obtains a degree even if most of it is done online as a backup plan. Could it be I get my independence from mom, not dad?

Kal is talking to the guys lightheartedly. They debate getting in a game of golf and if it will snow before Thanksgiving next week.

Suzy, and the hunk on her arm, Mitch, find us.

"Wow, you look stunning," I muse as I've never seen her dressed up. She's wearing an elegant blue dress with a slit up the side and a topaz necklace. Her usual ponytail is gone, leaving straight hair falling past her shoulders. Obviously flat ironed.

"Mitch," I introduce myself and Kal. After we've had a minute of sipping drinks, an announcement is made for us to be seated. We join my parents, and Carla at our table, Suzy and Mitch sit with us, as do Blake and Rachel.

Blake gives my mom a tentative hug and kiss and introduces his wife. I observe them, but it's clear she never heard about the incident.

I lean over to Suzy. "Did you see Dr. Dick?"

"No, you?"

"No, it's eerie. He's too arrogant to miss tonight, besides, he has a speech to make."

"Oh, boy," Suzy murmurs apprehensively.

I straighten in my chair as if nothing is out of the ordinary as our first course is served and prominent members with the hospital make use of the podium. All eyes are on Dr. Dick as he starts his speech, causing me to shift in my chair, my body becomes rigid. Kal is holding my hand, and I inadvertently squeeze it.

He's keen enough to figure out who the doctor is, and I have no desire for a run in with the handsy doctor or sewing cuts in someone's face.

"Are you okay?" Kal asks like a gentleman.

"Fine," I brush him off as I distract myself with the bread roll on my plate and focus my eyes on it. Presentations are over, and the crowd claps as Dr. Fluentes leaves the mic. Dinner music commences as the night carries on as entrees are delivered to our table and mom is suspiciously talkative, but I welcome it to keep Kal's attention off me.

I excuse myself to use the ladies' room. Kal stands to pull my chair out for me. He's become quite the debonair quintessential man taking care of me when clearly, I can stand by myself.

"I'll be right back," I whisper to him as he returns to his seat.

I exit the huge ball room and look for a sign with women's restroom on it and a hand slides under my elbow.

"Kal..." I turn, wondering what he's up to now.

Fuck, Dr. Dick.

"You never should have used the water. I'll show you what you need," his menacing voice scares me as he pushes me into a deserted conference room from the hallway. "Open your mouth and I'll slap it so hard you'll be unconscious," he snarls.

He manhandles me as I struggle to break free, it's my only chance at freedom.

He tugs at my arm enough to hurt and leave a bruise. His lips are on mine as he lurches forward so hard, I'm bent backwards over a long conference table. He had this planned.

I hear the door kicked open and a thunderous bang as the metal bar hits the wall so hard the noise makes me jump. Dr. Dick is being pulled off me, and in a flash, I vaguely catch the look on Kal's angry face.

Kal pulls his fist back, with one hand clenched on Dr. Fluentes' upper jacket as if it was a hockey fight, he punches him squarely in the face. I hear a crack and assume his orbital bone is bruised from the impact. The doctor falls back, landing on the hard floor covered with thin carpeting.

I process the sickening crack and hope Kal's hand is not hurt.

"You'll pay for that, you have a bad reputation, No one

will believe your word against mine when I sue you," the worm of a man crawls over his own leg to get up, holding his very bruised nose.

"I beg to differ," another voice is heard.

Dad!

Kal pulls me into his arms. "Are you okay?" His eyes intently check my body, my arms, and land on my face with concern.

"I am now. Thank you," my breath comes out in a rush.

Dad rushes to wrap his arm around me as he instructs Kal to call the police.

"Now, we have witnesses," I add.

"That won't be necessary," Dr. Fluentes' voice surprises me. "I'll resign, I have another job lined up out of state," he growls in defeat and sends me a menacing look.

Kal surmises Fluentes face and Dad tells him it's fine, we don't need to involve anyone else.

"How can we trust him?" I ask.

Dad looks at Dr. Fluentes, "Resignation in Mr. Barber's hand tonight, or we will call the police and we'll add a civil lawsuit to it as well. We can't be bought off."

My dad has my back! My eyes fill with mist. He loves me and wants to protect me.

Dr. Dick straightens himself into standing position, dusts his hands across his wrinkled pants and uses his free hand to smooth down his jacket. "Fine. I never liked Maine and your daughter is a whore," he nasal sounding voice comments. He's still holding the right side of his face. I assume his nose might be fractured.

Dad quickly drops his right arm to his side, turns his body before I know what is happening, and his fist flies past my head, landing on Dr. Dick's face and I watch the doctor fall to the floor for the second time tonight.

"Holy shit," leaves my mouth as my hands fly to my lips. I've never seen my dad hit anyone.

Fluentes scrambles to his feet, dazed, but he knows it's over for him, and he can't leave the room fast enough.

"Is your hand okay, Dad?"

Dad rubs his knuckles, "Yeah, he deserved more, but I think we're good. How about you, Kal? Are you good?"

"I'm good if you and Annie are, sir." Kal's words provide me with relief.

The two men exchange a knowing look of acceptance.

"How is your hand?" I ask Kal. Shit, they both could have broken a finger or knuckles as I heard the doctor's face crack under the punch. Maybe Fluentes has a few broken bones. One can hope.

"Fine," Dad adds before they both turn to me. "Are you okay, really?" The concern in my dad's voice moves me.

I pat my dress down and straighten my shoulders. "Fine, thanks Dad." I give him a reassuring smile. He runs his hand down the side of my face and cups my chin, our eyes meet. "I wish I had known. Why didn't you tell me?"

"I didn't want to bother you," I reply meekly and realize how lame of an excuse it is when I had so much at stake. "Besides, they don't make a greeting card for it."

His arms engulf me and mine automatically reach around him. "No matter what you might think, I love you, Annie. You were so independent as a kid that I didn't know what to do with you. I'm sorry I didn't push myself into your life more. You were a child, and I treated you like an adult. But no more secrets, ever," he warns. I know this voice, and it means business.

I wipe a tear struggling to break free. In one sentence, the past is explained, and an apology is given. He loved me, he just didn't know how to show me.

Dad drops his arms as he backs away. We've been gone too long. Kal moves towards me whereby he drapes his arm over my shoulders, pulling me into his chest protectively.

"How did you know?" I catch his greenish-blue eyes, instinctively I know they are filled with love.

"I was on the lookout and when your body gave me an indication of who it might be, I wasn't going to let you out of my sight." He brushes the few strands of hair from my face, tucking them behind my ear.

"We'd better get back," I state.

"We should." Dad turns to us. "Annie, I support you in your decisions. That's why I never brought up the fact Kal was dating you. However, seeing the way you look at each other, I think you made the right call." He sends me a smile filled with love.

I can't stop the tears. Dad approved of me all these years. He loves me. He fought for me, and he...holy shit, he approves of my boyfriend?

"I'll go back first, you kids take your time," he winks to Kal.

What is it with the inside track Kal has with my mom and dad?

"What is he talking about? I've gotten the weirdest vibes from my parents all night," I complain.

Kal turns me to face him, "I didn't see it happening like this; however, I love you, Annie." Our eyes meet and I'm under his spell. I can't fight the longing I have for him.

"I love you, too, Kal. Thank you for being here."

"I'm glad I was here, especially tonight. I promise I'll always have your back. When I'm away, I long to be with you. But know you are always on my mind."

"I know the feeling."

"We haven't known each other long," he drops to one knee.

"What are you doing, Kal? Are you okay?"

"Annie, this is not a practical joke," his serious tone takes away my glib comment.

"Will you marry me? I knew you were the one the minute you walked in the restaurant, I knew you were the one with the tickle fest, and the paint fight. You're a courageous woman, and so damn independent. And feisty! I want all our kids to be like you."

"Kal," I exclaim in shock as he holds a huge ring in front of him. And here I just thought it was his cock in his pants. "It's huge!"

"We're talking the ring, not my cock, Annie," he teases.

"Yes, yes, I'll marry you!" He slips the ring on my finger, and I'm impressed when it fits perfectly. He stands, profusely kissing me with deep throat action, until my lips are swollen. When he pulls away, I'm breathless.

My eyes once again fixate on the ring. I have no clue how many karats it is, and I decide I love bling now that I have this sparkler on my finger.

"What about. . ."

"There's enough time to figure out the rest of the details. We can have a small ceremony during the season, so no one has to know it's a shotgun wedding," his practical comment gives me pause.

"Really? You're okay with a wife and kid so quickly?"

"I hate to leave you for one day, Annie. I've never felt that with anyone else. You warm my heart, and the heart is where home is."

I stifle more tears, but they slide down my face just the same. Kal, the rouge player has become domesticated.

～

WE RETURN TO THE EVENT, and dancing is in full swing. Mom and Carla rush up to me.

"How are you, honey?" Mom asks. After I assure them, I'm fine. I decide there's no reason to burden them with the ugly incident tonight.

Carla grabs my fingers and shrieks, "Oh My, God, is that what I think it is?" She pulls my hand with the shiny object to her face and examines it closer.

"Yes," I can't hide my grin as my cheeks grow warm with self-conscious thoughts.

"Congrats, you two. Boy, what a shocker. That was fast!"

"When you know, you know," Kal smiles.

Dad comes over and shakes his hand, the transcendence look between them tells me Dad knew this was coming. He must have asked for his permission.

Blake comes over to see what we're being congratulated over, and Rachel gives me a warm hug and tells Carla she's in on the wedding shower.

"How exciting!" Suzy exclaims with Mitch on her arm.

"You two had better get out there and dance before the band stops playing," Mom interjects.

"I don't know."

Too late, Kal has grabbed my hand and leads me to the dance floor where we have our first dance to the slow song *Perfect*.

I trip over Kal's feet, but it's my fault.

"You really need to give me some credit, Annie. I need to lead on the dance floor," he says giving me a smirk.

"I don't know how." The years of being independent to the exclusion of giving up control is foreign to me. I take a breath, and let Kal take the first step on the next refrain.

"There you go, see, it gets easier. You just need some practice."

"I can adapt." I lift my head and give him a swoon worthy smile. I've given him control and nothing terrible happened.

"Are you thinking what I'm thinking?"

"I bet. I did all my fraternizing with co-workers waiting for you. I can leave."

"Say no more," he leads me back to the table where we grab my purse.

Suzy, Mitch, and I say goodbye. Blake, Rachel, and a few of the others in their group wave as they walk out the door. Everyone at our table is leaving, Carla is walking out with us, but Mom and Dad are on the dance floor. I stop in my tracks. They remind me of the elderly couple I observed at the Make a Kid Smile event.

They are just as in love today as ever. I can only hope to be so lucky. Mom is going to lose her shit when she finds out about the baby. I grin, it will be fun to grant her a wish.

MUCH LATER, after two rounds of the most intense sex, he hands me a square box wrapped in silver paper.

"What is this?"

"Don't be a kill joy, open it." He pulls the blanket up to cover me as we sit in bed.

I rip the paper and open the lid, it's a Mauler jersey.

"What is this?"

"The jersey the guys made landing me in front of your father, who read me the riot act. It's no act, he meant business Annie. It's what fathers do for their daughters. You might not have believed he loved you as actions mean more than words to you, but he's always loved you. He just didn't know how to show you. You don't have to change your name," he adds as I run my fingers over both our names on the back of the jersey.

"This jersey is cool. But Susneck can be my middle name."

I roll my eyes up to see his reaction and decide I made my fiancée happy.

He asks if I need anything, and seeing as how all I need is him, I say 'no', and we cuddle under the blankets. Thanksgiving is going to be interesting when we break the baby news to the family.

"What of your dad? Have you heard from him?" I ask, out of curiosity.

"No, it's more of a yearly thing with him. My mom will be ecstatic you've kept me out of the public spotlight. Now, it will be engagement news, a wedding, and a baby. She'll have nothing to complain about," and with that, he kisses my forehead, turns the lamp off and sinks under the blankets.

"I love you Annie." Kal drops a light kiss on my warm lips.

"I love you, too." Our lips meet again, and tonight when we make love, I realize he's always made love to me. Being with him is magical and I love when he wraps his arms me. I smile with contentment. He might travel a lot, but when he's with me, he's focused and he makes me complete.

For the Bonus Scene download Kal & Annie's Wedding or click this link: https://dl.bookfunnel.com/i99gkh53xh

If you enjoyed this you might like the next book
Pucking the Team Captain

TEAM ROSTER

TEAM ROSTER 2021-22 (subject to change)

C-Kal Kohlman #5, "A" Alternate captain as per Jagged Ice.

C- Jacques Bellare #65

C-Austin Martin, pronounces Maratn #38 is his lucky number

C-Eric Thomas #96

C- Finn Callahan #71

RW-Sean Ian #57

RW-Victor Karlsson "C" for Captain #90,

RW-Alexander Holloway #23

RW-Raymond Frick #73

LW- Wyatt Hildebrand #19 nicknames Hildy, Broomhilda

LW- Albert Bennett #86

LW-Sidney Roy #98

LW-Chandler Ross #49

D-Justin Puljujar #55

D-Colton Cermak #62

D- Simone Korhomen #77

D- Blake Gibson #45

D-Trevor Espisito #41 born April 1

D-Devin Coyle #68

G-Luc McDavid #23 f (or Patrick Roy)

G-Jason McKinney, backup #30 which is Martin Brodeur's number.

RESERVES

F-Greg Coture. #87 for Crosby, his idol as a kid

F-Douglas Wright #8 for Ovchekin

F-Michal Mitchell "#94 M&M" "Candy"

D- Georgiev Laurent #82 "Laundry" and at night "Dirty Laundry"

D-Roy Crug # 71 "Croog" is how it's pronounced

NHL TEAMS FOR THE SERIES

The NHL Team list for the Maine Maulers Series *subject to changes

Atlantic Division

    Fort Myers Gators (Jackson: Against the Boards)
    Buffalo Blazers
    Boston Sharks
    Detroit Brawlers
    Jacksonville Titans
    Ottawa Kings
    Toronto Twisters
    Wyoming Wolfs
    Metropolitan Division
    Washington Devils
    NJ Bandits
    Philly Flames
    Carolina Cobras
    Montreal Mounties
    Nashville Legends
    NY Renegades

Central Division

Calgary Oilers

Chicago Blizzards

Colorado Bears (Jackson: Against the Boards)

Dallas Bucks

Pittsburg Rockets

Quebec Pioneers

St. Louis Archers

Vegas Bobcats

Pacific

LA Thunder (Coach: Isak Sin Bin Series)

Edmonton Enforcers

Minnesota Mayhem

Phoenix Diamondbacks (Liam: The Enforcer)

San Diego Defenders

Seattle Whalers

Vancouver Cougars

Vegas Predators

FREE BOOK

Tyler, a college hockey player, is on a rafting trip and has no
expectations of meeting a hot chick.
Rebecca is recovering from a relationship that went
sideways and doesn't think she's looking for anyone.

But when Tyler pulls her out of the white water, what will happen next?
This is the Prequel to the Sin Bin Hockey Series
Hooked: Tyler

ALSO BY ZOE BETH GELLER

Tyler: Hooked (Free prequel to the series)

Sin Bin Hockey Series (10)

The Sin Bin Hockey Series

Jackson: Against the Boards

Alan: Between the Pipes

Erik: Fire and Ice

Blayze: Slap Shot

Paavo: The Defender

Spencer:Penalty Box

Isak: Coach

Kaden: Game Time

Liam: The Enforcer

Jake: Roughing

Sin Bin Series Box Sets (3)

The Sin Bin Hockey Series Box Sets

The Sin Bin Hockey Series Box Set Books 1-4

The Sin Bin Hockey Series Box Set Books 5-7

The Sin Bin Hockey Series Box Set Books 8-10

Zoe Beth Geller's Hockey Pond Fan Group

Maine Maulers

Maine Maulers Hockey Series

Rookie in Love

Jagged Ice

Hotter than Puck

Benched by the Nanny

Puck in the Oven

Pucking the Team Captain

Maine Megaladons (Football)

Faking it with the Football Star

The Dirty Series-Micheli Mafia (5)

Dirty: A Dark Mafia Romance Series (Micheli Mafia) Series of 5 books

Italian King: A Dark Mafia Romance (Micheli Mafia) Book 1

Dirty Vengeance: A Dark Mafia Romance (Micheli Mafia) Book 2

Dirty Bargain: A Dark Mafia Romance (Micheli Mafia) Book 3

Dirty Born: A Dark Mafia Romance (Micheli Mafia) Book 4

Dirty Deals: A Dark Mafia Romance (Michell Mafia) Book 5

Dirty Series Dark Mafia Fan Group

Volkov Brava (Standalone)

King's Promise

Brutal Promise

ACKNOWLEDGMENTS

Special thanks to my mentors, and close friends who are my support system. Thank you to the following ARC readers who helped with proofreading; Jeanne Jabour, Maureen Riley, Tinna Edna, Carol Jennings, Janet Greene, Nancy Lebel, Claire Trickett and Donna Bach.

ABOUT THE AUTHOR

I live in SWFL Florida with my grown kids and grandkids. When not writing I enjoy swimming, cooking, family nights and watching my son play ice hockey. I've kinda become the team mom which is cute because my kids aren't 'kids' anymore!

I am the author The Sin Bin Hockey Series which is a collection of 10 standalone novels. There is a bit of continuity across books and they do not need to be read in order.

My second series, Maine Mauler Hockey Series, is a pro team series based, obviously, in Maine! These are interconnecting romances and can be read as a standalone, but due to the interaction between players and a series arc it is best if you read it in order.

Other works include my dark mafia -The Dirty Series: A Dark Mafia Romance (Micheli Mafia). This was inspired by my love of Italy and I've visited family there many times. It's my home away from home.This series starts off with Italian King. These books should be read in order as the plots and romances are involved and carry through the series. This is a 5 book series. Book one is not as dark was it gets, it all builds. Book 2 is femme fatale because Francesca spoke to me and took off. If you know my books you'll know it's like a rollercoaster. Set up, get to the peak and then the Whoosh to the end. But this romantic suspense series builds as a murder mystery, and thriller with tension and plot expansion with each book! I consider this a Steamy Contemporary romance where the mafia aspect grows and grows and some characters and scenes are darker than others.

Want to sign up for the low down on my progress on the next book? Send me feedback?Want to join contests and enter for giveaways? Hockey fans can sign up here and get Tyler free. If you just want to sign up for the Newsletter for the latest releases and features, you can do so here. Or https://landing.mailerlite.com/webforms/landing/g4g1t8 for hockey NL.

What to be an ARC reader?

Email me at zoebethgeller@zoegellerasuthor.com You can review hockey or mafia or both. It's like shopping, tons of options!

Like to see eye candy and talk hockey? I have reader groups on FB and the link to them is on my website and listed below. If mafia is your jam, you can sign up here Newsletter sign-up or https://geni.us/MafiaSignUp

Fan Groups
Zoe Beth Geller's Hockey Pond
The Dirty Series: Dark Mafia Romances

Follow me on TT at zoebethgellerauthor20

ZBG Website

facebook.com/zoebeth.geller.96

instagram.com/zoegellerauthor

bookbub.com/authors/zoe-beth-geller

Printed in Great Britain
by Amazon

20777733R00153